SPE

The Novel

SPENDER
The Novel

Jimmy Nail

BANTAM BOOKS
TORONTO • NEW YORK • LONDON • SYDNEY • AUCKLAND

A BANTAM BOOK 0553 40502 0

First publication in Great Britain

PRINTING HISTORY
Bantam Books edition published 1992

This book is set in 11pt Linotype Sabon by
Phoenix Typesetting, Burley-in-Wharfedale, West Yorkshire

Bantam Books are published by Transworld Publishers Ltd., 61-63 Uxbridge Road, Ealing, London W5 5SA, in Australia by Transworld Publishers (Australia) Pty. Ltd., 15-23 Helles Avenue, Moorebank, NSW 2170, and in New Zealand by Transworld Publishers (N.Z.) Ltd., 3 William Pickering Drive, Albany, Auckland.

Made and printed in Great Britain by
Cox & Wyman Ltd, Reading, Berks.

*To all the people who helped
bring these characters to life.*

1

The bird tilted its head, fixing Spender with the shiny nugget of its eye.

'He can rip a rabbit's head off with them talons,' Mr Lee said, approaching the cage. 'Usually, though, they kill their prey by sheer impact.'

Spender glanced at the iron-black claws. 'It's a peregrine falcon, is it?'

'The male peregrine's a tercel, strictly speaking. The female's the peregrine falcon. That's one there, at the end.'

They moved along the row of slat-and-wire cages.

'She's bigger than he is,' Spender said.

'And browner. And smarter off the mark. You want to see one in action, lad. Talk about deadlier than the male. She comes curving down out the clouds at better than a hundred mile an hour. Smack. Right on the target. Fur, blood and shit everywhere.'

'How come these two are here?' Spender asked. 'Did the owners bring them in?'

'They're wild. A couple of schoolkids found the male flapping about down on the road. Hit by a car most likely. The female flew into telegraph wires and came down in a farmyard. Broken wings, both of them. They're on the mend but there's nobody I can bill for the treatment, more's the pity.'

'You could always sell them.'

Spender said it lightly, but the old man glared at him.

'Do I look soft-headed, or what? They're *wild* birds, for God's sake. I'd get done.'

'I didn't mean it, Mr Lee. No offence.'

The old man slapped the top of the cage, making the chickenwire rattle. The peregrine sidled away along the perch. 'The notion of people owning wild creatures makes me sick. What right's anybody got to take away their freedom and turn them into playthings and ornaments?'

'No right at all,' Spender said, realizing he had hit a nerve.

'Caged wild birds are a bloody abomination.'

Until now Mr Lee had conducted himself with an air of polite and modest proprietorship, showing Spender the scrubbed-and-whitewashed little out-house he called his surgery, then bringing him out here to the cages. Now, standing with his back to the sunlight, his white hair like a nimbus around his head, the old man suddenly had a look Spender recognized: it was the reproving glower a copper used when he was about to shove his nose in.

'You wouldn't have come up here expecting to buy a bird, would you?'

'Buy one?'

'That's what I said.'

'Well no, I told you I was joking when I said—'

'A young hunter, maybe?'

Spender shook his head firmly. 'Definitely not.' Earlier, before it became obvious that Mr Lee was honest to the bone, Spender might have nodded and said yes.

Lee was staring at him, perhaps reconciling the flowing hair and the ear-ring with the steady eye and the blunt sincerity of Spender's tone.

'Yes, well . . .' Mr Lee's voice trailed away. He cleared his throat. 'I like to know where I stand with people.' He waved a hand vaguely along the row of cages. 'Making chattels out of birds like these – peregrines, sparrowhawks, goshawks – it's against nature. And what goes against nature goes against life. I'll tell you this for nothing . . .' Mr Lee held up a finger close to Spender's nose. 'The penalties for trading in wild birds are tough, but they'd be a bloody sight tougher if I'd any say in it.'

He started walking back towards the house. Spender followed, feeling the sun warm on his neck. As dead ends went, this one at least had the weather and the scenery going for it. Mr Lee's bird sanctuary was on the sheltered slope of a wooded hill overlooking the straggle of Newcastle's north-western perimeter. It was a balmy Friday in May, the end of a week of wet, blustery weather. The lush scent of grass mingled with the fragrance of trees and the closer, earthier aroma of compost from Mr Lee's cottage garden. It was a good day to be out, although Spender would have enjoyed it more if the visit had pushed his enquiries forward even a fraction.

'Thanks for showing me the set-up, Mr Lee. It's nice to know there's still people here and there working to counteract the bad stuff.'

'I do what I can.' It wasn't a sanctimonious re-mark; Mr Lee was simply stating the case. 'At times I get despondent and it all seems pointless – I mean, for every bird I save there're thousands lost. But then I always manage to convince myself that any scrap of life's got to be worth the effort to save it.'

'Tell me something . . .' Spender tried to make his interest sound casual, 'do people often try to buy birds off you? Birds of prey, like?'

'They do. More often than maybe you'd think.'

'What kind of people?'

'Trendies, mostly. Hacking-jacket types. The kind that fancy showing off with falcons perched on their wrists.'

'I know nothing about it, but I'd have thought birds like peregrines would be hard to train.'

'Not so hard,' Mr Lee said. 'Not if they're young enough and the buyer's keen, and if they're trained to do what they like doing.'

'What kind of money do you get offered?' It was hard to keep the casual tone of a bloke who was only marginally curious. It was especially hard with Mr Lee, who seemed to take more notice of the words than how they were delivered.

'Nobody's ever got so far as making me an offer.' Mr Lee smiled faintly. 'I fly off the handle too quick. But I've heard tales. A thousand or fifteen hundred's not considered a lot for a young peregrine. Twice as much as that if it's been hand-reared right from hatching.'

'Hatched from stolen eggs?'

'That's right. It's a business with some folk.' Mr Lee scratched his nose pensively. 'Not that I know any of them,' he added, cancelling Spender's next question. 'If I did I'd shop the buggers without a second thought. Them *and* their punters.'

'Well, I'm not in the market,' Spender said, feeling the old man still needed reassurance. 'It's just like I explained when I came to your door – a friend told me about this operation of yours and I was curious to see it.'

Mr Lee nodded, clearing his throat again. 'Sorry I went at you like I did,' he murmured. 'I'm maybe a bit over-protective—'

Spender waved the apology aside and buttoned his jacket, signalling his departure. They walked together to the top of the narrow path where the black Cosworth was parked. Spender thanked Mr Lee again and as he got in the car he fished a tenner from his pocket. He handed it out through the window.

'Something towards the good work.'

'Oh. Cheers.' Mr Lee kissed the note and stuffed it in his shirt pocket. 'I'm obliged. I'll keep back enough to have a drink on you.'

Twenty minutes later Spender walked into a steamy café on Westgate Road in the centre of Newcastle. At the counter he looked around and spotted Detective Sergeant Dan Boyd, installed at a corner table with a coffee and a sugary doughnut in front of him. He looked every inch the seasoned desk-cop, despite his belief that his appearance was neutral to the point of invisibility. Spender ordered a tea and took it across to the table.

'Any joy?' Dan said as he sat down.

'I know a bit more about peregrine falcons, I suppose.' Spender took a tentative sip from his cup. 'Lee's as clean as a whistle. He's what he seems – a nice old guy doing something for the welfare of wild birds.'

'I've picked up a bit about peregrines myself,' Dan said, brushing sugar from the corner of his mouth. 'Did you know, for instance, that in the Middle Ages it was the death penalty for anybody taking one or interfering with its nest?'

'Mr Lee would go along with that.'

'It was only so they'd be left alone for the big nobs to use for falconry. Royalty had exclusive rights to gyrfalcons, peregrines were for noblemen, merlins for—'

'I get the idea, Dan.'

'I'm just showing off my homework.'

'Very impressive, but a lead's what I need. Did you get anything from Yellow Pages?'

Dan shook his head. 'One pet shop recommended a bird breeder out at Westerhope. I rang him and asked if he could fit me up with a falcon. He told me he wasn't licensed to breed them, so I said I wasn't that fussed about him being licensed—'

'And he told you to piss off.'

'More or less.'

'What a surprise,' Spender stared at Dan. 'There's ways of doing these things. Subtle ways. Hints and nudges, you know?'

Dan took a huffy bite out of his doughnut. 'Maybe you should make your own calls,' he muttered, spraying crumbs.

'Maybe I should.'

Spender gulped some tea and clattered the cup back on the saucer. They sat in silence, letting the mood die back to normal. Apart from the occasional spat they worked comfortably together, a blessing neither one of them took lightly. Between Spender's tenebrous undercover activities and the visible levels of policing, a link was essential, and Dan was the link. He made an excellent go-between. He was discreet, if a shade plodding and old-maidish, he was patient, and he was reliable.

'I'm going to look over that butcher's place out near Jesmond,' Spender said, breaking the small silence. 'You know the one I'm on about?'

'Gilbert Easton,' Dan said, keen to show he was up to speed on the case. 'Done in September eighty-nine for selling poached game. Got a fine and a telling-off.' Dan shrugged. 'He's not really a likely, but if we eliminate him from enquiries, it'll be something.'

'Shit!' Spender hissed.

Dan stared at him. 'What?'

'I've been clocked.'

'Who by?'

Spender nodded at the grimy window. 'Kid that just went past. Mickey Lawton. One of Ballantine's messengers.'

'You think he recognized you?'

'I'll take money on it. He put on the glassy stare, but he had a good look at both of us. He saw me shaved and wearing a jacket. Jesus.' Spender shook his head at the table. 'I could've done without this.'

'What'll you do? Lie low for a bit?'

'And let everything go cold? No chance, not after all the effort I've put in.' Spender stared across the road. 'I'll brazen it out with Ballantine, if I have to.'

Moments like these held Dan Boyd in thrall. If not entirely a Walter Mitty, he was a man whose real-life police duties sometimes fell short of his dreams; in his relationship with Spender he gravitated between bouts of envy and long stretches of being grateful he was a desk pilot. This was a grateful time.

'Brazening it out with a drug dealer isn't exactly a breeze, from what I've heard,' he said. 'I've also been told Teddy Ballantine's a fractionally bigger nutter than your average psychopath.'

Spender gazed quizzically at Dan. 'What kind of life would it be without challenges?'

Over another cup of tea he outlined his rough plans for the next twenty-four hours and suggested Dan keep hammering away at pet shops and aviaries. The illegal trade in peregrines was real enough; an absence of solid lines of enquiry was no excuse for taking the view that the source of supply was a mystery beyond the wit of policemen.

'Some bugger somewhere between here and Durham is making a mint out of these birds,' Spender said by way of summary, 'and I'm going to nail his arse.' He pushed back his chair and stood up. 'Here endeth the lesson, Dan. I'll be in touch.'

The sky had clouded over and it began to rain as Dan made his way round the corner to Clayton Street nick and Spender walked back to where the car was parked. Normally they would have made their rendezvous further from the centre of town, and as he legged it towards the car Spender cursed himself for agreeing even to a quick meet in that café. At his level of the business there were few rules, but the ones that existed were not for breaking or even bending; they were mostly unwritten, mostly sensible, and all inviolable.

He groaned softly, picturing Mickey Lawton shuffling past the café window, his mean little know-all eyes doing a deadpan scan, memorizing the interior faster than it took most people to breathe in and out.

'Crafty little bastard . . .'

Some aspect of Sod's Law seemed to govern the matter of surveillance skills. The police sorely needed personnel with Mickey Lawton's talent, people possessing the ability to glance into a place and come away with a roll-call of who was there. The irony was, men and women who were that gifted tended to favour crime as a career.

In the car Spender sleeved the rain from his face and took his portable telephone from the glove compartment. Before going to the café he had set the phone to divert calls to his messaging service. He tapped in the number and waited. After the beep there was the sound of a short peremptory cough.

'Gillespie speaking. My call is timed at fifteen twenty-one.' The Detective Chief Superintendent's voice was dispassionate, pitched close to hostility. 'I expected to hear from you before now. A fresh memo from Sir Reginald Monkton has landed on my desk. The gist of his whine is the same as before, only this time he's a lot more shrill. I don't need to explain how a pillar of the Police Authority – one with a knighthood, at that – can exert the kind of pressure that gives me blinding headaches, do I?'

There was a pause while Mr Gillespie coughed again.

'At the very least, I need a progress report on this toxic drug business. Try to remember what a sense of responsibility's like. Call me.'

Kalomp. The line went dead for a second; the beep sounded again and Spender heard the voice of Frances, his ex-wife.

'Hi, I'm calling to remind you Eric and I are out tonight. You promised you'd sit the girls. Seven o'clock latest. Fair warning – be ready for an ear-bending from Laura. She's got this new thing about saving dolphins. For three days now she's been full of it. She responds badly to anything less than a reasoned response, so bone-up. Try not to be late, huh? See you . . .'

Kalomp. This time the line stayed dead. Spender pocketed the telephone and started the car, wondering how much he'd be expected to know about dolphins. Even a little would be more than he could dredge up from memory. Maybe Laura would settle for a chat about birds of prey.

He parked the car in a side turning fifty yards along the road from the butcher's shop. Setting his pace at a stroll, he turned the corner on to the main street.

The village, for the most part, was a middle-class enclave, isolated by a system of residential values that took full account of prevention and cared nothing about cure, since the ills the community stood against had no chance of encroaching. The main street was like a sanitized and stage-managed effigy of the real thing, swept and spotless, with neatly painted shopfronts and tweedy, rosy-faced people coming and going. There was probably a lot more to it than that, more shading, but the relentlessly sunny, comfortably off image was what prevailed.

Trumpton, Spender thought.

The butcher's was the last shop on the left, a thirties' style double-fronted lockup, with real marble slabs in the windows and shiny chrome-and-steel implements on the tiled walls beyond. As ever, the joints and cuts of meat were a slight shock to Spender's eye, a measurable obscenity. That was the trouble with butchers' shops, they displayed their product at a point where it wasn't quite anonymous; you could see all too clearly where it had come from.

Spender paused by the open door, glancing up at the sign. In raised gilded letters on black glossed wood it said, *GILBERT EASTON, Choice Meat & Poultry.*

He peered swiftly into the shop. A blue-rinsed customer watched intently as a little man in a striped apron operated a bacon slicer. He had a straw boater perched on the back of his head at an angle that was less rakish than reckless, and he operated the machine with a certain flair, as if he were doing it for the customer's entertainment.

Spender moved on, strolling across the entrance of a cobbled alleyway beside the shop. He glanced sideways and counted the outbuildings, getting the gauge of Easton's operation. As reconnaissance went, this exercise had no particular plan. Spender liked to look first at whatever caught his curiosity. His next move depended on what he saw and how he responded to it.

He stopped in the mouth of the alley, listening, hearing the clank and rattle of human activity and the thrum of refrigeration motors from an outbuilding. Ahead of him, out of sight around a corner, a car door slammed; the engine revved, tyres squealed and the car appeared, swinging out on to the main street and accelerating past Spender.

He turned to watch, getting the registration number as a matter of habit.

Along the alley a woman cried out. The sound of motors became abruptly louder as a door was flung open. Spender strode into the alley and saw smoke billowing behind the woman as she rushed from an outbuilding and in through the side door of the shop. She came out again wielding a big red fire extinguisher. Spender took it from her.

'Are you OK?' he asked solicitously.

The woman nodded.

He snatched a chestful of air and ran into the refrigerated store, upending the extinguisher as he went. In the swirling smoky gloom the hanging carcasses looked ghostly. Towards the back, at floor level, Spender saw a guttering glow and headed for it. With the extinguisher held away from him he hit the cap and directed the spray at the flame, which hissed and began throwing off plumes of dense white smoke. Spender emptied the extinguisher then dropped it. He turned and ran outside, coughing violently.

The woman was standing by the shop wall opposite the door. The butcher was beside her, his hand on her shoulder.

'It's out, whatever it was,' Spender croaked, wiping his eyes. 'All taken care of, bar the smoke.' He saw the man and woman glance at each other, the kind of guarded look conspirators exchanged outside interview rooms.

'I'm very grateful, young man,' the butcher said.

As he came forward the woman leaned back on the wall and put both hands over her eyes.

'My wife's prone to panic . . .' The butcher smiled ruefully as he shook Spender's hand. 'I dare say you could use a drink after all that excitement.'

Spender thanked him but suggested they get the meat outside before it was spoiled.

'Oh Lord, yes, of course . . .'

The butcher managed to look suddenly flustered and helpless at the same time. In spite of his effort at brightness, he was clearly as shocked as his wife.

'If you've got a truck,' Spender said, 'we can pile it on that and get it out in two or three gos . . .'

Between them they had the meat transferred to the back shop inside ten minutes. By then the smoke had nearly cleared, but the store room stank of it. The last item Spender brought out was the source of the fire, a buckled metal container resembling a paint tin. Neither the butcher nor his wife appeared keen to acknowledge the object, let alone explain it. Spender put it down by the door.

'We'll let the wind blow through for a few hours,' Mrs Easton said, 'then we can hose the walls down.' The bustle and exertion of shifting the meat seemed to have restored her. 'You better get back into the shop, Gilbert.' She turned to Spender. 'I'm sure you really are ready for that drink now. What can I get you?'

'I could use a cup of tea, thanks.'

And a lot more besides, he thought, rubbing his greasy palms together. A bath would be nice for starters, and a change of clothes. He could smell the smoke and raw meat off himself.

Mrs Easton led the way to the house, which stood at the top of a long narrow garden behind the outbuildings. In the kitchen she filled a washing-up bowl with hot water for Spender to wash his hands, then busied herself with the tea things.

'It was lucky you were passing,' she said, plugging in the kettle and switching it on. 'My husband was right, I'm inclined to panic . . .'

'We all panic a bit when we're caught up in an emergency,' Spender said. 'It's different when you're an outsider. It's not your accident, you can be that bit more objective.'

He turned from the sink and saw Mrs Easton holding a knife poised over a fruit cake. She cut two neat slices and looked up.

'That was no accident,' she said. 'It was the liberationists, or whatever they call themselves. They did it.' She looked down again and cut another slice.

'Sorry, what was that?' Spender picked up the towel from the drainer. 'Liberationists, did you say?'

'Gilbert doesn't like me talking about it. He doesn't want trouble.' Mrs Easton put down her knife and looked at Spender. 'But people *should* know what they do, the wicked devils.'

Spender leaned back against the sink, folding his arms, doing nothing to disturb the mood. As Mrs Easton began to speak again, her voice low and confidential, he closed his eyes and made sure he remembered the number of the car that had passed him at the entrance to the alley.

2

Just as it was hard for most people visiting Newcastle to forget certain lasting impressions – the huge hump-backed structure of the Tyne Bridge, the imposing monolith of Earl Grey's Monument, the Norman Castle – so it was impossible for Spender to control the flow of his own special images. During his years in London with the Metropolitan Police the impressions had stayed rooted on the edge of his awareness, morning and night, markers of his source and identity.

Now he was back he still carried the same impressions of Newcastle, a series of images and imprints to hold up against present times. A lot of the places he remembered affectionately were gone now or painfully altered, but most of the people, the ones who mattered, had endured.

Stick was one of them. A man who managed to be wide-eyed and furtive at the same time, a quick-witted operator with a curious transverse scar bridging his eyebrows, he was not an easy character to classify. His tough, unconquerable spirit, plus a refusal to be dismayed by life, endeared him powerfully to Spender. The only aggravation was that Stick had taken to the path of crime early in life and had never strayed far from it since.

'There's some jammy bastards about,' he said now, nudging Spender. 'Get a load of that.'

They were leaning on the bar at the Builder's Arms, a smoky little pub along the road from the flat they shared.

'Who are you talking about now?' Spender said, looking up from a pamphlet on the bar in front of him.

'Him in the corner with the donkey jacket and the blonde tart giggling at everything he says.'

Spender glanced over. The man was fat, heading for gross, with a two-day stubble and a beer-gut spilling over his jeans. His lady friend, whose cough sounded like trodden gravel, had the remote, pain-free look induced by a lot of lager on top of hardly any food.

Stick shook his head. 'He's been seeing to her for a whole week now,' he said.

'So?'

'He's got a wife at home. Good-looking lass, too.' Stick sucked his teeth quietly. 'Jammy bastard.' He looked around, drumming his fingers on the bar. 'I fancy a Saturday night out.' He looked at Spender but got no response. 'What do you reckon? While away the afternoon with a few bevvies in here, toddle back home for a bit of kip, then hit the town and give the women a treat.'

Spender shook his head, studying the pamphlet again. 'I've got to keep myself available for other things.'

'You're no fun these days, you know.' Stick ran swift, expert fingers over the bulge in Spender's coat. It was made by a pair of 12 x 24 compact binoculars he had brought along. 'It's all this prying into other folk's lives. That's what you've been up to again, isn't it? Spying?'

'I've been birdwatching,' Spender said.

'Call it what you like,' Stick said. 'The point is, your own personality's getting shrunk from neglect. It's a serious hazard. Ask any peeping Tom.' Stick took a step back, appraising. 'You're pretty bloody scruffy looking, too. When did you last have a shave and change your shirt? There's more wrinkles in them trousers than you'll find on a donkey's dick. And your hair—'

'Don't push it, Captain Elegance. I'm in character at present. The gear and the general air of dishevelment are part of it. I'm striving to look a bit of a toe-rag. Fortunately my flatmate's the perfect role model.'

'Cheeky bugger.'

A youth in a boiler suit hailed Stick from the other side of the bar. Stick nodded and winked at him, tucking his chin close to his neck and glancing quickly left and right, a giveaway that suggested his business with this man was not above-board.

'See you in a minute,' he said to Spender, sidling off around the bar.

Spender decided this was an opportunity to move on. He pushed the dregs of his light ale away and put the pamphlet in his pocket.

'I'll catch you later, Stick,' he called.

Turning away sharply before Stick could try to detain him, he shouldered his way through the swing door and caught the wind's blast full in the face. Through slitted eyes he saw Keith Moreland across the road, leaning hard on his stick and hunched into the wind. This was another glimmer of old times, a commonplace Spender had forgotten: leaving the company of one pal, he had always been likely to spy another.

He crossed the road and fell in beside Keith.

'Got the price of a cup of tea, guv?'

'Yeah, *now* I have,' Keith said. 'I finally got the money for a pub gig we did weeks ago. The gaffer had cash-flow problems. I thought we'd have to gang up on him and hint he might get blood-flow problems if he didn't cough up, but one personal visit did it. Maybe he was sorry for me. You've got to admit I look pretty fucking pathetic.' Keith grinned and patted his pocket. 'It's got a nice warm feel, a little wad.'

'I've left Stick in the pub,' Spender said, as he led Keith through heavy traffic. 'He's in one of his hedonist moods. Wants to spend the day drinking, then do a bit of tailchasing tonight.'

Old times again, he thought. He and Keith had often put their heads together to bemoan or wonder at the life pattern of young Stick, nicknamed for the unvarying width of his body from shoulder to knee. Not that their behaviour in those days had been much different from Stick's. The difference lay in quantity; Stick was adroit at overdoing everything.

They chatted amicably until they reached Keith's guitar shop: it was only a mile or so from the flat occupied by Stick and temporarily shared by Spender.

Keith unlocked the shop door and they went in. The atmosphere of the place always soothed

Spender. In the magic years of the seventies when he had been an active muso like Keith – the times of performing at all-night gigs and crashing at whichever pad was nearest, then getting up after a few hours and chasing around and playing again as if energy was something that never ran out – there had been a cocooning atmosphere of *involvement*, of being where his unique edge on life was at its sharpest. That period was embodied in the paraphernalia, in the sight, smell and living presence of the tools and trappings of the trade. In those terms, Keith's modest shop was a shrine. It echoed a footloose era before Spender turned into a career cop and began avoiding – among other things – any instinct that had not been tamed.

Keith began rattling about making tea, Spender leaned on the wall and leafed through the pamphlet again. It was an animal rights propaganda handout that the butcher's wife, Mrs Easton, had told him to put in his pocket in case her husband walked into the house unexpectedly. 'I promised him I'd throw it away,' she had said, 'but I kept it to read. There's some sense in what they say, I suppose, but none of it gives them the right to punish my hubby for selling meat – what difference would it make to anything if he stopped, eh? That's what I'd like to know . . .'

The pamphlet was published by an outfit called Jude's People, an animal rights organization with a head office in London and twelve branch addresses throughout Britain. The nearest address was a few streets away from Keith's shop. Mr Easton had found the pamphlet on the doormat a few hours before he received an ugly telephone call warning him that stern action would be taken if he didn't urgently reconsider the way he earned his living.

'The pamphlet's very civilized and compassionate,' Mrs Easton pointed out. 'The threats all came over the phone.'

There had been three calls at one-week intervals, then a gap of two days before the fire had started.

The pamphlet opened with a chatty introduction outlining the group's aims – 'to challenge, oppose and enlighten the forces of government and commerce until the animals have a charter granting them the right to exist, unexploited and unharmed, in a world that was theirs in the first place . . .'

The remainder of the publication was an illustrated catalogue of the cruelties mankind routinely practises on other mammals. There were pictures of dogs and cats with wires attached to their heads and legs, stark images of mice and rats half gutted and apparently still alive on dissection blocks. Under the heading VIVISECTION Spender read,

This much overvalued procedure, where living animals are operated upon for alleged physiological investigation and the study of disease, is regularly carried out on conscious animals in circumstances causing unbelievable pain and suffering, in spite of guidelines that insist, repeatedly, that the procedure be performed under conditions similar to those carried out on human beings in an operating theatre of a hospital.

Spender was afflicted by a powerful imagination; sometimes it coupled with his excellent memory to produce images so vivid he would gasp out loud, forgetting himself in the onslaught of his reaction. Once, as an incidental aside to the line of duty, he had seen a rabbit being used for an experiment in a psychological research facility in London. The top of the animal's skull had been removed and probes were attached to its living brain. The sight of it – dumb, clamped motionless, able to do no more than blink its big dark eyes – had put a pain across Spender's heart that suddenly duplicated itself now. He slapped down the pamphlet and realized Keith was standing beside him holding out a mug of tea.

'You're getting the message, I see.' Keith nodded at the pamphlet. 'Grim stuff, eh?'

'Read it, have you?'

'On an empty stomach, thank Christ. I know the guy that runs the local chapter of that crowd. He gave me a bundle of leaflets and asked us to put them on the counter. They went fast. Cheaper than Stephen King and every bit as gruesome.'

'What's the bloke's name?'

'Jeremy Fuller.'

Bull's-eye, Spender thought. The PNC check on the car he saw at the time of the fire had come up with the name Desmond Fuller, who turned out to be a retired local banker.

Keith waggled his head loftily. 'We went to the Royal Grammar School at the same time, you know. Jeremy wasn't just a brainy scruff like me, mind. He's money from way back.'

'His old man was in banking, right?'

'That's the one,' Keith nodded. 'The old shit turned me down for a loan when I was after this prime condition Gibson I could have had for about half what it was worth, because the dummy selling it didn't know a fret from a freckle.'

'So what's Jeremy doing mixed up with—' Spender glanced at the back of the pamphlet '—Jude's People?'

Keith narrowed his eyes. 'What's he done, then?'

'Did I say he'd done anything?'

Keith sighed quietly. 'He's the joining sort. At school he was always getting involved with controversial causes. Not really an idealist, mind. More a compulsive rebel, all front and no substance. He'd get behind any outfit that needed a smart mouthpiece. A great talker, is Jeremy.'

'And a bit of a rabble rouser.'

'Maybe.' Keith shrugged. 'He's hardened up a bit since he was a lad, but I still get the feeling it's mostly mouth.'

Keith eased down on to a spindly chair, using his stick expertly, propping himself until he was properly seated. He shook his head, freeing his pony-tail from the collar of his jacket; in that movement Spender saw the Keith of fifteen years before, energetic and likeably self-assured, in charge of his talent, a guy going places.

Spender shifted his stance at the counter, edging away from the recollection. He had to stop these re-runs of the past. Most of the comparisons they threw up were too bruising.

'As it happens,' Keith said, 'I've got reason to be grateful to Jeremy Fuller. We did a gig for Jude's

People the other week – hey, know why they're called that?'

'No idea,' Spender said.

'Jude is the patron saint of desperate cases. Anyway, after the gig I met a very nice lass.'

Spender nodded approvingly.

'Her name's Dory. Dory Newton. You'll meet her soon.'

'I look forward to it.'

As Keith's MS had progressed by its erratic stages his wife, Astrid, had finally left. There was no acrimony between them; the simple fact was that Keith's diminished sexual prowess was incompatible with Astrid's needs.

At one point she had approached Spender, with a view to an arrangement whereby he might fill the deficit. He had turned her down as diplomatically as he could. Later Keith approached him on the same matter, wondering if an old mate would take on the physical duty that illness had put beyond his capability. Spender had said he would think about it; to his relief, Astrid left home before Keith raised the matter again.

After she had gone, Keith's incapacity seemed to get worse. Maybe now, Spender dared to think, there would be a turnaround, a phase of measurable and long-lasting remission.

'How are you keeping lately, anyhow?' he asked, by way of checking. 'You look well enough . . .'

'I could be worse,' Keith said. 'The specialist tells me there's definitely optic nerve, brainstem and spinal cord involvement, but the good news is I don't get any symptoms from those quarters.

Not yet. Also, my bouts of irritability are normal for a man in my abnormal condition, so I'm not going up the twist after all. My episodes of the wobbles and shakes are followed by periods of near recovery, as you know, which makes my type of MS better than the progressive kind, where there's just a steady decline into uselessness.'

Keith sipped his tea, considering a summary.

'I'd say I'm fine, thanks for asking. Some folk die a few months after they catch this lot, you know. But the average duration of the disease is more than thirty years. So I've a while yet to hobble across life's rich brocade.'

A small knot of punters wandered in, the Saturday kind, men in their middle and late thirties. They were ready to spring for the odd replacement guitar string or a packet of plectrums – Keith called it gate money – but they were really here for the rapp, the rhythm-and-blues scuttlebutt, ancient and modern. Spender felt it was time to move along, before he got so seriously stuck in the past he couldn't get out again. He winked at Keith, who was deep in conversation, and left.

Less than a minute after he hit the street his mobile phone rang. He slipped into a doorway and answered it. Gillespie was on the other end, curt as ever, demanding an immediate meet. Spender said he would think of somewhere suitable; meantime, Gillespie could establish a tail.

'I'll drift up and down City Road, sir. You'll not have any trouble finding me, window-gazing. I'll lead the way from there.'

*   *   *

The streets were filled with shoppers, the kind with money to spend and those without who nevertheless liked to come and look, gregariously thronging the pavements. Spender found himself moving against the flow, whichever way he went. He decided to anchor himself at a corner by an optician's, studying the spectacle frames. After a couple of minutes, above the clamour of voices and traffic sounds, he heard the rhythm of Gillespie's approach, the steady military clip-clop of his Oxfords on the pavement. Seconds later the cropped bullet head loomed into view through the crowd, the unforbearing eyes fixed straight ahead. Spender moved off, knowing Gillespie would follow at a circumspect distance. It was satisfying to fix a venue without specifying where it was.

He walked all the way down to the Quayside and on to a deserted stretch before he stopped and waited. When Gillespie finally came along he stopped two yards away, staring, his mouth a tight disapproving line before he spoke.

'Is there a reason for this, Spender?'

'For what, sir?'

'The way you look.'

'It's part of my cover,' Spender said, without blinking. 'Looking like a jumped-up bank clerk wouldn't get me anywhere,' he added, with the merest up-and-down glance at Gillespie's immaculate grey suit and Crombie overcoat.

'I've a meeting with Sir Reginald Monkton and a quorum of the Regional Police Authority in twenty minutes,' Gillespie said. 'Can we walk? I hate standing still in a breeze.'

They began to stroll, looking more like strangers incidentally taking the same route than men who were together. The appearance of detachment was enhanced by Gillespie's ability to talk with a minimum of lip movement.

'A girl died out on the streets in the early hours of this morning. Mary Louise Maxwell, a schoolgirl. A mobile patrol spotted her lying on the pavement near the bus station on Pilgrim Street. Mary was two months off her sixteenth birthday. An interim blood analysis shows she was poisoned by what the lab calls contaminated cocaine alkaloids.'

Spender stared straight ahead, taking the news in silence. He could feel Gillespie looking at him.

'That makes three deaths from the same apparent cause in a space of seven weeks. What do I tell the men from the Authority, Spender? That you've been on the case for more than a month and haven't got anywhere yet? That you don't know which way to move? Or maybe I should tell them you have your own system, and we should wait until a few more deaths have piled up and you've really got some material to work on.'

'That's not fair,' Spender said.

'Then give me an alternative scenario.'

'I'm in touch with one of the major pushers in our area,' Spender said, addressing the air above Gillespie's head. 'He's Teddy Ballantine, a freelancer who does business with a lot of suppliers. I've got reason to believe he deals directly with whoever concocts the poisonous batches of coke and smack that are leaking on to the street. I've passed myself off as a user to Ballantine and his people. Now, as well as being a punter, I'm one of their trusted part-time couriers. That puts me in a position where soon, I hope, I'll find out who the chemist is and finger him for you.'

'All that aside,' Gillespie said, his teeth hardly parting, 'you've really got nothing, have you?'

'Not yet. But I'm making progress.'

'Progress, you call it? We've had another death, and as yet you don't know the name of the perpetrator or even what he looks like. In the eyes of Sir Reginald and the other inquisitors from the Authority – not to mention any sane individual who can put two and two together – you've made damn all progress at all.'

'I'm doing the very best I can,' Spender said, his voice rising. 'If the gentlemen of the Authority think they can do any better, they're welcome to get off their fat arses and have a go.'

'That kind of talk is entirely counter-productive.'

'So is a load of bollocks about me making no progress, when I'm doing everything I can as fast as I can, without raising the villains' suspicions.'

'I'll ignore the insubordination.' Gillespie touched the neatly centred knot of his tie. He glanced up and down the river, sighing. 'In the absence of any headway to report, maybe you could prime me on what you know about this stuff we're trying to eliminate from the market. What makes it different from the other drugs?'

'It's been cut,' Spender said. 'Adulterated to make it go further and push up the peddler's profit . . .'

'That's hardly anything new.'

'No, except in this case batches of cocaine and crack have been found with traces of what our analytical bods call creative adulteration. The peddler's chemist—'

'So-called.'

'So-called, is a bit of a smart arse, or he thinks he is. He's cutting the coke with a cheaper drug called dipipanone, to cover the fact that there's been any adulteration at all. What he's done is make the coke and crack a lot more toxic than they were before. Worse still, he's added baking powder to the mix.'

'What does that do?'

'It's used now and then in the manufacture of crack—'

'While you're in that area,' Gillespie interrupted, 'and in case I'm asked, could you just crash-course me on what crack is and how it's put together, kind of thing . . .'

Spender nodded patiently. He was beyond the stage where the comprehensive ignorance of senior officers upset him. It was now something he accepted as inevitable.

'Crack is the street name for an almost pure form of cocaine,' he said. 'It's made from a solution of cocaine hydrochloride dissolved in water, with ammonia added and sometimes baking soda. The upshot is an alkaloidal form of the cocaine – do you want me to go into alkaloids, sir?'

Gillespie shook his head sharply.

'Well,' Spender went on, 'because the drug made from the process is not destroyed by heat, it can be smoked.'

'So what's the purpose of the baking powder?'

'Some people believe it's an accelerator – it gives the user a faster hit. But it intensifies the poisonous effect. According to our analysts.'

Gillespie was nodding. 'That gives me something, I suppose. A bit of a smoke-screen to soften the edges of the facts.' He stopped walking. Spender went on a few yards and did the same. 'Tell me straight,' Gillespie said. 'Have you any idea when you might get this bastard in the crosshairs?'

'These things take as long as they take, sir. There's no sense trying to force matters where drug people are concerned. They're mostly paranoid – they've got whole branches of their nervous systems tuned to catch false moves.'

'Even so, I want you to bear the urgency in mind. And remember the monstrosity of this business – the latest victim was no more than a child.'

'I'm hardly likely to forget it,' Spender said. 'I've got a daughter the same age.'

Gillespie looked at his watch, muttered something about keeping in touch, then turned and walked away. Spender stayed where he was for a few moments, watching the grey-brown water flow past, hearing the keening gulls. Finally he moved off, picturing his daughters with a sudden rush of warmth.

3

A sea wind blew in across the mouth of the Tyne, buffeting the slope where Dan Boyd stood, feet spread, facing south to keep the spray from his eyes. A few yards away Spender stared out at the North Sea, his coat collar turned up around his ears, his hair swirling across his face.

'This is taking caution a bit far, isn't it?' Dan yelled against the blast. 'First thing on a Monday I like to ease myself into the routine. Cup of coffee, warm office, you know?' He flailed his arms against his sides for a minute, like a man on a ski slope. 'I can see the point of staying away from the centre of the city – but here?'

'I fancied the drive,' Spender called back.

He pointed to a sheltered strip beneath them, cut into the leeward side of a jagged outcrop. They took the slope cautiously, Spender in front with Dan close behind, down on to the narrow, slippery platform. There was room for them to stand side by side if they put their backs to the rock. The abrupt absence of wind down there made the air seem warm; the drop in noise was like a vast engine being muffled. Dan passed his hand across his bald scalp and shook water from his fingers.

'Can't imagine what I liked about the seaside

when I was a kid,' he said. 'I used to dream about the annual bucket-and-spade trips for weeks ahead of time.'

'It was ships that got me,' Spender said. 'I only had to see them when I was a lad and I'd start dreaming about faraway places. Ships were magical, they were the nearest we ever came to smelling real adventure. You could look at the scabby paint on them and think, That's been to strange and dangerous ports, it's been round the world.'

'Nothing as exciting as ships, when you're a nipper,' Dan agreed.

'They all had exotic names on them, didn't they? And flags from countries straight out the story books.' Spender shook his head slowly, pointing towards the old ferry, halfway between North and South Shields. 'That's about all the traffic there is, now. That and the occasional coal barge.'

Dan was wiping his face with his handkerchief, nodding absently, shivering. 'On the topic of childhood,' he said, 'I suppose you've been briefed about the girl who died, have you?'

'Marginally. Did she have any previous?'

'Nothing official, although a couple of the WPCs knew her and they'd had occasion to warn her once or twice about the rowdy company she was keeping. She hung around with a largish crowd, no particular slant to them, but definitely a pattern of drug-taking under the surface. She was seen less than an hour before she died, talking to a man her friends know as Shanko. He's an elusive one, the drug squad have only ever heard of him, they don't even have a proper ID profile.

One of the kids we spoke to, a girl, said Shanko once told her he makes up the coke deals himself, out of stuff he imports directly.'

'An independent?' Spender frowned. 'He'd have a bit of a job keeping it all under his own umbrella. I mean, think about it – one man doing the buying, processing, packaging and peddling . . .' Spender wrinkled his nose. 'It's not likely. Have you got a description of him?'

'Caucasian, mid-twenties, short bleached hair, likes expensive clothes and has a thing about finger rings – wears lots of them and keeps changing the display – silver one day, gold the next, a mix of both the day after.' Dan dug his hands in his pockets and shrugged. 'Chances are he's nothing at all, of course—'

'Or he could be our chemist.'

'We can always hope.'

'I'll have a nose around.' Spender squared his shoulders against the rock. 'Meantime, in the interests of variety, tell me what you know about Jude's People.'

Dan did a quick eye-roll. 'That bunch. They're a Grade One pain in the bum,' he said flatly. 'They're animal liberationists, as you probably know. The local membership, about a hundred of them, are mostly young people. The movement's recorded history is clean, really. By policy they're peaceful types, passive resisters on principle, you know? But somehow or another, in recent times . . .'

'They've found themselves infiltrated by militants. Is that what you reckon?'

'I suppose so. They've turned kind of loud and

they've found their way on to our books, but we haven't given any of them a pull yet.'

'How come?'

'Lack of evidence.'

'So what are they supposed to have done?'

'We've got them down as implicated in three, arguably four, cases of arson in the last eighteen months – a pet-food cannery, a cosmetic manufacturer, a product-testing station, that kind of stuff. And they were definitely behind a raid on a private virology lab at Ashington, even though we could prove nothing. It was very nasty, that one. They let more than fifty animals go and about half of them were infected, two with anthrax.'

'How do they avoid getting caught?'

'No special technique. They make phone threats and if people don't respond, then the threats get carried out. Their basic guerrilla tactics are good. That and a bit of luck are all they need. So far they haven't left anything behind to incriminate them. The feeling is that we'll catch them eventually, if they keep it up. It's only a matter of time till somebody makes a slip.'

'Only a matter of time until somebody gets seriously hurt *before* they're caught.'

'Why the interest in them, anyway? Have they a connection with the trade in wild birds?'

'Well no, hardly that. Jude's People came up as a distraction. *A tangential line of enquiry*, as our Mr Gillespie would put it. Get me a print-out on what you have on them, will you?'

Dan made a note, then looked up. 'Any repercussions after that kid saw us together on Friday?'

'None. I put myself about a bit on Saturday night, all the usual haunts, but the drug squad's been doing the rounds. None of the faces were about.'

'So you've been having a quiet time. Unusual, for you.'

'I've kept busy,' Spender said. 'Saturday morning and most of yesterday I was out with the binoculars, eyeballing the gentry at play. I saw a bit of sport but nothing involving game birds.'

Dan said there had been an update on the record of wild birds sold locally. He fumbled in his raincoat pocket and took out a slip of paper.

'Two more. The teenage son of a wealthy farmer from Romaldkirk bought a young male peregrine. Paid eight hundred and fifty quid for it.'

'And I told Frances our pair get too much pocket money.'

'Eighteenth-birthday cash, apparently.'

Spender sniffed. 'I got a bloody pullover for mine.'

Dan explained how the boy's father had lost his temper when he found out. He confiscated the bird and reported the incident to the local police.

'Seems the lad was approached by phone after he'd talked to mates in the local about wanting a hunting falcon of his own. He was offered a choice – peregrines, kestrels, kites, all sorts. The bird he bought was delivered by a man with a black, high-sided van—'

'Same as the two cases last month.'

'Right, and the description of the vendor matches what we already have on file – tall, very fair hair, tattooed with daggers on both forearms and doesn't look directly at people when he addresses them.'

'What's the other one?'

'A sale made at Gateshead last week. Three sparrowhawk chicks. An off-duty nurse, who happens to be a member of the RSPB, saw the transaction take place in the reading-room of the public library, would you believe. A shoe box was put down beside the buyer, he handed over a wad of notes and the vendor – useless description, I'm afraid – took off. A minute later the woman heard the unmistakable sound of cheeping chicks and decided to alert the gendarmes. I don't suppose anybody else would have bothered.'

'What had the buyer to say for himself?'

'Swore blind he found the box lying on the table in the library. A search at his home revealed a small aviary in the garden with a pair of kestrels inside, trained and pretty vicious. Unregistered, of course. The man finally admitted he's a hunter and was keen to have a go with sparrowhawks. Said he answered an advertisement for the chicks.'

'But unfortunately he can't recall where he saw the advert . . .'

'Right. Forgets the address, too, and won't consider changing his story or even adapting it a bit.'

'Get me his details.'

As Dan made another note it began to rain. He put away his notebook and buttoned his coat right up to the throat. He glanced at Spender and noticed he was smiling.

'What's so amusing?'

'You are. You absolutely hated the idea of coming out here this morning, but you came anyway.'

'So?'

'You came even though it meant begging-off Mr Gillespie's departmental policy chinwag, which must have meant you losing a couple of class points.'

'What are you getting at?'

'I'm thinking you've more exciting stuff to tell me than the news about the bird sales – you'd have been happy to give me that kind of thing over the phone. There's something you definitely want to tell me face to face, isn't there?'

'Very astute, I must say . . .' Dan glanced at his feet and looked up at Spender again. He tried for a self-dismissing grin, but it didn't surface. Like any other cop, he hated being second-guessed. 'You're intuitively very smart, Spender. I'll give you that. But you should know this – it's an irritating trait. Nobody likes cheeky kids, or clever-clever ones.'

'I don't need people to like me, Dan. If it annoys you that sometimes I see through you, and other times I see through people you *don't* see through, remember what I told you a while back – I'm different from you, I'm half crook.' Spender held out a hand, palm up, testing the rain. 'I think we should go back to my car, or your car, before we tackle any remaining business.'

They clambered up the windy slope and dashed back to where the cars were parked. Opting for the Cosworth, they settled themselves in the front and sat in silence for a minute, watching raindrops explode on the windscreen.

'Are you going to tell me, then?' Spender said finally.

'Well, there is something, as a matter of fact . . .'

Dan cleared his throat primly. 'The whole up-and-down of it is, I think I got a possible source of supply on the wild bird thing.'

'Really?'

'Yesterday afternoon I was at a loose end, the Yellow Pages were lying there on the kitchen window, so I thought I'd make a few more calls. The second one was it. A breeder called Malcolm Heskett, out Consett way. I told him what I was after – a peregrine, I said, for hunting purposes. I made out I'd no idea how to go about it. Said I was badly in need of advice and guidance.'

'He bought that?'

'He was a bit cagey to start – pardon the word-play. But I think he finally believed he was dealing with somebody that really did want a bird. So suddenly I'm getting a pep talk and he's telling me how I don't want to go wasting my time with waiting lists and traipsing through all the rigmarole of paper-work and veterinary regulations that are necessary when birds are bought through registered channels. No sir, he told me, no need at all, especially when birds just as good and at competitive prices can be bought from this friend of his.'

'You got an address?'

'He gave me a number to call. After six, Monday to Friday, all day Saturday and Sunday. He emphasized I had to mention his name.'

'He likely fancies he's a judge of character, Dan. He'll front for the illegal vendors, and collect a bit of thank-you money on every referral that goes through to a sale.' Spender winked. 'They'll maybe not thank him for this one.'

Dan gave Spender the number and promised he would deliver the other stuff he wanted to Keith's shop before the end of the day. Business over, Dan got out and went to his own car.

Spender called a London number on the mobile. When a woman answered he gave her his Home Office clearance and asked for a name and address to tack to the number Dan had given him. It took less than a minute.

'The name is Adam Saddler,' the operator announced crisply, 'and the address is Moor Crest, Dovehill, Ebchester, County Durham.'

'Many thanks.'

He entered the details in his notebook and started the car. For a couple of minutes he stayed there, watching the sea, letting the thrum of the engine soothe a raw upsurge of memory.

He heard a small, inadvertent groan deep in his throat. It was not here that his brother had drowned, but the actual spot, further along the Northumbrian coast, was very much like this. The memory was painfully fresh.

It happened at a time when Spender had been in the Met only a short time, but even so he had begun to lose touch with his brother, Peter, and with his friends. So he had made a flying visit and it turned into a fine reunion, better than anything they could have planned. They had driven to the beach, played football and drank a lot, probably too much.

The sea always reminded him of Peter now. It was one of the unavoidable associations – the sea was where his brother's life had gone, that gleeful day that had turned suddenly into a nightmare. The memory hurt, but when it came Spender always bore it, like an act of penance for something important he had left undone.

Separating himself from the others, he had gone off for a walk along the beach, glad and sad to be there, using the solitude to gather his thoughts. Then they were calling him, and from the sound of it he knew something was wrong. When he ran back it had happened, it was over. Peter, somehow, had drowned.

Nowadays the sight and sound of the sea helped unlock things in Spender, pent-up things, none with names, none he could analyse even if he had wanted to. Whatever sense he possessed of the eternal, he could be in touch with it here.

He closed his eyes for a long moment and listened to the crashing surf. A minute later he was all business, gunning the engine, swinging the car round towards Newcastle and towards duty, whatever shape it would take today.

Even when Jeremy Fuller was alone he was conscious of how he looked. He believed, though he was careful never to preach the point, that seventy per cent of a man's potency came from the way he looked and how he carried himself. The rest was brain and delivery.

At the hall mirror he adjusted the collar of his Gianfranco Ferre cotton shirt. He flicked the wing of brown hair higher on his forehead. Once, years ago, someone had told Jeremy he looked like the young Terence Stamp. To this day he tried to maintain the resemblance.

He stepped back a couple of feet to gauge the effect: cool was how he read it, the blue eyes steady, incapable of surprise or panic, the firm mouth abetting the impression. Carefully husbanded stubble added the necessary earthiness, the mark of an activist.

As Jeremy stood there a tall, dark shadow fell across the front-door glass; a second later the bell rang. Jeremy glanced at the mirror again and adjusted the hanging end of his snakeskin belt. He went to the door and opened it.

'Yes?'

He disliked the look of his caller immediately. The eyes did it. They put Jeremy straight on the defensive. Eyes like that could look past what you were saying. The mouth was judgemental, set to deliver verdicts. In that facial setting the Byronic hair and the ear-ring added paradox. Jeremy hated paradox, or anything else that made him unsure of himself.

'Mr Fuller?' Spender came forward a fraction, making Jeremy step back into the hall. 'I just stopped by to have a private word.'

'About what?'

'It's to do with a fire and a bit of smoke damage in a storage building belonging to a butcher called Gilbert Easton. It happened on Friday afternoon. You know the incident I'm talking about, don't you?'

Jeremy shook his head, blinking coolly. 'Why should I know anything about it?'

'You don't deny you were in the vicinity of the premises at the time the fire started?'

'Who says I was?'

'A witness.'

'Does he have a name?'

'Of course he has.' Spender smiled with one side of his mouth. 'His name's of no importance to you.'

'So what's *your* name, friend?' He disliked it when members of the herd tried to act smart at his expense.

'My name isn't important, either . . .'

'Right.' Jeremy stuck out his arm, pointing at the street behind Spender. 'Since we've no basis for communication, just turn round and fuck off – OK?'

'I think you should listen—'

'I'm too busy to waste time playing silly buggers! I want you off my doorstep. Now.'

Spender continued to stare. Jeremy swallowed hard and wet his lips.

'The witness says you had a car with you on Friday. A ten-year-old Audi CD, dark green, in good condition. He got the number, of course.'

'I think your witness, as you call him, is just blowing through a hole in his neck, Mr Whoever-you-are. And even if I had been where he says, when he says, so what? How am I involved?'

'Well . . .'

'Listen, I was in a restaurant one day when there was an explosion in the kitchen, hell of a blast, took out half the wall. Now tell me, was my presence there enough to implicate me in the incident?'

'Not at all, no—'

'Right. And tell me this – why the fuck am I

bothering to waste more breath on you? It's not as if you're the police or anything.'

'I'm here,' Spender said, 'to have a few words with you about the fire I mentioned, because I happen to believe you had something to do with it – in fact I believe the sabotage was your idea and was executed by you and an associate.'

Jeremy stood shaking his head, hands on hips.

'Christ,' he drawled, 'you take a lot on yourself, I must say. I think you should just go away like I said, friend. Before I call the men with the funny hats.'

To Jeremy's surprise Spender took a long step forward that brought him into the hallway. Before Jeremy could regain his stance Spender grabbed him by the shirtfront.

'While we're in the house here with no witnesses, we'll play this your way, Mr Fuller – the small-time terrorist way. You're a fighter for animals' rights, or so you claim. Think of me as a fighter for the rights of honest human beings that get picked on by arseholes like you.'

Jeremy began to tremble. Beneath his anxiety he felt mad at himself for doing it.

'You've every democratic right to swing your arms,' Spender said. 'But your freedom to swing them stops where the next fella's nose begins.'

He did a half-turn to the left, swinging Jeremy with him and pinning him against the wall.

'What I've got on you is circumstantial, you're smart enough to know that. But if I decide to make this *really* personal, the way I feel like doing, it won't matter if I don't have a case to take to the law, for I'll not be bringing them into it.'

Spender let that soak in. The only sound in the hallway was from Jeremy, breathing through his mouth.

'How about it, Mr Fuller? How about laying off the soft quarry? You know who I mean, the folk that frighten easy and aren't geared to fighting back.'

'How about animals that can't fight back?' Jeremy spluttered.

'Point taken,' Spender said quietly. 'But scaring a soft target shitless doesn't change anything for the better, does it?'

Spender let go of the front of Jeremy's shirt. He took a step back, stared at him steadfastly, then turned and strode out of the house.

On the street he walked steadily without hurrying or looking back. At the corner he turned right, crossed the road and unlocked the Cosworth. He got in behind the wheel and started the engine.

'And life goes on regardless,' he murmured, pulling away from the kerb.

Until he laid eyes on Jeremy Fuller he hadn't known what tack he would take, since that had depended on the kind of man he would encounter. Jeremy was a surprise. He was a lot further up the effete end of the scale than Spender had expected, and it had taken no effort to unsettle him. The real surprise, he supposed, was that intelligent people with serious concerns allowed a man like that to be their leader. On the other hand, Spender's general impression of leaders and the led suggested the situation was hardly unique.

The confrontation with Fuller, on balance, had cured nothing. It hadn't been intended to. Jeremy had simply been shaken up and rendered less sure of himself, less presumptuous about his immunity from harm. Spender's best hope was that from now on, whenever an easy target presented itself, Jude's People would think twice before going on the offensive.

He drove past a hoarding with a picture of two leaping dolphins and the slogan, STOP THE SLAUGHTER OF OUR FRIENDS. He thought of Laura and wondered how she would have reacted to his behaviour at Jeremy Fuller's house.

There was nothing to wonder about. Laura would despise him for leaning on an animal liberationist – even a fart like Jeremy Fuller. Spender could picture how she would scowl at him if she ever found out. He had seen the disdain in her eyes last time he had sat in with her and her sister; when she talked about people who mistreated animals or took them too much for granted, she looked like she was discussing characters too vile to be allowed breathing space in civilized society.

Well, tough, he thought; if that was the way it was, he could do nothing to change it. He couldn't do this job and expect to be smothered with love and acceptance. He began humming as he threaded the car through the traffic, trying to put Laura's petulant scowl from his mind.

4

The week passed in a succession of false starts and missed opportunities. The Durham telephone number supplied by Dan rang out evening after evening with no reply. The drug scene, untypically, remained quiet, with only the dross of small-time dealers and a drift of hollow-eyed users hanging out in the cafés, pubs, clubs and parks that made up the market place. Spender found himself with enough slack in his schedule to back-track on old dead-ends and revise his list of official cases remaining unsolved. Glancing contact with day-to-day policing gave him a sense of proportion.

On Saturday at noon, following the strenuous ritual of his workout, he met Dan outside a small gym he used on the southern outskirts of the city. They walked slowly along the quiet streets towards the place where Dan had left his car, using the time and the relative privacy to make a review of case notes. As they parted company – Dan resplendent in sports jacket, crested tie and flannels, ready for a church fête in the company of Doris, his wife – Spender told him that he was determined the bird-traffic case wouldn't find its way on to the shelf, like too many cases did, just because clues were scarce.

'If I've to work on it round the clock until something turns up, then I'll do it.'

'I hope it doesn't come to that,' Dan said. 'I'm only sorry the lead I gave you turned out to be a dummy. I really had the feeling I was on to something with that number.'

'Maybe it's kosher even so, Dan. If I get no luck with it today or tomorrow I'll take a trip down Durham way and have a look for myself. Cautious like, a little bit of a recce, just to see how the land lies.'

'Best of luck.' Dan slapped Spender's arm. 'Have a nice weekend.'

'And you, Dan. Don't overdo the coconut shies or the home-made toffee.'

Dan crossed the road and got into his car. He was fitting the key in the ignition when somebody rapped the window. He wound it down and poked his head out. The round, fixedly jovial face of DC Kenneth Harrison beamed down at him.

'Nice to know you sometimes venture out where the CID riff-raff have to earn their crust.' Disconcertingly, Harrison's smile widened. 'On a Saturday, too. Surely you can't be working? I thought you were a five-day-a-week man.'

The cheery effect, Dan knew, was strictly an illusion. Harrison had the looks of a genial uncle or a jolly older brother, the kind of face and deportment that were typecast in a lot of PG films. The truth was wide of the appearance. An unwholesomely large part of Harrison's waking life was taken up with vindictiveness and professional jealousy. He was a profoundly unstable man who wrote impeccable reports and therefore had no difficulty holding on to his job. In the view of Dan Boyd, he was less equipped for the moral and emotional complexities of police work than the average cat burglar.

'I work Saturdays,' Dan said, holding on to his own smile, 'because it gets harder and harder to delegate. I just don't have the quality of support, Ken. You should realize that, since you're a major part of the problem.'

Harrison's eyes narrowed a fraction. He steadied his bulk with a hand on the side of the car and hunkered down by the window. When he spoke he exhaled a musty scent that Dan equated with chicken soup.

'I'd have thought you had all the help you needed, Sarge.'

'Meaning?'

'Rumour has it you're in cahoots with Freddie Spender . . . Is he still on the force, or what? He was with the Met, I know that much, and while he was there he was made up to detective sergeant. But then there was some stink about him dropping his oppo in it – another DS, wasn't it? Got his head bashed in with a wheel jack, had to be invalided out. They reckoned it was Spender to blame.'

'Who reckoned?' Dan snapped.

'Well . . .' Harrison shrugged. 'It's what I heard, right? I mean you can usually rely on a rumour that persists—'

'Bullshit!'

Harrison stared. Dan had turned very red. He was gripping the edge of the window to pull himself round.

'You're a bucket-mouth, Harrison!'

'Steady on, Sarge, I was only repeating what—'

'You were only perpetuating a calumny, lad, that's what you were doing.' Dan drew his head further through the opening. 'You're tragically typical of the muck-raking element, Harrison. You're one of the crowd that would sooner hear bad about a person than hear anything at all – especially when the person in question could out-police you with two broken legs and his hands tied behind his back.'

Harrison was trying to recover his grin, which had faded during Dan's onslaught.

'I don't know why you're taking this so seriously.'

'For the record,' Dan said, 'DS Spender was on a stakeout at a building site with DS Colin Driver when a robbery began to take place. The villains were team-handed and Spender called for backup. His mobile failed to connect. He left DS Driver in position while he went to use a pay phone. It's worth emphasizing that Driver himself agrees Spender told him to stay put until reinforcements arrived. If anyone was at fault in what ensued it was Driver himself, and he paid dearly for it.'

'Well fine,' Harrison muttered, 'OK . . .'

Dan put a stiff forefinger through the window and wagged it. 'Spender was absolutely in the clear. That's official. Now that you know it, I've every reason to land on you with both heels if I hear you've been at it again, further disseminating the slander you just tried out on me.'

Harrison stood up, no longer trying to look bright. He glared down at Dan.

'So what is Spender now, then? He's not on the official strength at the station . . .'

'He's nothing you need worry about.'

'Home Office, is he? Something like that?'

'Why don't you mind your own business, Harrison? You never know, the novelty might grow on you.'

Dan turned away and started the engine. As he nosed the car into the traffic he could see Harrison still standing there, watching him. It was a sight of which Dan had grown heartily sick over the years, a peevish, sick-looking plodder, harbouring one more grudge.

It would be nice, Dan thought, to know as much as some people thought he did. People like the obnoxious Ken Harrison, the kind who thrived on poisonous gossip and pined for want of it. Harrison no doubt believed Dan was in on the ground floor where Spender was concerned, fully clued-up on every aspect. The fact was, Dan knew very little. Following the attack on DS Driver, Spender's superiors in London decided it might be a good idea for him to get off the patch for a while. Spender had been reluctant, but he had finally come back up north, assigned to a case that needed initiative and a face unknown to the local villains. He had stayed to tackle more assignments and now he showed no sign of leaving. Not yet.

As to the precise nature of Spender the man, and the extent and limits of his authority, Dan could only guess. All he knew was that Spender, a lad with a degree of intellect and savvy not usually associated with fitness freaks, clearly knew a hell of a lot more than he ever acknowledged, paid little more than token allegiance to visible authority – particularly DCS Gillespie's – and could call on high-tech gear and a clutch of information services that Dan would have taken a drop in pay to access.

Eat your heart out, Harrison, he thought, pulling up at the traffic lights. And pray you never step on Spender's toes . . .

Ten yards from the door of a vegetarian café called The Happy Carrot, Spender stopped in his tracks and stared. He didn't even take the precaution of concealing himself first. At the door of the café Stick was standing with his arms around an attractive blonde girl. His face was very close to hers.

For no more than a second, Spender wondered if it would be in order to rescue the girl; the tableau was so odd, so unexpected. But it was perfectly clear that nothing was amiss, she wasn't resisting. Spender moved nearer, shaking open his newspaper and getting behind it as he walked. Passing the doorway he heard Stick clearly.

'I'd stop for the afternoon, pet, but there's business to attend to. Don't fret though, I'll pick you up in plenty of time for the meeting tonight. See you at seven.'

Spender glanced at them. They were kissing. Astounded he walked on as far as the corner and stopped. He waited, still behind the newspaper, until Stick drew level.

'Hey, Casanova.'

Stick stopped, came a couple of steps nearer, then grinned.

'Howway!' he said cheerfully. 'Stakeout, is it? Hoping to nab some big-time bookies' runners?'

'I just witnessed something I find hard to believe.' Spender folded the newspaper and stuck it in his pocket. They started walking. 'You were less than a yard away from a respectable-looking young woman, facing her, and she wasn't howling bloody murder for a polis.'

'Oh aye.'

'More amazing still, she was letting you *kiss* her – without a tetanus jab, for all I know.'

'That was Donna,' Stick said, with the merest husk of throaty pride. 'She's a mate of Keith's new lass, Dory. She works in The Happy Carrot there – well, she's a part owner, actually. It's run by a collective, six of them.'

'So you've taken up with a businesswoman.' Spender shook his head. 'I'm living through wondrous times, right enough . . .'

'I met her on Tuesday night. Dory introduced us in the pub. I've tried twice to tell you about her, but first time you were asleep and I didn't realize it, second time you were too wrapped up with momentous police matters to listen to an old mate.'

'So you're serious about her, are you?'

Stick nodded.

'And she's serious about you?'

'You saw us, didn't you?'

'Has she got something wrong with her, or what?'

'Sarcastic bastard. Mind you, I suppose a bit of hard feeling's in order, you being the only one of the lads I can think of with no bird.'

'You certainly know how to hurt a bloke,'

Spender sighed. He nudged Stick sharply. 'Give us the dirt, then. Is she single? Married? Ex-married? Any interesting tattoos?'

'She's a cracking lass,' Stick said, and his tone became more serious. 'Best thing ever happened to me, I reckon. She's even got me changing my habits after less than five days, and I'm actually liking it.'

'What habits?'

'Mainly the way I eat, and the way I think about certain things. You can laugh if you like, but that young lady's got a mind on her like a knife. Cuts straight through all the bollocks and gets right to the truth. Does a lot of public speaking, you know. She's talking at a meeting tonight. You should come, you'll learn something.'

'What's the meeting in aid of?'

'Animal rights. Dory's speaking too. Keith's coming along. Try and make it. You'll be among mates, even if you'll be the only one without a woman.'

Later, coming out of the Metro station at the Monument, Spender had a leaflet thrust into his hand by a young woman whose hair smelled disconcertingly of flowers. He had walked on a few yards before he remembered he was holding the leaflet. It was printed on green paper with the name JUDE'S PEOPLE along the top and their shepherd's-crook symbol underneath. A meeting would be held tonight at the Civic Centre, it said, and a number of speakers would take part. The public were welcome to come along and listen, and to take part in the question-and-answer session afterwards. Admission was free: there would be a silver collection.

Spender contemplated a few ludicrous episodes from a possible future. He saw Keith being led away from an animal rights demonstration, handcuffed, hobbling pitifully on his stick. Then there was Stick, pro-fox slogans painted on his naked chest and back, causing untold disruption at a Sunday-morning hunt.

It made for comic speculation, Spender acknowledged, but the satire wasn't too far from what was likely. Not that he wanted to be a wet blanket and go warning the lads about the kind of female company they were keeping. He had no right to do that. The thing he should do, honourably, was stand back, say nothing, and hope they would proceed without harm.

'Brycie. Hey, Brycie.'

Spender took a second to react. Brycie was him, it was his alias on the drug scene. Letting his face go vacant he turned, searching slow-eyed for the source of the call. From the corner of his eye he saw pinch-faced little Mickey Lawton. He pretended to miss him.

'Over here.' Mickey was leaning on a railing, staring at Spender with his steady, lifeless little eyes. 'I've been looking for you.'

Spender shuffled across. He wasn't entirely in character; his beard was only a day old and he was wearing clean clothes. But he believed he could still hack it; in London he had learned to go from bored cop to spaced-out junkie at a second's notice. It was a matter of *feeling* the part rather than just trying to look it.

'I've not been far away,' he told Mickey. 'I've

been needing some stuff. You lot were the ones that went missing.'

'Mr Ballantine wants a word.' Mickey pushed himself away from the wall. He looked up at Spender, a full foot taller. 'I don't reckon he's pleased with you.'

'Where is he?'

'I'll take you. Come on.'

Mickey led the way into the Metro station again. They travelled to Ilford Road, where Spender waited while Mickey made a phone call. Five minutes later they were picked up in an old station wagon driven by a woman who had yellow-and-green hair, a swollen neck and eyeballs that looked stuck on.

Thyrotoxicosis, Spender thought. She should have been in hospital. But she was a junkie, one of the only sick people who could walk around with illnesses that would flatten anyone normal.

He watched her as she drove. It was as if she were on remote, responding to impulses that came from elsewhere. She took them to a building somewhere at the back of South Gosforth. It looked like a boarded-up row of shops.

For the entire journey Mickey had said nothing. Spender could see he was high, but not so far up he didn't know what was going on. His eyes darted from side to side as he got out of the wagon and walked alongside Spender. He was alert and challenging, suspicious of blank walls. That was coke for you, Spender thought, it burned out nervous systems ten times faster than booze or good old-fashioned stress.

Ballantine was in an office one flight up at

the rear of the block. It was not an opulent room, Spender noted, memorizing details for future reference; nevertheless, it was better than anyone might expect in a rat-shit dump like that.

Mickey stayed in the office only long enough to see Spender seated on a rickety bentwood chair in front of the desk, then he left without a word.

Behind the desk Teddy Ballantine rocked back in his swivel, making the spring creak. He put on a hammy smile.

'Brycie. Nice to see you. I'd nearly forgotten what you looked like. What have you been doing? Who have you been seeing?'

Spender did a shiftless-junkie shrug and averted his eyes.

'You mean you've been nowhere? Doing nothing, seeing nobody? Is that the shit you're handing me?'

Ballantine continued to smile, and as he smiled he went on rocking the chair. He used his shoulders, too, swinging them forward fractionally by turns, working to exude menace. He was a fit-looking man in his early forties, given to wearing unfashionably tight shirts to show off his arms and his pectoral development. Today he wore a yellow polo shirt with the Lacoste alligator on the breast. Ballantine had money, serious money, but his shirt was a cheap fake. No amount of cash could stop him living up to the nickname he had among the halflight hoodlums of Newcastle: to them he was Teddy Tightarse.

'I'm told you were seen a week past on Friday, in a place near the city centre, all cleaned up and looking spruce, talking to a man with an official look about him. Do you remember that, Brycie?'

Spender stared at his fingers, knotted on his lap.

'I'm fucking talking to you.'

'Ah, well . . .' Spender looked up. 'That was Mr Fairbairn.'

'And who's he, exactly?'

'My parole officer.'

Ballantine stared. The chair stopped rocking. 'Explain,' he said.

Spender passed a hand across his mouth, a gesture common among people who were just frightened enough to tell the truth, however awkward it might be.

'It was a while ago he was my parole officer, years back. It was after I was handed this three stretch for theft. It was my second conviction, and the bench took a grim view of it. The place I screwed was a wholesale pharmaceutical warehouse, and they needed to make an example before somebody else got the idea into his head. That's what one of the screws told me after, anyway . . .'

'When did all this happen?'

'Eighty-three. I was put in Durham. Did nineteen months all told. October eighty-three to May eighty-five.'

If Ballantine was in a position to check – and he might just be – he would find that a John Bryce did spend nineteen months in Durham Jail during the specified period.

'So what did the parole officer want with you after all that time?'

'He thinks I'm worth rehabilitating. Been trying to find us a job.'

'And do you want him to find you one?'

Spender shook his head. Ballantine leaned forward and put his forearms on the desk.

'Are you sure, now, that this meeting you had was just about a job? I mean you didn't talk about other things? You weren't encouraged to do a bit of grassing on the side? Like coming up with a few names, venues, dealers, that kind of thing?'

Spender had wondered if the coincidence of the drug squad's recent on-the-ground activity would have struck a paranoid note with Ballantine. It clearly had.

'We just talked about a job. Well *he* talked about it mostly, I didn't say much. He was trying to talk me into going for an interview.' Spender shook his head at the thought. 'I hate things like that. I said I'd go, Tuesday last week it was, but I didn't.'

'And what about Mr Fairbairn? Has he been in touch?'

'No sign of him. I'm staying out of his road, anyway.'

The silence that followed was partly to give Ballantine time to weigh up what had been said, and partly to frighten Spender. It was old stuff, Spender had done it himself quite often. His view these days was that the procedure was counter-productive; now, sitting on the receiving end for once, he was gratified to learn he was right. Silence gives a man time to think. Silence *and isolation* are what put the wind up him.

'I'm not happy about this,' Ballantine said at last. 'Even if you're telling me the truth, I have to face the fact that you're the type that sits in cafés talking with *officials*, for Christ's sake. Men with offices and direct lines to the county courts actually know you, Brycie – they buy you cups of tea. I mean, if you look at it square, I shouldn't really be entrusting the likes of you with my delicate errands, should I?'

'I haven't let you down, Mr Ballantine.' Spender made the effort of speaking up for himself sound strenuous. 'Not once. And whatever happened, I'd never inform on you or anybody else. You can check on that. I've never grassed.'

Ballantine sighed theatrically and Spender knew that nothing was blown. His story had been bought, no matter how much longer Ballantine might want to pretend otherwise.

'If I let you carry on doing courier bits for me, Brycie, I want you to remember it's a big favour. Do you get that?'

'Absolutely, Mr Ballantine.'

'If I'd any sense, you'd be out on your arse. But I'm taking things into account, things other people might not. You've never fucked-up, you've always done just what you were told, and I've not heard a bad word about you, outside of this once, this titting around with the bloody parole officer.' Ballantine held up a warning finger. 'No more of that, understand? If he comes near you, this Fairbairn, tell him to sod off, you don't want to know.'

Spender nodded and touched his mouth again.

'I might have a little job for you on Monday night. Be at Chumley's round about eight o'clock. Somebody'll get in touch if you're wanted.' Ballantine pointed at the door. 'I'll be seeing you. And remember, keep your nose clean.'

Going down the dark stairwell, Spender realized that getting off lightly could be almost a disappointment. He had prepared himself for a serious confrontation with Ballantine, and he had been ready to take a hammering if his story wasn't believed. He had known, too, that an excuse which passed muster could still earn him bruised ribs or a broken arm. Ballantine was a believer in the salutary properties of a good kicking; pain invigorated the memory and ensured that mistakes and errors of judgement didn't happen twice.

Coming out from the gloom on to the street, Spender shielded his eyes from the onrush of light. He simultaneously bumped someone with his elbow.

'Sorry . . .'

Passing on, he heard a swift movement at his back and took his next step sideways. A blow clipped his shoulder and trailed down his arm. He turned and saw a young man regaining his balance.

'I'll make you sorry, arsehole . . .'

Spender saw the right fist coming, but missed the bottle that thudded up into his crotch. Pain flared and he felt his knees give.

The man came at him hard, swinging the bottle shoulder-high. Spender braked his impulse to hit back. This was one of Ballantine's apes, had to be . . .

Through the enveloping nausea he read the face – coked-up, jumpy, ready to risk everything. He memorized it too, the blue, watery, unfocused eyes, the cracked lips, the stubbly off-white hair.

Something hard hit Spender in the chest and he fell back. He felt his shoulder strike the corner of the wall and noted dimly there was no pain. He was hit again, in the stomach this time, and again on the side of the head. There was a harsh ringing in his head and a scuffle somewhere off to the side.

'That's enough, for Christ's sake! Leave him, leave him . . .' Spender dipped down into darkness, taking the tail-end of a girl's ragged, pleading call with him: 'Shanko, for Jesus' sake, come on – will you leave him alone before you bloody kill him . . .'

5

'Since I switched to the new bait,' Stick said, 'I don't get that blown-out feeling any more.' He slapped his stomach with both hands. 'It's great, man. I go about feeling like a soddin' evangelist – I want to tell everybody and get them converted straight away.'

'Well lay off me,' Keith told him. 'I've seen the light already.'

Keith turned to the bar and paid for the two pints and two halves the barman had pulled. As he handed a pint to Stick the door swung open and Spender came in.

'I've got to hand it to him, he's got magnificent timing,' Keith muttered, fishing for more change.

Spender was clean-shaven and smartly dressed, which would have made him stand out in that pub anyway; the dark purple bruise on his left cheek was another attention-getter, together with the limp he tried to disguise as he stepped up to the bar.

'Decided to show your face at last, then,' Keith said, signalling the barman for another pint. 'If I was you, I'd have waited another couple of days.'

It was Monday night. Spender had lain low at the flat since late Saturday, nursing his injuries. Through the panelling of his bedroom door he had promised Stick he would come along to the

Archer's Arms tonight and meet the girls. In spite of the fact that he resembled an ambulant casualty he had obviously taken care over his appearance, and Stick was grateful he had made the effort to get here.

'Glad you made it, mate.'

He slapped Spender's shoulder, a mistake, since beneath the jacket and the shirt, directly under the spot where the hearty palm landed, was a thin dressing covering an area of serious bruising where Spender had come into contact with rough brick.

'Christ almighty,' Spender hissed through his teeth, swinging away from Stick. 'Lay off, will you?'

'All right, all right . . .' Stick stepped back, hands raised defensively. 'Just doing a bit of male bonding. I didn't mean to hurt you.'

'What happened, anyway?' Keith asked, passing Spender his pint. 'Was it a big building that fell on you, or just a bungalow from a great height?'

'It was business.' Spender raised his glass. 'Cheers.'

He took a gulp of beer and savoured it. Normally he could take drink or leave it. He was, on the whole, an indifferent fan of alcohol. Tonight, though, he looked as though he really needed a pint. He took another giant swallow and looked around, smacking his lips.

'Where's these women that have changed your lives so miraculously, then?' he demanded. 'Thought better of it and gone after a couple of real men, have they?'

'They're in the ladies,' Stick said.

All three turned and stared at the door of the women's lavatory.

'Birds always go there in pairs,' Keith observed. 'Funny, that. If men did it there'd be a right buzz of speculation, but with birds it's all right.'

As they watched the door opened. They turned back to the bar at once. When the girls came across Keith made the introductions. Close up, Donna was stunning. She had rich amber eyes and a delicately oval face; her features were even and her hair, fine and golden, gave off the same scent Spender had noticed on the girl handing out leaflets by the Metro. Dory, Keith's girlfriend, was taller, darker haired and noticeably more positive and less delicate in her movements. She had the kind of mouth Spender associated with the word *sybaritic* – devoted to sensuous luxury – but her style suggested that wouldn't be accurate.

'So what line are you in?' she asked Spender, staring pointedly at his bruised cheek.

'I work for the Government.' It was his usual answer, and he followed it with his customarily sharp footwork to get the topic away from himself. 'What's your game, Dory?'

'My whole working life is conservation, the planetary kind.' She said it disarmingly, without a trace of pomposity. 'I'm not aligned with any of the bigger movements – they tend to get too political and lose sight of the real concerns. I like to keep it small. It's not much of a living, but I confess to a small annuity, plus I scrape a wage from journalism, and from giving talks to women's groups and anybody else who'll pay to listen to me. Then of course there's The Happy Carrot. Do you know about that venture?'

'Stick gave me the outline. It's a vegetarian place, right?'

'Right,' Donna chipped in. 'And we follow an adapted form of the Hay diet. *Proper* food-combining. Do you know the system?'

Spender shook his head and admitted he knew nothing about it.

'It's great, man,' Stick told him. 'You should try it. Just look at me – the picture of health, right? Or I'm heading that way, any road. It's all down to good diet. I do most of my eating at The Happy Carrot these days and I'll tell you this, the sense of well-being is cracking.' He slipped his arm around Donna's waist. 'Dr Hay and Donna here have changed my life.'

'Isn't it just sickening?' Dory said. 'His bad eating habits might be cured, but his crappy sentimentality's still intact.'

'I'm told you've a special interest in animal rights,' Spender said.

Dory nodded. 'That's the heart of it all,' she said, and Spender saw Keith squeeze her arm. 'Since I was a little girl, I could never bear to see people take advantage of animals. Now I'm older and I've stuck my nose into all the areas of animal exploitation, I'm one of their champions. I couldn't *not* be, any more.'

Spender narrowed his eyes at her. 'Who's being sentimental now?'

'Not me,' she said. 'Affectionate, loving even, but I'm not sentimental about animals.' She grinned. 'I'd just die for them, that's all.'

'Which reminds me,' Donna said.

She waved to the barman and when he came she asked him something, pointing to a carrier bag she was holding. The barman went away and came back with the landlord. Donna spoke to him, using her smile, and he gave her an avuncular nod.

'OK,' she said, turning back to the group, digging in her bag. She brought out a wad of leaflets and handed half of them to Dory. 'I'll take this side of the room, you take the other.' She beamed momentarily at Stick and kissed the end of his nose. 'I'll be back soon. Try not to forget me while I'm gone.'

'A belter, eh?' Stick said as the girls moved off. He looked at Spender, who was glumly observing two men who had seated themselves at the other end of the bar. 'We'll have to find you a woman. You look like you cured a headache and caught the black death.'

'You're imagining things,' Spender said.

'Cobblers.' Stick appealed to Keith. 'It's right what I say, isn't it? He looks bloody tragic. His glands are drying up from lack of action. He's turning sour.'

'Don't push it, Stick.'

Spender watched Donna approach the pair at the end of the bar and hand each of them a leaflet. The younger one said something to her; Spender could imagine how much it would lack by way of sophistication or subtlety, but it seemed to bounce off Donna and she laughed as she moved on. Spender felt a small relief. The MacIntyre brothers were trouble, and occasionally, depending on how they felt, they would treat even a cordial approach harshly.

'I see the MacIntyres are having a night off from charm school,' Keith said.

'They make me look like class, them two,' Stick muttered. 'That Gerry, he was barred out the Brass Cannon for taking a swing at a bloke in a wheelchair.'

Gerry MacIntyre, the youngest of three brothers, was the nutter of the family. The eldest, George, was in prison serving a five-year sentence for transporting stolen antiques inside cattle carcasses. The family business, a large and lucrative abattoir founded by their late father, was run by the middle brother, Alfie, with less than able support from Gerry.

'I hear they re-applied for membership of the human race,' Keith said. 'Turned down again, of course.'

'While Donna and Dory are busy,' Spender said, 'and if you don't mind suspending this re-run of The Comedians, can either one of you help me out on a small matter? Does the name Shanko ring any bells?'

Keith and Stick looked at each other, then at Spender. They both shook their heads.

'I'm talking about a man in his twenties, bleached hair, blue eyes. He's into flash threads and he wears a lot of rings.' The shapes of a few were printed on Spender's breastbone. 'I need to find this bloke. He could be a link in a handful of murder enquiries. If you pick up anything, let us know, eh?'

Earlier that evening Spender had put on grubby old clothes for his Brycie guise and gone to Chumley's as

Ballantine had told him. It was a sleazy drinking hole on the quayside, one oblong, blue-lit, low-ceilinged room frequented by introverted single men, disaffected married women, downmarket whores and closet junkies, some of them businessmen. The place operated as a lonelyhearts interface and a courier point, know to pushers as Wells Fargo. The closing of deals of any kind on the premises was vigorously discouraged, but body-language soliciting, low-key touting and the transferring of small packages between sender and carrier were permitted activities, so long as discretion was exercised, and on condition that everybody present drank plenty of the vile, overpriced cocktails.

Spender waited and was eventually passed a packet to deliver to a hotel in the city centre. Judging by the size and weight it was a modest cocaine deal, to be left with the man on the door for delivery to yet another Mr Johnson. The kid who passed it to Spender wasn't prepared to talk; he wanted to make the drop and leave, so there was no opportunity for Spender to start a line of conversation that might have been angled to finding out the probable stamping ground of the man called Shanko. Wherever he hung out, it *wasn't* at the place where Spender had been beaten up.

That afternoon, Dan Boyd had the block checked over. He called back to report it had probably been a floating venue, used for a few days then abandoned. It was completely deserted. Even the office Spender had been able to describe was no more than a shell.

'I won't be able to stop long,' Spender told Keith and Stick now, as he gathered their glasses and put them on the bar. 'I've got a bit of business to attend to.'

'At this time of night?' Stick shook his head.

'Well, it passes the time,' Spender sighed. 'Me not having a girlfriend, and so forth . . .' He turned to the bar, tried to catch the barman's eye. While he waited the girls came back and Dory insisted it was her turn to buy a round.

'I won't hear of it,' Spender said.

'Don't you believe in women standing their corner, then?'

'It's my turn, that's all,' he replied, smiling. 'When I'm going to say anything sexist, or chauvinistic or fascist, a little bulb lights up on the top of my head.'

Dory was about to come back at him when there was a shout from the far end of the bar. They turned and looked. It was Gerry MacIntyre, standing on the spar of his stool and waving the leaflet Donna had given him.

'Hoi, you . . .'

'Oh, boy, I think he means you, Donna,' Dory said. 'Who's a lucky girl, then? I'd say you've really scored there . . .'

'You believe this shit that's printed here, darlin'?'

Stick flushed and made to push along the bar past Keith. Spender caught him by the elbow of his jacket and pulled him back.

'Don't go making yourself a martyr, man. Let him shoot his face off. He's a balloon. This is his idea of banter.'

In the meantime Donna had walked calmly forward and stopped a couple of yards from Gerry MacIntyre. She propped her elbow on the bartop.

'Yes, I believe it,' she said. 'And so should you.'

Spender, alert for the first sign of mayhem, was aware of a pause, a gap in Gerry MacIntyre's forward flow as he overcame the small shock of being answered back by someone he didn't impress.

'You're telling me what I should do and shouldn't do, are you?'

Gerry's eyes flicked towards his brother Alfie sitting beside him, like a street thug checking his Rottweiler was awake. The brothers were similarly square-headed and dumb-faced, the type Spender once heard a commander in the Met describe as slow-blinking mouth-breathers. There was a difference between Gerry and Alfie, however; Gerry was precisely the social bear he appeared to be and he was fond of a vendetta, whereas his brother Alfie, a violent man too, rarely played the bully and had never been known to hang on to a grudge for longer than a couple of days.

'I'm simply a person who has taken the time to examine the facts,' Donna said. 'I've arrived at some conclusions and I feel I should share them, because they're based on careful thought and balanced consideration.'

As Donna spoke Gerry MacIntyre made a sour face and waggled his head. His brother did the same.

'Big kids,' Keith muttered. 'They're embarrassed and that's how they cover it. I bet arse-face is wishing he'd kept his mouth shut.'

'I *do* think you should believe what's in that leaflet, and you should act on it,' Donna was saying, ignoring the face-pulling, 'because it offers a humane antidote to some of the casual brutality we all condone, practically without noticing, every day of our lives.'

'And it says here,' Gerry yelled, waving the leaflet again, 'that people should take steps to stop the trade in animals for profit.'

'That's right.'

'Would that include the trade in beasts for meat?'

'In my view it would,' Donna said. 'It's up to the conscience and beliefs of the individual – I'm one of the people who believe animals should be respected and left alone, not tortured and murdered and then eaten by so-called enlightened human beings.'

The clarity of her responses and the out-of-the-ordinary sound of her middle-class voice in that bar was having a quenching effect on Gerry MacIntyre's anger. It was obvious he wanted to get mad and was trying to whip himself up; it was just as clear he couldn't – not when he was being doused with so much civilized charm.

As Donna finished, Gerry's fretting gaze switched to the group she had stepped away from. 'Your pals think the same way, do they?'

'I can't speak for all of them.'

'Well *I'll* speak for me and my brother here.' Gerry stood up on the spar of his stool again. He looked straight at Spender. 'No sheep-shagging animal fanciers better decide they want to interfere with *our* business,' he said. 'Not ever. Anybody damages us, we damage them twice as hard. So the do-fucking-gooders better not get it into their brainy little heads to try anything on with the MacIntyres. Not if they want to go on breathing, got that? Not if they don't want to wind up on a kebab pole.'

Gerry sat down again and snatched up his drink. Donna came back looking bemused. Stick put his arm round her.

'He's roughly one chromosome short of being a pilchard, that one. Who is he?'

Stick explained about the MacIntyres and their abattoir. Donna stopped smiling. She turned and looked at the brothers for a moment, watching them gulp their beer.

'God, think of it,' she said. 'They actually torture and kill animals for a living.' Her tone conveyed the precise weight of the atrocity. Spender could imagine how easily she would hold an audience. She looked at Stick. 'Can you imagine what it must be like, waking up in the morning and realizing you're one of those two?'

Dory was writing something in her diary.

'A note for Jeremy,' she said, winking at Donna.

Spender missed none of it but wouldn't let himself speculate. He finished his drink, ordered a round for the others, then asked to be excused.

'I've an appointment, one I shouldn't break,' he said. 'It was nice meeting you Dory, Donna . . .'

'We've hardly had time to say hello to you,' Donna complained.

'Let him go, love,' Stick said. 'He gets to be a right drag after a while.'

Donna and Dory laughed, and Spender saw Gerry MacIntyre glowering, trying to take it personally. Spender advised his friends to move on to another pub.

'You don't need the strife.'

Keith and Stick promised they would when they had finished the fresh round. Spender left them then, feeling the eyes of the MacIntyre brothers on him all the way to the door.

He drove to Low Fell on the far side of Gateshead and parked the Cosworth two streets away from the address Dan had written down. The terraced house was easy to find from the details supplied by Dan. Spender let himself through the front gate with a minimum of sound. On the top step he heard a laugh-track from behind the lighted curtain. This was always the best time to get people off their guard, when the day was over and they were using TV instead of their brains. He gave the doorbell three sharp prods and squared his shoulders.

The door opened with a rush of warm air and a whiff of furniture polish. A man stood there in shirtsleeves. He was tall and wiry, with not a trace of stubble on his face even so late in the day. An old soldier, Spender guessed.

'Mr Holmes? Derek Holmes?'

He nodded slowly, peering. Spender imagined the reaction. This man had seen a punched face before, who hadn't? What was someone with long hair, an ear-ring and a recently duffed face doing on his doorstep at this hour?

'Sorry about calling so late. I wanted to be sure I caught you in.'

'What's it about, then? If you're selling anything I can save you the trouble now, I never buy at the door.'

'No, I'm not selling, Mr Holmes. Giving away, more like. Replacing, to be accurate.'

Holmes looked deeply suspicious now. 'What are you on about?' He stepped back.

Spender looked left and right, as if somebody might be listening. He narrowed the gap between himself and Mr Holmes again.

'It's about the birds. The sparrowhawk chicks. We heard what happened and we didn't want you to think we were callous about these things.'

Holmes blinked. 'Who are you?'

'I represent the people you bought the birds from. I'm authorized to offer you replacements.'

Holmes lost his remote look. Suddenly he was alert. 'I'd sooner have my money back.'

Spender pretended to think that one over. 'Well . . .' He shrugged. 'I don't suppose there would be any objection to that.'

The start of a smile tugged the ends of Holmes's mouth. 'I'll admit this much, I thought I'd heard the last of you, and my money.'

'We're not villains, sir.' Spender said it with trace of hurt in his tone. 'Far from it.'

'Oh, I didn't mean to imply that, no . . . It's just that I rang a couple of times and got no answer . . .'

'We're people dedicated to seeing certain traditional sports kept alive in this country of ours, no matter what idiot laws our masters pass through parliament.'

'I'm right with you there.' Now it was Holmes who looked from side to side in the darkness. 'Would you like to come in, Mr, ah . . .'

'Gutteridge. No, I won't, thanks all the same.' Spender took out his notebook and appeared to write something in it. 'Just noting that you'd prefer to be reimbursed.'

'Well, I'm very grateful, I must say.'

'We're grateful too, Mr Holmes. You obviously didn't tell how you came by the birds and we appreciate that.' Spender stuffed the notebook back in his pocket and buttoned his coat. 'I'll be off, then. Somebody will either get in touch with you in person, or you'll get your refund in the post. If there's any query, just ring the number you've already got – oh, hang on, you've been getting no answer, right? Maybe you've got the old number, we had it changed not long ago . . .'

Like a dog trained to respond in an exact way to a precise stimulus, Mr Holmes turned away for a moment, fished through scraps of paper lying on the hall table by the telephone, and picked out one. He held it up. Spender had no difficulty reading the thick black numerals. With a small sensation of uplift in his chest, he registered the bonus; there was no need to memorize the number.

'That's the old number, Mr Holmes. Put an eight in place of the four and you've got the new one. OK? We'll be in touch soon. Good night to you.'

Back in the car Spender called Dan at home on the mobile. Without going into detail – it saved time and he enjoyed puzzling Dan – he explained that Holmes had contacted the dealer who sold him the sparrowhawks by using the same number Spender had been trying all last week. So it wasn't a dud and he was more determined than ever to pay a personal visit to the dealer's HQ.

'If you care to turn up at Holmes's house pretending to be a man bringing him a refund for the chicks, which you'll hand over just as soon as he can prove he's the real Mr Holmes, I think you'll have enough for a collar and a solid link with our vendor in Durham.'

'Great stuff,' Dan enthused. 'How did you get all that sorted out so fast?'

'By making myself available to luck,' Spender replied, confident that Dan would dismiss the truth as just so much horse shit.

6

Jesmonde Dene is probably Newcastle's best-loved park. Once it had been no more than a narrow, steep-sided river valley, formed by streams from receding sheets of ice towards the end of the last Ice Age. A number of similar places had been filled in long ago to make way for city development, but Lord William Armstrong, a lawyer turned engineer and industrialist, bought all of Jesmonde Dene in gradual stages and had it laid out as a park. At first the public were charged a small fee to visit, and the funds collected in this way were donated to a local hospital. Later, Armstrong gave the park to the people of Newcastle.

Spender knew the history of the Dene and he liked it; the story-book details fitted the character of the place. He also thought the park a pleasant setting for a clandestine meeting with DCS Gillespie. At that time of year the spot was magnificently green and tranquil – wandering through the woodland Spender found it hard to believe he was actually at the heart of the city. The only thing spoiling the visit was the nagging possibility that he wouldn't be able to find Gillespie.

After half an hour of strolling and recovering forgotten snatches of childhood along the way,

Spender sat down on a rock at the side of a stream. As if that were the move necessary to make the marvel work, Gillespie emerged from the trees twenty yards away.

'You picked a nice day for it,' Spender called.

He tried to read the expression on Gillespie's face as he picked his way over the grassy thickets and rocky mounds. There were no clues; he looked querulous and slightly preoccupied, the way he usually looked.

'Nice places, parks,' he said, when he was close enough to speak without shouting. By the edge of the stream he stopped and carefully wiped the toes of his shoes on the grass. 'They make me feel better.' He drew back his lips, exposing strong teeth. It might have been a smile, Spender couldn't be sure. 'I think there might be a streak of claustrophobia in me. I get the impression my heart beats a lot slower when I'm in a park, or any other open space. Tight interiors and narrow streets make me jumpy.'

It was a rare flash of candour from a man whose reticence about himself amounted to a fixation with secrecy. He eased down on to the rock next to Spender's.

'Pleasant as this is, however, I didn't invite you here for a picnic. We've got a serious problem, and I don't think it's unfair to place responsibility for clearing it up – or trying to clear it up – on your shoulders.'

'Why's that?'

'It's largely your fault the problem exists.'

So what else is new, Spender wondered. He clasped

his hands around his knees and waited.

'I'm being threatened with the incursion of an *ad hoc* drug investigation team,' Gillespie said. 'Have you ever encountered such a beast?'

'Once, sir. In London. A twelve-man unit. They were drawn from teams all over the place, but they all seemed to share a certain, well, togetherness . . .'

'A stiff-backed loyalty to governmental brass. How did you find them? To work with, that is?'

'Intrusive,' Spender said. 'Bulldozing. Offensive and red hot at planting blame. They were total bastards. And they did nothing to clear up the case they took over.'

'From what I've heard elsewhere, I'd say that's probably a balanced evaluation.' Gillespie folded his arms and stared at the water. 'You realize why they're being imposed on us, don't you? Three deaths, drug-related. No traceable line of enquiry unearthed by our own drug squad, and you, having decided in your quasi-autonomous way that you'll take on the investigation as a personal project, have come up with as little as the others.'

'I told you, Mr Gillespie, it takes time.'

'So does an elephant's pregnancy. We don't have time, Spender, not the kind of sit-on-our-butt-and-let-things-develop time you're talking about. The deaths of these young people are a matter for grave concern. We have an emergency here, it's our direct responsibility and it's an emergency in red letters, as in a state of affairs requiring immediate action.'

'Action.' Spender shook his head. 'You'll get that from your *ad hoc* boys, all right. They'll not be in the station five minutes before they're victimizing any poor sod that obstructs them and generally kicking up buggery like a school trip.'

'You paint a vivid picture when you care to.'

'Heads will roll,' Spender said darkly. 'That's a key feature of the action. Government-appointed investigation units generate vacancies. The trick is, they make sure they never leave a situation looking anything like the way they find it. Change equals progress. That's the motto. Bullshit baffles brains.'

'Yes, yes, so I've heard . . .'

'That way they look as if they've achieved something, don't they? It's like running at a big pile of manure and shovelling it all over a nice green lawn. It looks as if a lot's happened, but all you've done is shift the shit.'

'Well, I hope you'll be taking the hazards of the situation seriously,' Gillespie said. 'You're not immune from everything, you know. These people could reshuffle your future.'

'I know that. Where they're concerned I'm as humble a foot soldier as anybody.' Spender looked squarely at Gillespie. 'It's not just lowly heads that roll during these operations, though. Nobody *at all* is safe.'

Gillespie's frown tightened.

'They lost us a deputy commander once,' Spender said. 'One back-stabbing memo to Whitehall was all it took.'

Gillespie stood up and walked along the bank a few paces. He picked up a stone and threw it in the water.

'We've got maybe a week,' he said. 'Probably less. Then they move in.'

'Unless we get lucky.'

'Or smart. And a lot more diligent.'

Spender thought about that.

'I think I resent the implication,' he said. 'I've been *smart* enough to make contact with the hard core of the city's drug-peddling element without them realizing I'm the enemy.' He pointed to the bruise on his face. 'My *diligence* in maintaining said contact got me this, plus some sore ribs and a severely twisted knee. You might not like the pace of events on this enquiry, but I'm the one that's catching the consequences.'

'I can appreciate your point of view, Spender, but—'

'So I'd respectfully suggest you save your criticisms until such time as your arse is in as much jeopardy as mine.'

They fumed silently at each other. Gillespie dug his hands into his pockets and kicked another stone out into the middle of the stream.

'I don't want strangers running my show,' he said flatly. 'Whatever line you're chasing on this case – and I don't expect you to tell me everything – I'd be grateful if you would find some way of speeding it towards a result.' He moved closer to Spender and stood looking down at him. 'I suppose I'm asking it as a favour.'

Spender nodded. 'If I can gee things up I'll be doing us both a favour. I'll try everything I can.' He stood up. 'Sorry if I seemed to be suggesting you're good at covering your arse . . .'

'I am good at it.' Gillespie switched on his smile, flicked it off again. 'I remember too well what happened when I wasn't.'

Later, driving south, Spender did one of his periodic re-thinks. From the first day, his relations with DCS Gillespie had been less than cordial; even so, when he compared the association now with the way it had been in the beginning, he could see progress. Today, Gillespie's admission that he was professionally in a corner, and that he wasn't enjoying it, marked a breakthrough. He was admitting that he was human in spite of all the signs, a man with normal limitations, a normal capacity for anxiety, and a perfectly human tendency to worry over his future.

Spender smiled, remembering Gillespie's uneasiness as he came clean. He had admitted nothing Spender didn't already know, but the admission made all the difference.

As Spender approached Durham he slowed the car and wound down the window. For anyone needing a spiritual lift, he could make no better recommendation than to breathe this air and simultaneously let the eyes be ravished by the scenery.

Inhaling deeply, he thought of Gillespie again and wondered if he had tried this. It just might put some warmth in him for a while, long enough for other people to glimpse the human, vulnerable bloke behind all that ironwork.

The house called Moor Crest was old and rambling, built in the lower sweep of a west-facing hillside with a scatter of outbuildings and two acres of fenced land at the rear. The sandstone ashlar frontage had been darkened by time and weather; a network of cracks and fissures patterned the softer stone around the windows and the entrance to the deep-set porch, enhancing the charm of a place which, a hundred years earlier, must have looked striking in that setting.

From his position in a hedgerow two hundred yards from the house, Spender could see part-way into a high-doored building at right angles to the house and standing partly in its shadow. Using the polarizing ring on his binoculars he was able to cut the glare created by shafts of sunlight across a couple of puzzling vertical surfaces in the dark interior of the building. When he had made the adjustment he turned his head aside from the eye-pieces for a moment, blinked a couple of times and looked again. What had been a mystery before was perfectly clear now. It was the rear end of a black, high-sided van.

Pocketing the binoculars, he lowered his head and pushed his way bodily through the hedge. The field on the far side was soft and undrained, catching at his feet and making him walk unsteadily.

He crossed the field at its narrowest stretch, stepping carefully all the way, but still managing to soak his feet. As he drew near the road separating the farmland from the low front wall of Moor Crest, he tripped on a half-buried tree root and landed face-down in the wet earth.

'Nice one, Spender,' he muttered, getting up and shaking clotted dirt from his jacket and trousers. 'Sketchley's dream come true . . .'

Somebody shouted from the direction of the house. Spender turned. A tall, wide-chested man in a checked shirt and a waistcoat was standing at the gate. That was bad. Spender had wanted to arrive, reconnoitre, and leave again without being seen.

'What are you doing over there?'

Spender went forward, still shaking dirt from himself. He got to the road and stood at the edge, stamping the mud off his shoes.

'I got kind of lost,' he said, pointing back towards the hedgerow. 'I was trying to take a shortcut to Dovehill, as a matter of fact . . .'

'You're a couple of miles out of your way then.' The man pointed to where the road dipped and curved out of sight behind the hillside. He had fair hair, Spender noted, but there was no trace of tattoos on the arms. 'That's the way you want. And I wouldn't try any more shortcuts if I were you. It's all private land round here. Step on any of it and you're trespassing.'

Spender thanked him and started walking, cursing quietly. He had left the Cosworth in a lay-by half a mile down the road from the hedgerow he had pushed his way through. To get back to it with his credibility intact he would have to go right round the corner, get fully out of sight, then double back across open land, keeping to the cover of high ground.

'Just the way I like to spend an afternoon,' he grunted, feeling the mud drying on him.

At the corner he stopped and looked back at the house. There was no sign of the man. Spender took a closer look through the binoculars. Nothing. He stepped smartly across the road and leapt the fence into the thick grass at the bottom of the hill. A few minutes more scouting could at least justify the trip.

Strenuous uphill progress brought him out at a point where he overlooked the back of Moor Crest. From the new vantage he could see two rows of cages with chickenwire fronts, running all the way from the rear of the house to the side of a barn fifty yards away. The binoculars picked up more cages in the barn's shadowy interior. The cages on the outside, he assumed, had legitimate birds in them; he had checked and found that Adam Saddler was a licensed supplier of exotic and semi-exotic breeds.

For a couple of minutes he stayed where he was, listening to the faint sounds of machinery working, straining his eyes to see if anyone was moving in the vicinity of the house or the outbuildings. He noticed there was a low electric fence running around the perimeter of the house and its grounds, and there was a small compound, locked at present, with four big black dogs inside. That would be the night-time security, he presumed.

A hand landed on his shoulder with a thump. He turned and found himself staring into the dour face of the big man with the checked shirt and the waistcoat.

'Shortcut my arse,' he said. 'What's the game, pal?'

'Mr Saddler? Adam Saddler?'

'What about it?'

'You're not answering your phone lately.'

Saddler's jaw slackened the smallest fraction. The

point of the *non sequitur* technique was to buy time, confusing the target with remarks that made sense but were not appropriate to the circumstances. It worked with some people.

'I tried to call,' Spender said. 'Night-time.'

'There's something wrong with the—' Saddler cut himself short. He grabbed Spender by the arm. 'I want to know what you're doing up here.'

'I had a word with Jonathan.' It was the first thing that came to Spender's lips – pure autospeak, which was faster than consulting his head. He was preparing to run and he needed Saddler properly off guard. 'Mad as ever,' he added, realizing the technique wasn't really working with this man.

'Just cut the crap . . .'

With his free hand Saddler drew something from his trouser pocket. Spender glanced down for a second. It was a sap, the real business, flexible with the tell-tale imprint of lead shot under the stitched leather casing.

'Oh dear, Mr Saddler . . .'

Without knowing it, the man had put himself in a position where harming him became a priority instead of a last resort.

'I don't think there's anything more I want to say to you,' Spender said, spreading his feet imperceptibly.

'Sure about that?' The brass glint of thuggery was there, right behind Saddler's eyes, gloaming through the civilized sheen. 'I've got my ways of dealing with trespassers and other awkward bastards . . .'

Saddler adjusted his thumb through the loop in the thong and swung the foot-long instrument out and upward, beginning the curve that would bring it down on the side of Spender's neck. It reached its highest point and flexed with a crack. Spender set his teeth in careful alignment and tensed his neck. As Saddler leaned inward a fraction to bring down the sap Spender's head came forward at speed. The broad front of his skull struck Saddler's nose at the junction with the brow, driving the nasal bone inward and splitting a lachrymal bone.

Saddler jerked back, mouth open and silent. He dropped the sap as his system went into shock and his left eye bulged.

Spender was off and running towards Moor Crest before Saddler hit the ground. At the bottom of the hill he jumped a wall, cleared the electric fence without touching it and ran for the cover of the nearest building. There were two elderly men inside, working at opposite sides of a bench. Spender gave them a thumbs-up and charged on past, out the far door and into the yard again.

To his right was the barn with the cages inside. He ducked down and ran in there, keeping his head below the level of the table tops. When he was sure no-one else was in the building he straightened and looked around.

Forty or fifty cages were set out on long tables and on shelves, each one fitted with a heavy padlock and none of them empty. On a swift scan he recognized an eagle owl, three kestrels, three or four peregrines and a bird with short rounded wings and a reddish barred breast that he believed was a sparrowhawk.

'Bingo,' he whispered, going back to the door and looking out.

The air between the barn and the building he had run through was rich with the smell of wood shavings and something else, linseed oil perhaps, and paint or varnish. Now that he was actually here among the buildings, he could tell from the steady noise that he was at the heart of some kind of small multi-unit enterprise, maybe a factory.

He stepped out into the yard and crossed to a wooden building with a bright light inside. On tiptoe he looked through the tiny window and saw what looked like two identical *chaises-longues* and beyond them a beautiful Victorian sideboard. A man wearing a protective mask was spraying a pair of identical carvers, very new-looking, with something that gave them a dark crackled finish on contact.

Turning away, Spender saw three lengths of thin rope stretched between hooks in the rear wall of the house and poles set in the ground twenty feet away; at roughly six-inch intervals along the ropes small copper hunting horns dangled.

Suddenly it was perfectly clear to him. He ran around the side of the house, setting the dogs barking, and out on to a clear stretch of ground at the front, where the mobile would be likely to work without interference. He punched in the number of the Clayton Street nick and was talking to Dan in less than a minute.

'We've got our bird man,' he said, and read out the full address from his notebook. 'No alarm's been raised, and I reckon if I make myself scarce you'll get here before anybody twigs. There's one casualty, he's on a hill, south-east side of the property, you'll likely have to pick him up. He'll need expert attention. A bit of the old intraocular haemorrhage.'

'You nutted him,' Dan said.

'Unavoidable. I'll explain later. Make sure you bring plenty of people, it's an Aladdin's cave set-up. Game birds aren't the half of it.'

'How do you mean?'

'They're faking antiques.'

'Good God.'

'There's some cracking bits of pseudo-Sheraton knocking about. And you'll love the Chippendale. Good old private enterprise, eh?'

They met up late that evening in a quiet pub near the university campus. Dan got the first round in and they took their drinks to a corner table. Dan had been containing himself since he arrived, but as soon as he sat down opposite Spender he had to let it out.

'It was *incredible*,' he said, his eyes wide, like a jubilant child's. 'I mean, I've been on some raids in my time, but that place – utterly fantastic. There's a full team of specialists out there yet, you know, cataloguing, photographing, going through the computer records of customers. It was an export business. The entire top floor of the house and three other buildings were packed with stuff destined for Berlin, Hong Kong, New York . . .'

'I guessed it might be like that,' Spender said.

'The odd part, the big irony, is that the bird

trade, the thing that got us on to Saddler in the first place, was practically a hobby. He's a hunting freak and he operated the business for people like himself. Delivered birds from the same van he used to take his crates full of fakes to the shippers.'

'What about the description we got of the guy with tattoos and shifty eyes and so forth?'

'He's the brother-in-law. A bit soft in the head.'

This calibre of irony was never lost on Spender. How often, he wondered, had one crime and one suspect led to the uncovering of another felony and a different villain? He had even whimsically formulated it into a law of life: *Evidence is uncovered indirectly; truth abhors direct lines.*

'I don't reckon Adam Saddler's the most balanced individual in the world either, to be frank,' Dan said. 'But he certainly has an eye for business.'

'Speaking of his eye . . .'

'He's going to be all right. Sore as hell for a long time, but he'll mend. He was ga-ga when we picked him up. Kept trying to give the uniform boys a description of his assailant until they managed to get it into his head that he was under arrest, and that he needed a lawyer as badly as he needed a doctor.'

Dan waxed on for another ten minutes about Saddler's team of fakers and the magnificent replicas they had produced. In the corner of a barn he had found a Hepplewhite chair, he said, that he'd have sworn was the real McCoy if he had seen it anywhere else.

'And those chaps are all craftsmen, you know. Time-served, dedicated, skilled people. Driven to crime because of the declining market for handmade furnishings and cabinet work.'

'And because of the good money fakers make,' Spender said, 'and because they don't give a monkey's about duping the public.'

'I suppose so.'

Spender swirled his drink. 'You'd never guess what made it all click for me,' he said. 'The clue that made me realize what their game was.'

'So tell me.'

'It was those little copper trumpets. The ones hanging on the clothes-lines.'

'Yes, I saw them,' Dan nodded, frowning. 'Can't say I caught on, though.'

'It's a sideline that practically every antique-faker indulges in,' Spender told him. 'It's such a sure-fire number, you see, and a doddle to do, they can't resist it. The trumpets are new, of course, and they're cheap. Made in Taiwan for the most part, but not stamped. So your faker gets hold of a few dozen, and he hangs them up outside and leaves them there for three or four months. What happens?'

'They get pinched.'

'You're not really interested in hearing, are you?'

'Sorry. Tell me.'

'They get weathered. They start to get the old verdigris look and that scummy patina metal objects have when they've lain about undisturbed for a long time. After a while you wouldn't be able to tell one of them little Taiwan hunting horns from an eighteenth-century original, hand-crafted in the Home Counties.'

'That's fascinating,' Dan said.

'That's not all. When the time comes to take them off the ropes, the faker doesn't simply untie them and put them in boxes. He cuts the ropes and lets the trumpets come rattling down on to the concrete or the paving stones or whatever he's got under the ropes. The result is a series of random scratches, bashes and dents, the final authentic marks of age. Brilliant, isn't it?'

'I can see the fascination in certain kinds of crime, the non-violent kind, the quirky stuff.' Dan shook his head slowly. 'Today, until about ten minutes before you called in, I had been getting a statement off a daft old flasher. I wasn't dealing with a crime, I was there to chide a man for giving in to a weakness. Somehow the areas are linked, moral weakness and the desire to hoodwink. I'd sooner get wrapped up in all that, full-time, than face some of the sewage I have to sift to earn a living.'

Spender grinned. 'I'll agree with that.'

'So how did you know about the hunting horns?'

'When I was a kid I used to help an old fella that faked them and sold them off a barrow – one at a time, mind, in among other fake items like Tudor offertory boxes and Elizabethan tortoiseshell combs.'

'A rascal in the old sense.'

'Right. He always made out he'd no idea of the value of anything, and he never made extravagant claims for any of the merchandise. Smart bastards used to give him about a third of what they thought the things were worth, and he'd go home at the end of the day with five and six hundred per cent profit.'

'Brilliant,' Dan said. 'I have to admit it, even though I shouldn't – I always like to hear about a good scam.' As he sat back he appeared to make a buzzing, rattling sound.

'What the hell's that?' Spender said.

Dan turned a delicate pink as people at the bar stared.

'It's my pager,' he said.

'Is it supposed to do that? It sounds like a robot farting.'

'I dropped it and cracked the casing. I meant to hand it in for fixing but I forgot . . .'

The pager rasped again and Dan fumbled it out and switched it off.

'I'd better call in and see what they want.'

'Use this.' Spender handed him the mobile. 'I'll get us another drink.'

When he got back Dan was rising and buttoning his jacket.

'What are you doing?'

'I have to get to the office. There's been another drug poisoning, or that's what it looks like.'

'Any details?'

'Just that it's another youngster, a boy this time.' Dan took the half of beer Spender had brought and swallowed it in three gulps. He patted his stomach absently as he put down the glass. 'He isn't dead, not yet anyway. They've pumped him out and got him on life-support.'

'Let me know what's happening,' Spender said.

'Yes, I will, don't worry.' Dan put down his empty glass and sighed. 'Life really *would* be less of a pain if all we dealt with were fakers and flashers, eh?'

7

The security of drug dealers, Terry Knowle observed, depended on the organization surrounding them being so fragmented that nobody could make sense of it. Or make a case of it, for that matter.

'Everything happens in little bits,' he said to Spender, who was looking at a museum catalogue, examining a delicate pre-Raphaelite painting. 'There's no such thing as a line leading back to the source. With those bastards the line leads back only as far as the line before it. How many people does it take to get the hard stuff on the streets?'

'Quite a few,' Spender said. 'When I'm delivering, I'm the third or fourth man in the chain, as far as I can tell, and I'm not handling serious amounts.'

'There you are. It's all down to numbers, and to each person in the chain supplying only his titchy bit towards the overall action.'

'You're not wrong, Terry . . .'

'And I'll tell you this, mate – if every villain operated his business the way the drug boys run theirs, we'd feel a hell of a lot fewer collars in a year.'

'Sure. But it's the profits in drugs that make it possible,' Spender pointed out. 'Other lines of crime don't have the mark-up that lets them use dozens of personnel to set up mazes and smoke-screens.'

'You've thought it all through, then.'

'Of course I have,' Spender said. 'Like every other cop in the world, including you, I'm an expert on the logistics and economic structure of organized crime. Goes without saying.'

They had been wandering in the University Precinct for almost an hour, discussing business as they strolled around.

'Looking for one man in a drug set-up and hoping to find him,' Knowle said, 'especially if he's not a key figure or a pivot in the operation, can be handled only two ways. The first way's impossible, the second way's *bloody* impossible . . .'

'I'd still like you to try. Even if all you do is keep your ears open.'

'Oh I'll try all right. I was only reminding you it doesn't do to hold out hope.'

They wandered along to the rear of the Hancock Museum and stood there, letting the afternoon sunshine warm them. Because they met only occasionally, much of the time was taken up with back-tracking and updating on topics that didn't find their way into official summaries. Knowle held the rank of detective constable; his role in police work, like Spender's, was covert, and both men served the same ultimate masters. Since they were the only two of their kind in the region they felt a kinship that had a lot to do with being disliked by other policemen. Today though, just for once, the personal complaints had taken second place to Spender's pressing need to make headway in the drugs case.

'The kid that was found last night has definitely fingered Shanko,' Spender said.

'In bad shape, was he?'

'It was touch and go for a while. He was semi-conscious when they got him into hospital. The overdose team did a stomach washout then hit him with intravenous Valium. After half an hour his heart started acting up and they put him on something else intravenous—'

'Propanolol?'

'That's it. I bet you're glad you went on that course. Anyway, with the medication, plenty of oxygen and a couple of hours deep kip, he was fit enough to speak to Dan this morning. He was too sick to put up resistance, so it was a straight question-and-answer session. He said he was in a games arcade last night, trying to score crack. He was approached by a man answering Shanko's description who sold him a lump that made him feel very peculiar about ten minutes after he'd smoked it. It wasn't the kind of peculiar he wanted to feel. Then he went into a semi-coma.'

'Do the tests confirm it's the same stuff that killed the other three?'

'They certainly do. They also confirm the chemist works to the exact proportions each time, which isn't all that usual. Could be an obsessive type, they make good criminals.'

'And you're positive the ID is a ringer for your man Shanko?'

'What is this, Terry? Do you hit a gong if I slip up and answer yes or no?'

'I'm asking you to be sure. You've done the same with me.'

'I'm sure all right. Short whitish hair, the kid

said, and bleary blue eyes. He remembered the rings, too. But long before that boy turned up I was convinced Shanko was nearer the source of the toxic stuff than Teddy Ballantine. My reasons for thinking it weren't all that logical, mind. If you'd asked me why I was targeting Shanko, I'd have said, because there's just something about that bastard that convinces me he's extra-specially shitty.'

'You can't beat clear deductive thinking.' Knowle looked at his watch. 'I've got to shoot.'

'Me too. Remember, let us know if there's even a whisper.'

'If I get anything at all, you'll hear.'

When Knowle left Spender decided to go back to the flat and see if there were any letters. Re-organization at the sorting office had meant the mail arriving later and later, until it wasn't practical to hang around in the morning waiting for it. Usually he was content to leave it until evening, but today he was expecting a letter from his London solicitor with the details of an upset over the leasing of his flat in Hampstead. Ever anxious to put troublesome news out of the way, he drove across town and parked the Cosworth opposite the flat.

Keith was visiting, leaning on the wall by the living-room window with a steaming mug.

'Split that tea in two,' he yelled to the kitchen. To Spender he said, 'I was in the district so I thought I'd drop in. Makes me really appreciate my own place, this gaff.' He smiled. 'I've just been talking about you.'

'That's right,' Stick said, coming from the back with two mugs.

'I was talking to a punter about harmonicas,' Keith explained, 'and I told him what you've always reckoned, that a mouth organ's the ideal musical instrument, you can always have it on you.'

'And join in with anybody at the drop of a hat.' Spender slapped the bulge of the B-Flat Hohner in the pocket of his denim jacket. 'Or entertain yourself when you're on your tod, wherever you happen to be.' He took a mug from Stick and gulped the hot tea. 'Nectar. With the accent on tar.' He pointed to a fan of envelopes on the table. 'Is that my mail, by any chance?'

'All yours,' Stick said. 'Four items and not a whiff of scent off any of them.'

Spender reached across and lifted them. The one he had been expecting was on top. He started to rip it open, then decided to wait, in case Stick got nosy. The business surrounding the flat was delicate; Spender didn't want to talk about it.

'Anyway, Keith, as I was saying before we were interrupted,' Stick said, 'Donna put it nice and simple for me, in a way that made me actually think for once, instead of sailing through my life not bothering. She looked me straight in the face, the way she does, and she says, "Surely we're clever enough to fight disease without abusing dumb animals in the process." And that did it. It's so obvious, isn't it? How can any outcome be called good when some poor bloody creature's gone through hell to make it happen?'

'Vivisection's not just barbaric,' Keith said, 'it's

useless.' He looked at Spender. 'Did you know that big-time developments like cataract operations, gas anaesthetics, locals, heart drugs, kidney and gallbladder ops, caesareans, breast surgery and a ton more were all perfected from work done on human beings, not animals – and they were all in regular use by 1900?'

'No, I didn't know,' Spender said.

'Yet blood transfusion was delayed two hundred years because of animal experimentation. They finally got it working when they switched to research on people. And Florey, the guy that refined penicillin, he said it was a lucky thing it wasn't tried out on guinea pigs, because it kills them. The evidence is blinding. Animal research doesn't help progress, it holds it back.'

Spender glanced at a poster beside the door that had appeared there overnight:

IN THESE ENLIGHTENED TIMES PEOPLE STILL HUNT ANIMALS FOR FUN; THEY DEBASE THEM FOR AMUSEMENT, BLIND THEM FOR VANITY AND SLAUGHTER THEM FOR FUR. MAN CAN HAVE NO DIGNITY OF HIS OWN UNTIL HE GIVES DIGNITY BACK TO THE ANIMALS.

'You two are really getting into this stuff, aren't you?'

'You could say that,' Keith murmured.

'A real pair of converts.'

Keith looked at Stick, then at Spender again. 'Do you disapprove, like?'

'I didn't say that.' Spender nodded at the poster

by the door and at another one further along – END DISCRIMINATION AGAINST ANIMALS. 'I'm just surprised at the speed of it all. I'm not objecting or criticizing. As far as I can see it's a good thing. Admirable. As long as it doesn't elbow your sense of humour.'

Keith frowned. 'What makes you think it would do that?'

'You do, the way you're getting the needle over nothing.'

'Look . . .' Keith put up a hand like a policeman controlling traffic. 'If I was getting defensive just then, it was only because I could see the scope there is for you to take the piss.'

'And you think I'd do that.'

'Well yes, I do, as a matter of fact.'

Spender rubbed his nose thoughtfully. 'You're not a bad judge, as it happens,' he said. 'I suppose I *would* be inclined to take the piss out of a bloke that spends years of his life mercilessly battering catgut, then turns round and tells me it's cruel to eat a beefburger.'

It was a relief to see Keith smile. He had always had the gift of timely derision, laughing at the pretentious and the stuffy, never acknowledging that the society he lived in could be much more than an elaborate farce. It would be a small tragedy, Spender believed, if his mate ever lost his amused distance on life and got so one-sided that his sense of humour could no longer breathe.

'Are you going to tell him then?' Stick said, addressing Keith.

'Tell me what?'

'It's nothing,' Keith said, shaking his head, his pig-tail swinging. 'Nothing to go making announcements about, anyway.' He shrugged, making light of the moment. 'I joined up with Jude's People, that's all.'

'How about it?' Stick said. 'Him that never joined a thing. Mr Independence, the man that reckoned the Boys' Brigade was too militaristic.'

'I wish you'd told me when you were thinking about it,' Spender said.

'Oh aye?' Keith stared at him. 'What for?'

'Because I'd have advised you against it.'

'Eh?'

'You heard me.'

'Are you telling me I'm not capable of making up my own mind, for Christ's sake.'

'I'm saying there's things about Jude's People you maybe don't know. They're implicated in a fair bit of crime, Keith. Associating with that crowd could mean trouble for you.'

Keith looked affronted. 'What the hell are you on about? You're looking at me like I'd joined the Hole-in-the-Wall Gang.'

'I'm a mate and I'm concerned—'

'You're a copper and you're over-reacting. What I've done is simple, Spender. It's sunny and wholesome. My lass is a member of an animal welfare group, she asked me to join and I did. What's the big deal? Where's the calamity?'

'They've got militants at their core,' Spender said, 'and militants are always trouble. CID have got them on the books already—'

'Oh, I'll bet they have. It's par for the course, isn't

it? Shake up the status quo and you'll find yourself on some bureaucratic bastard's little list.'

'It's not like that at all—'

'Of course it is. Keeping tags on the malcontents, that's the game, right? Well fuck the list, Spender, they can put me on it if they want. In fact I'll likely insist, in case there's any danger I get mistaken for one of society's *respectable* people.'

'You're taking this all wrong, Keith. I'm just trying to warn you what you're getting into.'

'I know what I'm into and I've no qualms about it.'

Keith put down his mug with a bump, snatched his stick from against the wall and hobbled out through the door. Stick went with him.

'I'll catch you both later,' Spender said, putting his mug on the table. 'I'll be here for a while if I'm wanted.'

He sat at the bare kitchen table for a while, the letters unopened in front of him. Taking stock of himself, he faced an old enigma: he had no fixed sense of where he stood in relation to other people. Keith's anger had hurt him, and now he was alone the silence and bareness of the flat were superimposing themselves on his mood, making him feel more alienated than ever. There was a hazy parallel with the way he felt when his brother died.

Cautiously he checked for traces of self-pity, which he despised. He found none. He was simply aware of his solitary nature, the monolithic self, the enigma he presented to other people and occasionally to himself. Self-awareness was not comfortable. There were reasons for the way he was, for being the gregarious loner; he knew all the reasons and no longer chose to confront them. He understood too much about people to find mankind lovable, and in truth he was more comfortable living at a distance from them. But he was not without a need for people; it hurt when any of the few he called friends turned on him.

'You're just a lad that needs his pals,' he told himself, getting it into proportion and slamming a door on the bleak mood.

He opened the letter from the solicitor. It was informal and chatty, and the news wasn't so bad as he'd been expecting. The worst of it was in the second and third paragraphs:

Your tenant, Ben Ingram, has been posted to Manchester, as he feared he would. Sadly, given the added financial burden inevitable with such a move, plus the cost of setting up another home base, he doesn't feel that he can afford to hang on to the lease of your place and asks, accordingly, if you would be willing to let him surrender it to you without incurring any penalty – or, for that matter, any liability to pay the few hundred pounds rent that would be due if he continued in residence at Western Avenue.

It is a matter entirely for you, Mr Spender, though I see it as a small duty on my part to point out that Mr Ingram has been an excellent tenant, and he *is* a former colleague of yours; in the circumstances, I think that a minimal upscaling of the rent you charge the next tenant would take care of the shortfall under the present arrangement, and the outcome would be an amicable conclusion to what has been an agreeable undertaking. Do let me know what you think.

'I think,' Spender said, 'that Inspector Ingram has got you in his pocket, pal.'

He put down the letter and thought about it. Ingram had been in the flat for approximately two years. It had been a handy arrangement. The rent paid the mortgage and other upkeep expenses on the flat, meaning that Spender still had a place in the Smoke, which kept him from feeling cut off in Newcastle. He would have to go through the palaver of getting another tenant now, just when he could ill afford the time to do it. On the other hand, he couldn't afford to let matters ride, either; if he didn't do something soon, the flat would start to cost him serious money again. That had to be avoided.

'Bull by the horns,' he murmured, folding the letter and putting it back in the envelope. 'Do it and get it over with.'

He would telephone the lawyer and make arrangements for an immediate re-letting, subject to a revised rent plus the usual guarantees and Spender personally vetting the applicants.

He was opening the second envelope when Stick came into the kitchen. He had a bulky jiffy bag under his arm.

'I think you were a bit hard on Keith, you know,' he said, sitting down opposite Spender.

Spender studied Stick's face. 'Are you winding me up, or what? I thought I was perfectly reasonable.'

'He took it bad. I mean he was feeling all kinda proud and warm, joining a cause he believes in, giving himself one more thing in common with Dory. It was a real romantic scene. He was long overdue for one. Then you come in off the street and throw cold water over everything. Very inconsiderate, that.'

'Jude's People are trouble, Stick. That's all I was telling him. The bulk of them are nice people like Dory and Donna, I'm sure, but that doesn't make a damned bit of difference when arson and suchlike are getting perpetrated in their name by the militant minority.'

'I'm sure you're right about that. He just took it bad.'

'But that doesn't mean I was hard on him,' Spender insisted.

'OK.' Stick shrugged. 'I take it back.'

Spender stared at him. 'What's the game?'

'Game?'

'Don't piss me about, Stick. You've turned all what's-his-name. Acquiescent.'

'There's no need to be abusive.'

'What's that there?' Spender pointed to the packet under Stick's arm.

'Oh, aye . . .' Stick made a show of remembering it. He put it on the table. Staring at the packet he suddenly looked sad. 'I hate doing this, really.'

'Well, don't do it,' Spender said, impatient with

the heavy-handed theatricals. 'It's no skin off my arse . . .'

'It was a legacy, you see.' Carefully, Stick eased a padded leather book out of the bag. 'My Uncle Archie left it. You remember I told you about him.'

'No, I don't. What is it?'

'It's the only thing he owned that was worth anything. When he died he left a letter saying I was to have it. I was sixteen at the time and my mam hung on to it till I was of age, like.' Stick pushed the volume towards Spender. 'It's his stamp collection. He spent his lifetime on it.'

Spender opened the album, smelling the richness of the leather. The binding alone was an expensive item – a thick unflawed hide, the endpapers cut from genuine vellum; the blue-and-yellow head-band and the marker-ribbon were silk. The stamps themselves, five to a page, were mounted with meticulous care in transparent mounts on quality moiré board.

'Where's it been hiding all this time, then?'

'Auntie Ellen looked after it when the old lady passed on. I forgot she had it, till last week, when I was sitting through in my room there, wondering what I was going to do to get myself on my feet.'

'If you hang on a minute, I'll nip downstairs and see if I can borrow a violin.'

A flash of annoyance crossed Stick's face but he controlled it.

'I need some readies to get myself looking half-way decent and generally smarten up my act. I mean I've landed the right way up, haven't I?

With a lass like Donna looking after my interests I'm bound to thrive for a change. But I need a boost, Spender, a bit of decent gear on my back and a bob or two in my pocket to give me some momentum . . .'

'And you want to sell the stamps, is that it?'

'Right.'

'It must break your heart, parting with a collection like this. I don't know anything about philately, but just looking at them I'd say this lot's worth a small bomb.'

'Well, I hope so. They're all I've got that can be turned into cash.'

Spender closed the album and pushed it back across the table. Stick left it lying there.

'I was wondering if you'd get them valued for me.'

'How am I supposed to do that? I told you, I don't know a thing about stamps . . .'

'But you can walk into a shop with something like this and put it on the counter without the manager getting an armlock on you and the place suddenly filling up with bobbies.'

Spender didn't feel like arguing. He didn't feel like challenging Stick with what he really thought, either, which was that the album was stolen property and was probably the subject of a circular that was even now doing the rounds of the city's stamp dealers.

'Leave it with me,' he said.

'Thanks a lot. I really appreciate it.' Stick rose and went to the door. He turned. 'You won't take too long, though, will you? I mean, the sooner I've got a bit of wedge behind me the quicker I'll start getting myself on the right road and—'

'Just leave it with me, Stick.'

'Aye. Right.'

When he had gone Spender called Dan and asked if the boy in hospital had said any more.

'Nothing. I think we got all there is. Mr Gillespie appears to be very fretful about this one. Is there something I should know?'

'You'll know it soon enough if it happens. Otherwise there's no point getting yourself in a lather. Listen, Dan, I think I'm going to put in some night shift, proper *dead-of-night* shift, when the parasites are crawling back to where they come from. I might get lucky. In case anything happens that needs an upfront presence, will it be OK to ring you at home?'

'Certainly – in fact I look forward to the recreation.'

'Don't build your hopes up.'

'Does this mean I shouldn't disturb you during the day?'

'My insomnia's as bad then as it is at night. If anything's urgent, call me.'

'Fair enough. Speak to you soon, I hope. Be lucky.'

Spender stared at the stamp album and the solicitor's letter lying beside it.

'I'll do what I can,' he said.

8

'I'm beginning to feel sorry I took on this job,' the
young man said, looking up from his clipboard
and speaking for the first time. 'No kidding, it's
a real pig. I've not been given the staff I asked for
and already this week I've put in more overtime
hours than I'm supposed to.' He sighed and shook
his head, heavy with resignation. 'Next time I'll
take a desk assignment. This outdoors stuff's too
exhausting.'

They were sitting at opposite sides of a chipped
Formica-topped table in a café with steamy windows and an ingrained smell of greasy cooked food.
The faded floor-covering was worn into ragged oval
holes in front of the chairs where people shuffled
their feet. Depressing enough to make you cut your
throat, Spender thought. Even three cold, fruitless
hours on the streets didn't make this place anything
like a haven.

'Must be tough for you,' he said to the youth
opposite. 'Still, we have to get on with what we're
good at, eh?' He glanced at the battered clipboard,
probably rescued from a skip, and the defunct old
calculator taped to its edge. 'Lots of people would
be glad of a job, these days.' He pushed back his
chair and stood up. 'I'll get us both a cuppa.'

'Oh, cheers.' The youth smiled and rubbed his unshaven cheek. 'You're a livesaver – I forgot to pick up my wallet before I came out tonight. There wasn't time to go back . . .'

The proprietor, a glum, silent, hoody-eyed man known to the regulars as Sunny Jim, dispensed tea from a tall, rust-pocked chrome urn fitted with pipes that forced steam through cold water and turned it scalding hot in less than five seconds. Spender paid for the two cups and took them back to the table. The young man was earnestly writing something on the grubby sheet of paper on his clipboard.

Spender sat down again and looked around him. At that hour there were only a few people in the place, the kind who rarely moved in daylight – winos, junkies, superannuated prostitutes, people not so much marked by life as worn characterless by it, huddled in units of one, glad enough to be warm and breathing.

'It's probably one of the longest statistical analysis reports ever undertaken, you know,' the young man said, gesturing with his stub of pencil. 'My name's Simon, by the way.' He started writing again, clearly not interested in a two-way introduction.

Spender noted the dirt caked under Simon's fingernails. He must have been living rough for weeks. His hair was matted and his putty-grey skin had a flaky texture resulting from a depletion of vitamin C and too much exposure to cold air. Like many in his situation he had made a partial retreat into fantasy, reality being too bleak to withstand. The job with the clipboard was probably as real to him as anything else in the world.

'Do you get in here a lot at night, then?' Spender asked him.

'Most nights. My area of analysis is this quadrant of the city, you see. Right here, on this street, we're at the heart of the zone I measure.'

'And what is it you measure, exactly?'

'Time-stretches of vacancy.' Cleaned up and wearing a suit, Simon would have been completely credible at that moment. 'I monitor given lengths of city pavement, you see. I time the stretches during the night hours when no-one is walking on them. It's a long-term project, operating on a national scale. It's aimed eventually at rationalizing the layout of urban footpaths.'

Spender nodded, feeling that anything more he said would be patronizing. He drank his tea slowly, conscious that he was being sized-up by the regulars. In his black crewneck, grey trousers and black raincoat he didn't present a picture that could be evaluated at a glance, and that was the idea – he didn't want to invite ready-made labels. The less people could assume about him, the more likely they would be to talk, if only to make him spill something about who he was.

Two girls came in, one an exaggerated blonde, the other with unbelievably bright chestnut hair. They sat at the table nearest the door, directly in Spender's line of vision. They were young, no more than twenty, both wearing too much make-up and mini-skirts that measured maybe ten inches from waist to hem. In this setting they looked almost attractive. After they had discussed what they would have – two jam doughnuts and two coffees – one of them, the blonde, went to the counter. Her companion looked round the café swiftly, her gaze lingering for a second on Spender. She looked away sharply and fumbled a packet of cigarettes out of her tiny handbag.

'Streetwalkers,' Simon said in a hushed voice. 'Steer well clear, that's my advice.' He made a slow sideways movement of his head, indicating the glum individual behind the counter. 'He shouldn't let them in here. They spread disease, after all, and hygiene's of paramount importance in an establishment like this. I mean even their hands . . . Well, you don't know where they've been, do you?'

Spender finished his tea, wondering idly what a lab culture from Simon's grubby paws would turn up. Everything but Lhasa fever, he mused, then stiffened in his chair. The girl coming back from the counter had stumbled and spilt tea on the redhead's skirt. It was the redhead's voice that startled Spender, the precise sound of it as she pushed her friend away. 'Don't mop it,' she had yelped. 'You'll ruin the velvet! Leave it! Leave it!'

Spender had a good ear for pitch and inflection. Like a cross-reference he heard the modulation and tempo echo back from memory: *That's enough, for Christ's sake! Leave him, leave him . . .*

He listened harder, staring at the table top, trying not to let the concentration show.

'You're a right dizzy bitch . . .'

'I said I'm sorry, Margo. It was just one of them things, I couldn't help it.'

'You couldn't help it because you were born bloody clumsy. Oh, for Jesus' sake, look at it . . .'

For Jesus' sake, come on – will you leave him alone before you bloody kill him . . .

There wasn't a doubt. She was the one. That girl's voice had followed him into the dark when he went unconscious.

'Working yourself, are you?' Simon enquired.

Spender looked at him, not comprehending.

'Sorry? Oh, working . . . Yeah, I've got a job, thanks . . .'

Margo was determined not to be consoled. She was on her feet, dabbing at her skirt with a paper napkin, heading for the door and ignoring her friend.

Spender waited until she had gone, then he stood up.

'I'll see you around, Simon.'

The blonde girl had sat down again and was drawing both doughnuts towards herself. Spender went outside and looked along the street. Margo was standing a couple of doors away, still dabbing her skirt. He approached her.

'What would it cost to buy a new one?' he said.

She looked up. Spender smiled. Margo scowled at him.

'Was that a proposition?'

'I suppose it might be.'

'Well, is it or isn't it? Are we talking business or what?'

'Sure, it's business . . .'

'Fair enough.' Margo straightened and threw the balled paper napkin into the gutter. 'It's twenty quid a short time, forty-five all night, specials are extra and you have to use a rubber.'

'That's fine.'

'What is? Twenty? Forty-five?'

'Let's just see how long it takes.'

She asked him if he had a car. He said no, so they caught a mini cab which took them to a place that looked like a boarding-house. At the small desk behind the front door Margo collected a key from an old woman and led Spender up to a room on the first landing.

'Cosy,' he said, as Margo switched on the blue-shaded bedside lamp and knelt to light a gas fire. He took in the cramped proportions. There was room for a three-quarter-width bed and a walkway beside it, carpeted with a strip of threadbare runner. In the corner by the window was a basketwork chair, painted bilious green, with two fresh towels draped over the arm. Above it hung an incongruous photograph of sheep grazing on a misty hillside.

'I'll want to see the money first. Twenty, for starters.'

Spender detached two tenners from the wad in his pocket and put them on the chair. Margo snatched them up and put them in her bag. Without further preamble she lifted her skirt to undo her stockings.

'Hang on.' Spender leaned on the door and folded his arms. 'No need to do that.'

Margo looked at him suspiciously. 'If I keep them on it comes under the heading of special.'

'I mean I don't want to do anything with you.'

'Christ, I really get them.' She sat down on the bed and let her hands dangle between her knees. 'Is there a weirdies' convention on in Newcastle tonight? Less than an hour ago I was with a bloke that wanted me to force potato peelings in his gob while he played with himself. He brought a whole bloody big bag of peelings – and *he* didn't want me to take off my clobber either.'

'I want to talk.'

'Talk.' Margo looked thoughtful. '*Taxi Driver*,' she said. 'Ever see it?'

'Pardon?'

'Robert de Niro, Jodie Foster. He goes back to the room with her and all he wants to do is talk.' She ran her gaze up and down Spender. 'Explain it to me – are you saying what you mean, or is there more to it?'

'I want to ask you a couple of questions, that's all.'

'Questions,' Margo said. 'You don't look like a cop. What are you? Social worker? A reporter? Or just a nut case like I thought in the first place?'

'You don't need to know who I am. Just bear in mind I won't do you any harm, plus I'll be a lot less trouble than most of your customers.'

'And I keep the money? All of it?'

'Plus a bonus, if you help me enough.'

'Is this research? One of my mates got a researcher one night. He worked for one of them polls. She reckoned it was interesting.'

'You could call this research, yes.'

'Right, then.' Margo brightened. She pushed herself further back on the bed and crossed her legs. 'Fire away.'

'I want you to tell me all you know about Shanko.'

Margo was silent.

'Did you hear. I want to know about—'

'I don't know anybody called that.'

'Yes you do.'

'So? I don't have to answer any bleeding questions about him.'

'I only want to know a few little things. What can it hurt to tell me? It'd be more painful giving me the money back.'

Margo looked up at Spender. She was uneasy. Seeing the tension of her neck as she shifted on the bed he was struck by a terrible memory: a girl dead in a room like this one, blood in a fan across the wall and half her brain on the headboard. Her neck had been stretched back taut like Margo's, a disquieting counterfeit, a sign of strength in an inert body.

'A few questions, that's all.'

The memory of the murder modified Spender's feelings. He was reminded how much Margo had in common with the dead girl; enough to earn her a similar exit. Through his sympathy for her he sensed her fear.

'He wouldn't know you'd spoken to me.'

'If you knew one thing at all about him you wouldn't say that.'

'You mean he's got you believing he's psychic?'

'I mean I just know it's not a good idea for me to say anything.'

'But you'll admit you know him? He's a friend?'

Margo bounced up off the bed and grabbed her bag. She took out the cigarettes, lit one and stood directly in front of Spender.

'Make it fifty.'

'Fifty would make you feel safer, would it?'

'It makes the risk less stupid.'

Spender nodded. 'You've got it.'

He peeled off three more tenners and handed them over. Margo put them in her bag and sat down again. Spender passed her an aluminium ashtray from the narrow shelf above the gas fire.

'How much do you know about him already?' she asked.

'Hardly anything. But he did give me a duffing up recently, so I know a bit about his fighting style. Basic pit-bull, with a trace of kick-boxer influence.'

Margo was staring at him, her head on one side.

'Christ,' she said after a minute. 'It was you, wasn't it? I don't usually remember faces, but now you mention it . . .' Her expression changed. 'You're not thinking of going after him, are you? That would be real silly.'

'Margo, I just need to know about him. My plans needn't concern you.'

'Well, one thing you should know about him is he's a head case, but you've likely worked that out already. He's a real header, mind – been inside one of Her Majesty's facilities for the criminally insane.'

'Quite a mouthful.'

'I learned it through seeing it so often – on forms, on applications to visit, on other forms to sign so I got my sharp objects when I was leaving.'

'You're a close friend of his, then.'

'He used to call me his old woman. We lived together for a bit, but that all changed after he got me on the game. Strictly business after that . . .'

'He runs you?'

'He's my pimp. It doesn't offend me if you say it.'

'Give me it from the start. Who he is, how you met him, what he does these days – everything you know.'

She was silent for a minute, agitatedly puffing on the cigarette.

'His name is Billy Shanks. He hates the Billy bit and doesn't like people knowing about it. I think he was the one that started the Shanko nickname. Introduced himself as that at a few places, you know, until it caught on. Anyway he's twenty-six, and he's been doing time of one kind or another since he was fifteen. I've known him three years, and he was already running a couple of girls and doing a bit of drug pushing when I came on the scene. He's a smart dresser and he's got a lot of charm under the temper . . .'

'You don't have to justify anything to me.'

'I was passing it on for your information. I always give a punter his money's worth, whatever the service.'

'Does Shanko work for Teddy Ballantine?'

'As a puncher,' Margo said. 'He puts the hammer on credit customers that get slow or try to renege. It has to be done with a bit of showmanship.'

'So the word gets around and Ballantine saves face?'

'Right. You can't be in that business and let junkies shit on you. Shanko does a thorough job. He does some bodyguarding for Ballantine, too.

That's what he was hanging about for the other day when you ran into him. You caught him at a bad time.'

'So I gathered.'

'He was tripping on two or three things at once. That always makes him jumpy.'

'Is he still peddling drugs?'

'Sure. Once somebody starts that he doesn't really pack it in. It's easy money.'

'Does Shanko do pushing for Ballantine?'

'He does the heavy courier stuff, which is just delivering really, except it's big amounts to big-time clients. When it comes to direct selling, which he still likes doing, he's an independent.'

'Who supplies him?'

Margo stubbed out the cigarette, looking sidelong at Spender. 'You're determined to get your fifty's worth, aren't you?'

'Well, you *did* say that's how you do business . . .'

'He tries to make out he doesn't have a supplier,' Margo said. 'It's a vanity trip with him, he's always fancied being different from the other guys in the business. So he puts it about that he imports, processes, distributes – but he really buys his deals ready made. I know that. But I don't know who he gets them from.' She looked at Spender. 'That's straight. He's got his own bloke, a tame chemist I reckon, and he's keeping him to himself.'

'Where does Shanko hang out?'

'All over the place. He doesn't have a pad – he reckons that keeps the law in the dark about him, because he can't be pinned to an address.'

And he's right, Spender thought.

'When he's pushing he doesn't stick to one place, either. He spreads it around. Calls himself the moving target.'

'If I want to get hold of him, where do I go?'

Margo fished out another cigarette, lit it. 'To be sure of finding him you might have to wait for a while, but as long as you're waiting in the lounge bar at the Three Elms, he'll show up sooner or later. It's the only place he uses regularly.' Margo blew a long plume of smoke at the ceiling. 'I imagine I've dropped him right in the shit, now.'

'It didn't seem too hard, once you got started.'

'That's because getting started was all I had to do. Apart from fighting down the fright, I'd nothing to think over.'

'What do you mean?'

'Nearly every day I try to talk myself into doing something about getting out from under Shanko. Maybe this is it. You look like you might be able to do him a bit of harm. I was surprised you didn't fight back when he jumped you.'

'There were reasons. And the reason I'm after him now isn't revenge.' Spender made a mouth. 'Not all of it, anyway.'

'I don't want to know.' Margo got off the bed. 'Are we finished?'

'I think so.'

'How was it for you?' She drawled. Laughing suddenly, she betrayed plenty of girlish lightheartedness under the whore's crust.

As Spender opened the door she became serious again. 'Listen, there's a bit more I should tell you. It's about his mental trouble. The shrinks got him under control with medication, but that was inside. The way he abuses other stuff now he's out – well, he's not really under control at all. They had him classified as APD – I don't know what that is, but it was in big red letters on all his records.'

'It stands for Antisocial Personality Disorder,' Spender said. 'It's the polite new way of saying he's a psychopath.'

'Well be warned, anyway, whoever you are and whatever you want with him. He can be crazy. One of the blokes he was bashing up for Ballantine started to fight back once, when Shanko was going through one of these funny low spells he gets. Calm as you like, he took out a knife and sliced the bloke's lip off. He told me after that if he'd really been mad it would've been his balls.'

'I'll bear the story in mind,' Spender said. 'Is that everything?'

Margo nodded. 'Except you won't be able to find Shanko for a couple of days. He's in Birmingham. Visiting his mother. Can you believe he's sentimental about his old mum? It's her birthday day after tomorrow. He'll be back the day after that.'

They parted company at a taxi rank. Before she went, Margo stood on her toes and kissed Spender's cheek. 'Best of luck,' she said, and hurried away.

Spender got back to the flat a couple of minutes after four. He managed three hours of on-and-off sleep, then got up and had a hot shower, which refreshed him more than the sleep. After breakfast he called his solicitor in London, then made tea and took a mugful to Stick's room. He opened the door carefully, ready to withdraw if Stick wasn't alone. Listening carefully, hearing only one breathing rhythm in the semi-dark, he moved silently to the curtain, grasped the edge firmly, then yanked it back.

'Up! It's morning! Every bugger up!'

Stick was on his elbows before he was properly conscious. He screwed up his eyes against the light and shook his head from side to side, whining.

'Sadistic *bastard*!'

'Here's a lovely cup of the stuff that gets you going!' Spender thrust the mug at Stick. 'Extract of linoleum, the way that only your best mate knows how to make it.'

'Piss off, will you?' Stick grabbed the mug and gulped some. He roared. 'Christ on a bike! It's took the skin off the roof of my mouth!'

Spender sat on the foot of the bed and waited for Stick to settle.

'You look horrible when you've just wakened up. You look like a man desperately in need of a good night's rest.'

'What's this in aid of, anyway?' Stick peered at the clock. 'I should still be dreaming.' He took a cautious sip from the mug. 'I dream a lot better at this time of the morning than I do during the night. There's more erotic thrust to the plots, somehow . . .'

'Listen,' Spender said, 'how do you fancy a couple of days in London?'

'London?' Stick pushed himself up to a sitting position. 'When?'

'Today and tomorrow. My treat, just bring pocket money.'

'Why London?'

'I suddenly got a bit of free time, so I decided I'd use it to go and see to my pad down there. My tenant moved out at the weekend so it'll want a little bit of a tidy round, then I'll have to talk to a couple of people that want to take on a lease. You could give me a hand, and we could have a bit of time on the town, just for a change. What do you reckon?'

'I'll have to see Donna, first,' Stick said.

'Right, I realize that. But it won't take more than five minutes, will it? I want us to be away before noon.'

Stick looked doubtful. 'It'll be our first separation,' he said. 'I can't just rush things. It calls for a proper farewell, doesn't it?'

'It's two days you're going for, not two bloody years.'

'All the same, the lass is sensitive, and I dare say she'll be a bit tearful at the thought of me leaving for a couple of days whooping it up while she's working away there in The Happy Carrot. I'll have to break it gentle, and stay with her for a bit till she gets used to the idea.'

Spender stood up. 'I'm going to phone Dan now. When I'm through, I'll pack a small bag, and when I've done that, I'm out that front door. If you're not around to join me at that point, then too bad.'

Stick watched Spender stamp out of the room. He sipped his tea thoughtfully.

'I suppose I could just give her a ring,' he said, and yawned.

9

'It's quite sad to think your friend's gone now,' Mrs Lomas said. 'I got used to seeing him every morning.' She was seventy, with arthritis in both hips and a degree of deafness that was more a nuisance to other people than to herself. 'He was such a cheerful soul, for a policeman.'

'I'm sure somebody just as nice will move in soon,' Spender said.

'His friends were pleasant too. Always very polite.'

Mrs Lomas's eyes were not too good either, so she hadn't noticed Spender's lips move; his words were lost in the general buzz of traffic noise from the road behind him. It was raining and Mrs Lomas's generous width was blocking the entrance to the building. She didn't appear to notice Spender's discomfort, or Stick's open annoyance.

'I wonder if I might just get past,' Spender said, gesturing with his bag.

'Slide her to one side with the bloody thing,' Stick muttered. 'We'll be here till teatime if she doesn't shift.'

'He forgot to cancel the milk.' Mrs Lomas pointed to two pint bottles standing in the porchway. 'I told the milkman he shouldn't leave them, but he said that since nobody had told him not to leave any, he was leaving them, and furthermore there's four pounds owing.'

They finally managed to negotiate a route round Mrs Lomas, who had wrapped up for the weather and then seemed to have forgotten she was going out. As they got in the lift she was wandering back into her flat without a drop of rain having touched her plastic coat.

'She's one of those fixtures you get used to,' Spender said as they rose to the second floor.

'Maybe *you* would. She'd drive me daft.'

'I wish you'd cheer up. You've done nothing but moan since we got underway. It can get to be a habit – God knows what you'll be like when you're Mrs Lomas's age.'

Stick's mood had darkened while he was calling Donna to explain he was spending a couple of days in London. She told him she hoped he would have a nice time, and added that she was sorry they weren't going together. Then she asked him if he would write down the titles of three books she wanted from a specialist address at Shepherd's Bush; while he was at it, she wondered if he would also pick up some boxes of leaflets from the offices of the National Anti-Vivisection Society.

'I wish I'd never rung her,' he told Spender. 'I hate being saddled with responsibility. I hate it especially when I've got to go into strange places and struggle with the resistance. It's the same every time. There's always some toffee-nosed bastard or other that can't believe I've got legitimate grounds for being there.'

'Here we are, then,' Spender said, putting down his bag in the hallway outside the flat. 'This was home, until I returned to the backwoods of my youth.' He fished among his keys and found the right one. 'It feels odd, letting myself in here again . . .'

He turned the key twice and pushed the door. It swung inwards on a darkened hallway. He sniffed, then sniffed again and looked at Stick.

'Chinese,' Stick said. 'And Indian. There's a trace of pizza too, if I'm not mistaken.' He poked his head into the hall as Spender went in. 'Your mate left at the weekend, did he? That lot's had plenty of time to mature, then. I'd open a window for starters, if I was you.'

Spender walked along the hall and opened the sitting-room door. He stopped abruptly and stared.

'Jesus Christ almighty.'

Stick peered past him. 'Amen,' he breathed.

It was as if a powerful wind had swept through the room, picking up everything, scrambling it among alien debris, and dropping it again. The floor was littered with squashed takeaway containers and pizza boxes. There were beer cans in groups on every flat surface, including the top of the television set. Plates with the forks still on them were stacked in a leaning pile on the carpet beside an easy chair. The couch was a tangle of assorted bedding with three sticky beer mugs in its midst.

'They're a great laugh, farewell parties,' Stick said. 'Especially if you're the one going away.'

A bar towel hung from the ceiling lampshade. Three more were draped around the frame of a long mirror on the wall by the door. On the same mirror, under a matchstick drawing of a cat, somebody had written LOVE IS A WARM PUSSY in orange lipstick. A variety of good-luck cards were scattered about the carpet; a placard over the fireplace said, GIVE THEM HELL BEN! in tall red letters. Spender stared at it.

'If I had the bastard here right now I'd show him how it's done . . .'

Stick had gone along the hall to assess the rest of the damage. He came back with one hand tentatively raised, the thumb pointing in the direction he had come.

'I think you want to have a stiff drink, or a strong coffee, before you go through there.'

Spender stared at him. 'At least give me a bloody clue. Don't let it be a total shock.'

'Well, somebody was sick,' Stick said. 'In the bathroom.'

'Aw, God . . .' Spender buried his face in his hands.

'And in the bedroom.'

It took two hours and most of the available cleaning materials to make the flat habitable again. When they had finished, Spender and Stick sat on the couch with big mugs of tea, admiring the gleaming transformation around them.

'It's a very nice place you've got here,' Stick said. 'When did it last look like this?'

'Years ago,' Spender admitted. 'I suppose I've that much to thank Ben Ingram for. The shitbag.'

'People are savages where other people's property is concerned, aren't they?'

'Well you are, certainly.'

'You know what I mean. They've no respect. Did you ever speak to anybody that hired out cars for a living? Those guys can tell you stories that would turn your hair white. Taxi drivers, too – the things people will do in the back of a cab, women included . . .'

'Don't get too specific,' Spender warned. 'My stomach's been put through enough today as it is.'

'It just doesn't pay to own anything. It ends up owning you, doesn't it? I mean, you get a decent bit of property, the last thing you dare to do is leave it unattended. Look what happened here.'

'He that hath nothing is frightened of nothing,' Spender said. 'I'm beginning to see the point of that one.' He looked at his watch. 'Listen, how do you fancy we go out now, get them books and other odds and ends for your lass, so that's off your plate, then I'll drop in on my solicitor and give him a rocketing? That way we've the evening to ourselves with nothing pending. Sound like a good idea, does it?'

'Brilliant.' Stick rubbed his hands. 'What'll we be getting up to tonight?'

'Nothing too unwholesome. I have to bear in mind you're a reformed individual these days – vegetarian, attached – so I'll not be leading you into anything hedonistic.'

'Rotten bastard.'

'We'll have a good dinner somewhere, then maybe I'll take you round a few places I used to haunt. Give you a flavour of London. There's an idea I've had, too – we can talk about it as the night wears on.'

'And if I'm too pissed to concentrate you can tell me about it in the morning,' Stick said cheerily. 'When do we get started, then?'

The remainder of the afternoon sailed by. Stick got the books and pamphlets and Spender was able to impress his displeasure on his solicitor, together with instructions to extract rent from Ben Ingram and every additional sum due under the leasing arrangement; in addition, the solicitor was to have the best prospect for a new tenancy ready for vetting by noon the following day.

They had dinner in a superb Indian restaurant in Hampstead. The food was accompanied by a good full-bodied Chianti and Spender's edited highlights of his time as a beat constable in the very area where they sat.

'Those were good times, Stick. Things seemed very clear cut, there was a distinct path to follow, if you see what I mean. I suppose what I'm saying is, I had an uncomplicated sense of purpose, the clearest kind of ambition . . .'

'Aye, and while you were following your sense of purpose your marriage was dying from neglect.'

Spender mopped at the dregs of the mutton vindaloo sauce with the remains of his paratha. 'I don't know why I bother talking to you,' he said.

'Maybe it's because I'm not a yes-man.' Stick patted his stomach gently. 'I'm glad I settled for the vegetable curry. Really nice it was, and it keeps my conscience clear.'

'I'm glad to hear it. Come on, drink up and I'll take you somewhere that's more your speed.'

Half an hour later they were entering a club tucked along a side street off the Fulham Road. It was called the Time Machine, a cramped, overheated cellar where men and women in fifties clothes danced under a spotlit mirror-globe to records by Frankie Laine, Billy Daniels and Dean Martin, interspersed with lively instrumentals by Billy May's Orchestra and the George Melachrino Strings.

Stick loved the place on sight. He nodded and smiled to people he had never seen in his life before, and he hadn't finished his first drink before he was arguing with another man, an Eden Kane lookalike, about the dates of Guy Mitchell hits.

'"Singing the Blues" came out in nineteen fifty-seven,' the man insisted. 'I remember buying it.'

'No it didn't. "Knee Deep in the Blues" was fifty-seven. "Singing the Blues" was nineteen fifty-six. December.'

'Well, I'd have to see it in print,' the man said, but he was backing away, realizing that Stick was right.

'How come you know so much about that old stuff?' Spender asked him.

'You know me,' Stick said. 'Find anything worthless and completely without uplifting content, and you can guarantee I'll be the oracle on all there is to know about it.'

They eventually moved on to a basement club with a small band that played jazz standards and had a clientele mature enough to keep from twitching while the music played. Stick ordered the drinks – a Perrier for Spender and a pint of lager for himself – and had to be placated over the price.

When he had quietened down, Spender broached the idea he had hinted at earlier in the day.

'The national headquarters of Jude's People isn't far from here,' he said.

'What about it? I've got all the books and leaflets I'm going to hump back with me, ta very much.'

'I thought it might be a worthwhile exercise – and a bit of recreation, too – if we did a Watergate on the premises. Just to see what we can find out.'

'What do you want to do a thing like that for?'

'Because they're going to make more trouble in our area before long. I can see it coming. It pays to be well informed about organized groups when they're restless and likely to make waves.'

'It pays the likes of you, maybe, while you're being a cop. Just remember our mate Keith's a member of Jude's People. So's my girlfriend. The outfit's no enemy of mine.'

'But you're not a member, I notice. How come?'

'The dues, that's how come. It costs. I've made out I'm weighing up the moral pros and cons and that stuff, just to buy a bit of time until I can afford the membership.'

'So what are you saying? You don't want to come with me on my little adventure, is that it?'

'I didn't say anything of the sort. I'm just curious about why you want to do it.'

'I'm a cop, like you reminded me. Jude's People are likely to do things that become cop business. I'd like to know the full strength of what I'm up against.'

Stick shrugged. 'It's something to do, I suppose. When were you fancying having a bash?'

'Tonight.'

'Ah, well hang on, now, just hang about – I like to have plenty of warning—'

'Bullshit. You're an opportunist if ever I met one. In on an impulse and out again, that's you.'

'I've told you about reading my diary.'

'Are you game, then?'

'I suppose so.' Stick took a long swallow from his glass. 'I'll have another couple of these first. Wash my dinner down. Can't go breaking and entering on a full stomach.'

The building was on the end of an Edwardian terrace, with wide steps in front and spiked iron railings mounted in ornamental brickwork four feet in front of the tall windows. They drove past it three times, the last time very slowly.

'I don't fancy it,' Stick said. 'I bet it's alarmed better than a bank. You can tell looking at the place. I'd lay money there's businesses in that block that have paid top whack to keep ragged-arsed villains like me from poking about in their secrets.'

'The ground floor isn't alarmed at all,' Spender said. 'Jude's People are on the ground floor. I don't reckon there's anybody on the premises, either, or we'd have seen something by now.'

'How do you know it's not alarmed?'

'I just do, that's all that matters.'

'Bloody police state,' Stick muttered. 'You know everything, don't you? Nobody can fart but it goes in the ledger.'

Spender put the car in a quiet court on the street behind the building. They approached along the side and walked around to the front at a strolling pace. When Spender was sure no-one was around he nudged Stick, who ran up the steps and inserted a long pick into the brass door lock. Using it to stabilize the mechanism, he put a shorter pick alongside it and located the first lever. It cleared the bolt with a soft click; so did the second one. The third was stiff and sprang back with a *clunk* that vibrated across the broad door like a drumbeat. Both men froze, playing shadows for a count of ten.

'Right then, Stick. Let's get at it.'

Spender turned the handle and the door opened. They crept inside. Stick closed the door carefully behind them.

'Straight ahead.' Spender took two high-energy halogen torches from his pocket and passed one to Stick. 'Remember to give me that back.'

The office door, its etched-glass panel painted with Jude's People's name and crest, was harder to open than the front door. When they were finally inside, Spender shone his torch on the beige-tiled floor, creating an ambient glow that would not look unnatural from the outside. He looked round the office rapidly and pointed to a bank of filing cabinets.

'I'll take those. You go through the desks on this side, and be careful you put everything back as you find it.'

'What do you want me to look for?'

'Anything with people's names, or lists of organizations. Use your common sense. If it looks interesting it probably is. And just remember, Stick, don't swing the beam of your torch anywhere near the windows.'

'Try not to insult us any more than you can help, eh? I mean who's the amateur on this job, you or me?'

Going through the cabinets, Spender found that Jude's People's files were neatly and methodically organized, but in the main they appeared to be scrupulously impersonal. Individuals were hardly ever mentioned in reports or research summaries; instead, government and the larger institutions came in for the heaviest criticism on the issues of vivisection and support for product-testing on animals. Twenty minutes of searching turned up nothing Spender had not come across already, elsewhere.

Then Stick found a file containing a list of the charities supporting animal experiments.

'I'm going to memorize this,' he insisted, 'and when any of them rattle their tins under my nose I can tell them to bugger off, I don't give to sods that exploit animals.'

They worked on for another half-hour, discovering that much of the information stored there was duplicated, whether Jude's People realized it or not. It made for tedious searching.

'I think we should have a look on the computer,' Stick suggested finally.

Spender didn't think it was worthwhile trying. 'Their files are probably password protected.'

'You'll never know till you look.'

Between them they got the PC on to the floor. Spender switched it on and booted up the system. He put in a disc marked, DEMOS – DIARY

OF EVENTS; a menu of files appeared immediately on the screen. He opened the first file with no difficulty.

'There you go, then.' He put the box of discs on the floor beside Stick, who was already sitting cross-legged in front of the screen. 'Call up the files one by one, exactly like I did just now, and read them. If we need a print-out of anything I'll have to fiddle with the printer, as and when. If you need me I'll be on the other side of that row of green cabinets.'

For ten more minutes Stick scrolled through list-ings of research groups that used animals, those that didn't, and two whole files crammed with the names and addresses of laboratories where the exact nature of business was still not clear. It had been a long day and Stick began to wilt, mesmerized and lulled by the upward tracking of line upon line of type on the luminous screen.

Spender, meanwhile, was picking up pointers on the organization of protests, with emphasis on the deployment of short-range signal generators to destroy communications between police radios. He also learned that classes in unarmed combat were planned for that summer at a venue in Yorkshire. Attached to the sabotage and combat documents was a letter from the National Director of Jude's People, expressing regret that such activities should be thought necessary by the younger element of what was, essentially, a movement traditionally allied to a policy of peaceful protest.

Reading through the documents, Spender won-dered how many Jeremy Fullers had entered the top echelons of the organization, bent on moulding it to their own style of dissent. In a few years the whole face of civil protest could change dramatically. Then he wondered vaguely if he really cared, or if it was just his training that did the reacting for him.

'Ah, if you've a minute, Spender,' Stick called in a harsh whisper. 'I think you should see this.'

'What is it?' Spender queried, crossing the floor at a crouch.

On the screen in front of Stick was a close-typed listing headed, JUDE'S PEOPLE: NATIONAL MEMBERSHIP. Stick pointed to a name and address halfway down the screen. The type was small; Spender had to get close and peer. When he finally saw it he stared for a while, then sat back on his heels.

'Well,' he said.

'A surprise, I suppose?'

'You could say that. What's the date of joining?'

'About five weeks ago.'

Spender nodded, still staring. There was no way he could mistake it. The name Stick had found on the membership list was Laura Spender, his own daughter. It was confirmed by the address.

'Do you reckon we should tidy up now?' Stick said.

'Not a bad idea.'

Spender crawled back to the filing cabinets. Stick closed the membership file, took the disc out of the drive and switched off the computer. With an effort he lifted it back on to the bench.

'You know I could have kept that to myself, Spender? I wondered for a bit if I should show you, or what . . .'

'Don't worry about it. You did the right thing.'

'Aye, maybe,' Stick muttered, pocketing a fountain pen.

After three hours back in Newcastle, Spender discovered Keith was talking to him again. Like all reconciliations it began coolly, polite and considerate, with the three of them in the flat having coffee. Keith wanted to hear about where they had gone during their time in London, and what they'd got up to.

They filled him on the highlights, entirely omitting any mention of Jude's People, both saying how relieved they were to get back to the relative sanity of the north-east.

'Do you really mean that?' Keith said. 'Do you truly find London insane? I've always thought it was exciting. I spent a lot of time regretting I never went there to live in the early seventies, when I had the chance.'

'I don't think it's mad,' Stick said. 'But it's hard to live up to.'

'That's it,' Spender agreed. 'You have to get into the pace. The rhythm. That takes more time than we had, so coming back to what we're used to was bound to be a relief, wasn't it?'

'The big question is,' Keith said, addressing Spender, 'would you want to go back there again and take up the life you had?'

'I really don't know,' Spender said.

A few minutes later, when Stick had gone out to give Donna a call, Keith turned and gave Spender's shoulder a quick squeeze.

'I hope one day, when I ask again if you'd ever go back to London, the answer can be a sincere and resounding no.' He smiled, not quite meeting Spender's eye. 'I realized, these last couple of days, that if you stayed away again I'd miss you.' He grinned. 'It's a terrible truth, but I'm stuck with it.'

10

Dan Boyd had to go out and take statements at a petrol station in the north the city where forged banknotes had been passed three times in four days. Accordingly, to save time, Spender had suggested that he go out there and meet Dan to discuss upcoming business. They arranged to have a pub lunch at a place called the Parish Arms.

Spender arrived just after one o'clock. He stepped into the comfortably furnished lounge bar and saw Dan leaning on the curved end of the bar by the bay window. Spender moved towards him, then pulled back suddenly; Dan was nodding, obviously being spoken to, but from the door the person addressing him hadn't been visible. Now Spender could see who it was: Kevin Gunter, Detective Inspector, something of a specialist in fraud cases with a roving commission that kept him moving between Newcastle, Gateshead and Durham. The broad sweep of his activities also meant he was hard to pin down and therefore, according to internal gossip, he sailed through his week by delegating carefully and doing practically nothing in the way of productive work. He was known to be cunning.

'DI Gunter,' said a certain desk sergeant, 'could

play tag in a cage full of monkeys and never be it.'

Gunter was a handsome man, not even his most mean-spirited colleagues nor the jealous ones would ever deny it. Older women said he resembled Ronald Colman, the younger ones said he was a dead ringer for Michael Caine. The truth, according to a lady detective sergeant at the Clayton Street nick, was that Kevin Gunter looked like a cross between Colman and Caine, with his wavy fair hair, nearly lilac eyes, straight nose and sensuous mouth. He was also, the lady insisted, a complete shit.

Spender went along with that, and his own experience of Gunter had taught him that the man was also a tedious, trivializing bore. His obsession with the superficial aspects of sex didn't help. Gunter was to be avoided; Dan hadn't managed it, but Spender was determined he would. He slipped outside again, opened the car boot and took out a small box from a combination-locked leather case. He slipped it in his pocket and went back inside. He ordered a tomato juice and sat at the bar, ten feet from where Gunter had Dan cornered.

When he had erected a newspaper in front of himself as a blind, Spender reached into his pocket and thumbed open the spring lid of the box. The contents, a dark-pink object the size and shape of a medium, rather battered garden pea, was a listening device called an AuroMag. In the ear it was practically invisible, and when the position of the head was adjusted, the narrow listening angle could isolate and amplify a conversation thirty feet away. Spender tapped it into position. He moved his head from left to right then back again, slowly, until Gunter's voice came over loud and clear.

'I was on to the little tit weeks ahead of anybody else,' he was saying, and beside him Spender could here Dan's automatic 'Uhuh, uhuh,' a sign to those who knew him that he was seriously bored. 'Maybe it's just me, Dan, but I could see Dummock was our man a mile off. He started behaving all wrong, it was like waving a banner that said he was guilty. I mean, just look at it front-on – there's a blag at a wholesale jeweller's, they get away with thousands, and days later a man who's never had any money to talk of is suddenly spending like an Arab and driving around in a new Rover. I ask you. Plain as the nose on your face, right? But I had to go it alone, Dan. Nobody else would wear it, they all said he was too stupid to carry out a raid. Now you tell me – how bloody clever do you have to be to point a shooter at somebody and say, "Hand over the goods or I'll blow your arse off"? Eh? Hardly an Einstein job, is it? So anyway, I thought to myself, sod the others, Dummock was my target, and I stuck to the little turd, like glue. I shadowed him and got copies of every bit of paper he passed, every transaction he made, tallied it against his pittance off the DSS and got myself enough to bring him in on suspicion. The rest, as they say, is history.'

Spender glanced round the side of his newspaper and saw Dan try to move away. But Kevin Gunter actually grabbed his sleeve.

'Come on, have another one, it's not often we get a chance for a chinwag – certainly no hope of it down the bloody nick, eh? Drink up, it'll put roses in your cheeks. Miss, I say, Miss – same again here, please. Come to think of it, make mine a large one.'

Spender decided that lunch with Dan was out of the question. He couldn't approach him while Gunter was there – it would be awkward, since Spender was a topic of speculation among certain higher ranks and Dan was supposed to know as little about him as anyone – and there didn't seem much chance that Gunter would be moving along in the next few minutes.

Spender ordered a sandwich and settled to reading the paper. After a while, as Gunter continued to drone on about his prowess as a detective and an unfaltering judge of human nature, Spender changed the angle of his head, picking up other conversations from around the room. A man leaning by the door was telling his companion, in throaty confidence, that if business continued to shrink and fall off the way it had been doing, he would have to cancel the annual holiday in the Seychelles and drop his membership of the golf club; he had already thought it out and had decided to use gout as his excuse until things started looking up again. At a table near the window a young woman was telling an older one that she hadn't had sex – 'not proper sex, anyway'– for six weeks, and frankly it could have been six months for all she cared about it. Near them a man and his wife were arguing back and forth, in an unsynchronized way, about her financial extravagance and his over-attentiveness to the barmaid when he got the drinks.

Sex and money, Spender thought, money and

sex, the eternal preoccupations. When he shifted his head back to the original angle, Inspector Gunter, too, had finally got around to sex as a talking point.

'I never made any bones about it, Dan. They can say all they like about the superior wisdom and experience of the older woman. I know blokes who make a fetish out of it. Older women, they get het up about them, got to be older women, mature, talented in the sack, all that. It's crap. Give me a healthy young bird with a strong back every time.'

There was a rustling and Spender took a quick look. Gunter was opening his wallet and sliding out a photograph. He passed it to Dan.

'She's my latest. Twenty-eight years old, which is as old as I need them.' Gunter winked. 'Her legally-wedded is inside.'

'She's very nice,' Dan muttered.

Spender got back behind the newspaper. Like Dan, he knew the implications of Gunter's remark about the woman's husband being in prison. There was a practice, not uncommon, of certain policemen having affairs with the wives of jailed felons; in most cases the game was more political than opportunistic, because the wife would eventually be told that if she didn't co-operate by providing details of her husband's associates and his future criminal activities, he might just find out how she had been behaving while he was inside.

'She's a real cracker,' Gunter enthused. 'I'll tell you what, though – she looks a lot better without the clobber.'

There was rustling again; Spender looked. Dan was trying to hand back the picture, but Gunter, out of a bizarre misjudgement of generosity, was pushing it back at him.

'Hang on to it, mate. I've plenty more. Keep it to remind you what she looks like, so you'll be nice if you ever run across her.'

Gunter lingered for another twenty minutes and one more drink before he left. Dan frowned at Spender as he finally edged along the bar.

'I clocked you earlier, sitting there with your newspaper. I got the impression you were amused.'

'That's paranoia, Dan. I was sorry for you, but there was nothing I could do to help.'

'I've just been through a very unpleasant experience.'

'I know. I was listening.' Spender took the AuroMag from his ear and put it back in the box. 'That Gunter's the pits.'

'He's the kind of man that the word *scumbag* was coined for. Worse than half the garbage I have to lock up. But what can you do, Spender? You can't choose the people you work with.'

Spender looked at the picture lying by Dan's elbow. It showed a young woman photographed in a bar, grinning glazedly behind a Tequila Sunrise. He committed the face to memory from sheer habit. Having known Gunter for several years, he could still wonder why a man so presentable, so laden with charm, should find that his relish lay in that direction, in habitual associations with outright bimbos and the sluttish wives of other men.

'Things are never what they seem,' Dan said.

'Gunter, you mean?'

'Yes. The smoothest operator around. That's what you'd think, looking at him.'

'You're invading my thoughts, Dan.'

'It's the same thing everybody thinks after they meet Gunter and realize, after five minutes, what a slime he is. It seems such an incredible waste of physical resources. We'd all like to look like him. Well I would, anyway.'

Dan glanced at the clock above the bar.

'That's lunch hit on the head,' he sighed. 'I've got to get back. Was there anything pressing?'

'Not yet. But I want you to be ready for a swoop. Have a good team on standby.'

'Drugs?'

'I hope so. I can't say when it'll be of course, but I don't want there to be too much delay between me blowing the gaff and the troops turning up.'

'You've obviously got hopes, then. Thank God.'

'You've found out about the *ad hoc* merchants, then?'

'I've lost sleep over them. The rumour is they'll be with us some time next week, unless we make a better showing.' Dan took out his notebook and flipped it open. He removed a folded slip of paper and handed it to Spender. 'I don't know what that is, and life being complicated enough already, I don't want to know. It was phoned through to me direct, by a very breathless caller, and I was asked to pass it on to you.'

Spender opened the paper. It said:

Royal Vic three days max. I have dark warnings. Come soon.

Roadrunner.

'Cheers, Dan.' Spender put the note in his pocket.

'Who's Roadrunner?' Dan asked, eyeing Spender's pocket.

'A cartoon character. A big kind of hare thing. He tears across the desert roads going, "Beep! Beep!" You must have seen him.'

'Yes, I've seen him,' Dan said patiently. 'That wasn't what I was asking, and you know it. But if it's top secret then forget it, I'll survive without the knowledge.'

'A minute ago you said you didn't want to know.'

'I was lying.'

'Oh. Well in that case, Roadrunner's Terry Knowle. It's his code-name. He picked it himself.'

Dan nodded thoughtfully.

'Don't think I'm prying, but does the note mean—?'

'Aye, he's in hospital. I better get along and see him.'

The doctor was attractive but rather forbidding. She waved the chest X-ray as if it were damning proof of a terrible misdeed.

'This is clear,' she said, 'no sign of cracks or fractures, and frankly it's a miracle. He was severely kicked about the ribs, flanks and stomach.' She picked up another radiograph from the table and held it in front of the ward-room window. It was a grinning frontal short of a skull. 'No serious head damage either, even though the bruising suggests that a number of very heavy blows were landed in the region of the face, the back of the head and the neck.'

'Well, I suppose we can only be grateful it wasn't worse,' Spender said.

'No, there's more than that to be done, I think.' The doctor set her jaw for a second, choosing her words. 'Your brother should be taught that fighting achieves nothing, and that it could quite probably cost him everything if he carried on as he's been doing in the past.'

'He doesn't actually do it from habit,' Spender said.

'Really? Then how do you explain the presence of so much scar tissue on his chest and back? Or the extensive old muscle damage present in most areas of his body, and the healed fractures in his ribs, arms and legs?'

'Well, he used to fall down a lot when he was a kiddie . . .'

'Your brother is a man who gets into fights on something like a regular basis, probably because it fulfils his notion of what constitutes manly behaviour. I've seen it before, I've met the type and I've had to patch them up more often than I would have chosen.'

'I'm sure it's not wilful, doctor . . .'

'He should be persuaded that it's a pathetic and extremely hazardous way to conduct his life. The Health Service has quite enough to contend with, without having to put him to rights every time he decides to take on someone bigger and smarter than himself.' She slapped down the X-rays. 'You can go in and see him now. Remember what I told you – make him understand he has to change his ways.'

The ward was half-empty. Most of the other patients seemed to be old, the kind who tended to whinny when they breathed. Terry Knowle's bed was at the far end. He was propped up on an unpadded back-rest, his chest and arms bandaged, his face puffed and bruised.

'You've to stop fighting,' Spender told him, throwing a bag of seedless grapes on the coverlet. 'It's not manly, even if you think it is.'

'Dr Graham,' Knowle grunted. 'She thinks I'm a thug.'

Spender pulled out the chair from the side of the bed and sat down.

'I told her I was your brother, thinking it would mean I'd get in a bit easier at this time of day. I wasn't ready for the lecture on responsible citizenship. What happened, anyway?'

'Your mate Shanko, that's what.'

'Eh? When?'

'Night before last.'

'Christ, my information must have been wrong. I didn't think he would be back in Newcastle until today some time. How did you get on to him, anyway?'

'I asked around, mostly out Gosforth way, where I've a long-term snoop going . . .' Knowle moved his back and winced. 'Jesus! I feel like one big bruised dislocation . . .'

'Gosforth, you say . . .'

'I was sounding at random, not expecting

anything, then this Asian kid approaches me and asks if I'm the one that was asking about Shanko. I said yes, and he told me my message had got passed on. I asked him what message but he ignored that and told me to be at Neville Street, Newcastle, near the entrance to the Central Station, nine o'clock. That was two nights ago. I tried to call you, but I got no answer.'

'I was in London, and some of the time I didn't have the mobile with me. I wasn't expecting anything urgent.'

Knowle attempted to yawn, but the thickened tissue of his face made it impossible. His mouth did no more than twitch a fraction at one side, causing him pain.

'After what I'd said to you, about one man in a drug set-up being impossible to find, this seemed miles too easy. I didn't know what to expect, either. In the end I decided to be there, but out of sight, just to see what was supposed to go down. But the bastard was too cute. I was grabbed from behind and marched to a car-park near the station. Shanko was there. He got a couple of his lads to search me – I'd the usual ID, John Higgins, Private Investigator.'

'Oh, dear . . .'

'Sure,' Knowle said, 'I should have left that one at home. But I didn't, so I got a terse little lecture on over-reaching myself, then they tied my hands behind my back and Shanko personally worked me over.' He paused and moistened his lips. 'I think he's a nutter, Spender.'

'He is. It's official.'

'Now you tell me.'

Spender thought about what Knowle had told him.

'Somebody must have rung Shanko – he was supposed to be in Birmingham. They must have thought your snooping was important enough to disturb him with. And *he* must have thought it was important enough to justify cutting short a visit to his beloved mum.'

'Well, whatever. I found him and I lost him again, and in the meantime I got the crap beaten out of me. It's a full old life in today's police force and no mistake, guv.'

'I'll get him, Terry,' Spender promised.

'Just watch out for him. He's unhinged enough to do the unexpected.' Knowle moved again and this time it hurt so badly he cried out. Spender got out of the chair, hovering helplessly as the spasm died away. 'Jesus Christ on a crutch.' Knowle lay panting. 'I've got some exquisite nerve responses going for me. I'm getting agony in places where I didn't know I had places.' He looked at Spender. 'I'm truly sorry if I've screwed this one for you.'

'I'm the one should be sorry. If I hadn't mentioned Shanko to you this would never have happened. But I think you might have done me a favour, at some cost to yourself.'

'What favour's that?'

'You've put the bastard on the boil. Psychos don't simmer down very fast, and I've always found it's best to go after them when they're jumpy. They don't calculate too well when they're like that, their responses are all to hell, too.'

'You said all that to make me feel better, didn't you?'

'Just get some rest.' Spender rose and pushed back the chair. 'And remember what I told you, no more scrapping with big boys.'

At ten o'clock that evening Spender was at a table in the darkest corner of the Three Elms, an extensively gloomy club where everybody seemed to mumble or whisper and most of the light emanated from behind the bar. In the past he had known this to be the haunt of small-time traders and minor executives of a certain self-deluding kind, who met in here to ogle each others' wives and tell prodigious lies about astronomical deals they had in the pipeline. Spender couldn't imagine what made it Shanko's favourite hangout.

Towards eleven, when nothing of note had happened and he could no longer pretend he found the far corners of the ceiling fascinating, he was joined by a young woman. She sat down opposite him and nodded amiably. Her smile was open and genuine, and her dark intelligent eyes held his effortlessly.

'I'm Cynthia. I've been sent over to speed you up a bit. They don't think you're spending enough.'

'I see.'

'I'm not supposed to tell you that, of course. My job's to engage you in conversation, get you to buy me a drink which will actually be an imitation of what you pay for, and then I've to keep your interest by letting you talk suggestively to me, while I drink more and vaguely imply that if you play your cards right you can get inside my pants before the night's over. Except you won't, I promise you.'

Spender grinned. 'You must do a hell of a lot for trade if you're that candid with every punter you speak to, Cynthia.'

'Oh, I usually play the game according to the rules. But this is my last night. The management don't know that yet, but I've had it. There's got to be something else I can do, something more challenging with a bit more money than they pay me here.' She leaned across the table briefly, gazing closely at Spender. 'You don't look like the usual zombies that come here to sit in the dark.'

'You don't sound like the usual hostess, either.'

'Would you believe I have a BA in European Studies? It's about as much use as a condom in a convent – at the moment, anyway, although I have hopes. I took this job to pay the rent. After my years of schooling and all that time studying at university, it was the only employment I could get.' She sat back in her chair, looking rather sombre. 'That's something that doesn't bear too much thinking about.'

Spender had no response, beyond a strong pang of sympathy.

'But you don't want to hear my problems,' she said, turning mock-bright. 'Do me a favour and spring for one of their lousy coloured-water drinks, so I can stay here for a while.'

Spender beckoned the waitress and ordered a light ale for himself – 'and whatever the lady wants . . .' The waitress seemed to know what that was. She went away. When she came back she brought the light ale and a liqueur glass full of yellow liquid. The scribble on the tab said it was Drambuie. The charge was three pounds.

'It's not even cold tea,' Cynthia said when the waitress had gone. 'At least that would be stimulating.' She sipped without seeming to swallow any of the liquid, then put the glass down. 'Now, how can I repay you for this? Smutty talk? Or should I just sit and nod while you tell me how your wife's appetite for the physical side of marriage seems to have died away lately?'

'Maybe you could give me some information.'

She shrugged. 'Try me.'

'Does a man calling himself Shanko come in here?'

Cynthia nodded. 'He's a regular.' She leaned forward to look at Spender again. 'Are you a policeman, by any chance?' She put up a hand at once. 'Don't tell me. I don't want the responsibility of knowing.' She sat back again. 'What else do you need to know about him?'

'As much as you can tell me, I suppose.'

Cynthia thought for a moment.

'He's not a real human being. You get the impression he's pretending, and doing it very hard, but he's not quite convincing, you can tell he's something alien and definitely nasty.' She smiled. 'That's me being facetious. But he really is an odd person. More than a social misfit, even.'

'Why does he make this place his hang-out, do you think?'

'He meets Reginald here.'

'Who's Reginald?'

160

'Another oddball. He usually sits alone at the bar, waiting to catch the barmaid when she's not busy, and telling her a lot of lies about the kind of day he's had – he makes out he's a theatrical director, something like that, but he's just another misfit. Whatever it is he and Shanko have in common, it binds them. They get into a huddle regularly.' Cynthia tapped the table. 'Usually they sit right here.'

'Do you think there's any trading going on?'

Cynthia smiled. 'I've wondered about that. Twice I've been sure Reginald came in here carrying something under his coat, but didn't have it when he left. He probably thinks he's good at concealing things, but he's not, he's awkward, he's not good at anything human – like Shanko, only worse. Yes, I reckon there could be some sort of trade between them. I'd hate to speculate about what it is, though.'

'Will either of them be in tonight?'

'No. Tomorrow they'll both be in. The night after it'll be Reginald on his own, then that'll be it for another week. They're like clockwork.'

Spender sipped his drink. 'It's a pity you're packing in tonight, Cynthia. I'd have been happy to buy you a coloured water again tomorrow.'

'Promise you'll be here, and I'll definitely show up.'

'I promise.'

'Right then, my swan-song will be postponed for twenty-four hours. If you want, you can kid yourself I'm doing it because of your charm, and the way I'm smitten with your graceful profile and the slow, powerful way you move.'

'You mean that's not the reason at all?'

'Nope. It's because I want to be around any time Shanko's here and somebody shows up wanting to do him harm.' She raised her glass. 'That'll really make my day.'

11

'Sometimes I think you're the perfect public servant,' Frances said, lightheartedly. 'You respond to nothing but your programming, unless somebody forcibly overrides it.'

Spender had bumped into her at a corner, said sorry, and had been about to move on before she stopped him.

'I had something on my mind,' he said.

'A curse of modern living,' Frances sighed.

'What is?'

'Preoccupation. We've got so much distracting us, so much pure trivia in most cases, that we don't actually *do* much of anything. We just let it all dominate our heads.'

Spender raised an eyebrow, amused. 'Is it anything I can help with?'

Frances smiled, took a deep breath and released it slowly. As he watched her Spender felt an old pang, the remains of what had been. Frances was once the most important person in his life, the centre of all he was and did . . .

'Sorry,' she said. 'Bad morning. There's class notes I can't find, I've lost the ticket for shoes I'm having mended – you know the kind of morning I'm talking about. Then I was digging for change at the baker's and I found that Polaroid of you and me at Whitley Bay, the one I never chucked away. I stood there having a little daydream about the fun it once was, and then here I am walking along the pavement and you bump into me and nearly pass on without seeing who I am . . .'

'Do you fancy a tea or a coffee or something?' Spender asked.

'I've no time. I wouldn't want to be seen having a coffee break with somebody looking like you, anyhow.'

'The crappy clothes are cover,' Spender explained. 'I often get spotted in this part of town – in fact it's why I'm here right now, to get spotted – and the people that spot me don't expect to see me in a Giorgio Armani jacket and Gucci loafers.'

'Listen,' Frances said, 'I've just thought, you'd be doing me a big favour if you could sit with the kids tomorrow night, between seven and nine.'

'Well, as long as you're back on time – I might have work to do after.'

'I'll not be late. Cross my heart.' She made it her parting shot and moved away swiftly, giving him a little wave.

Spender moved to the edge of the pavement and checked the traffic. He was about to step into the road when he saw someone else waving to him, over on the other side of the street. It was Mickey Lawton, Ballantine's gimlet-eyed errand boy. There was nothing casual about the wave. It was a come-here job, Mickey wanted to talk. Spender stepped into the road, grateful to himself for taking time to put on the scruffy cover. He pointed to a café on the corner. Mickey went in ahead of him.

'Mr Ballantine wants you to do a job for him tonight,' Mickey said when they had sat down with a Coke apiece. 'It's important business. Big courier stuff.'

'Where?'

'Just be at Chumley's at ten.'

The action rate on this job of his, Spender had often observed, was either a feast or a famine; it was never anything in between.

'Any idea what the scale of it is? I mean, will I need a bag, or will my pockets do? I have to think of things like that if I'm to do a good job for the man . . .'

'Just show up and do what you're told when the contact speaks to you. It's very big, I can tell you that, and the reason I know it's big is because Mr Ballantine took a long time deciding who should do the delivery bit of the operation. When he takes a long time it's always a serious deal. You should do all right out of this one, Brycie.'

'I hope so.'

Mickey pushed his Coke away and left without saying any more. Spender left his too and went out by another door. Turning along the first side street he came to, he got out the mobile and called Dan.

'Things are moving,' he said. 'I think we can do a lot of damage to an area of the city's drug trade tonight. Maybe even two areas, if I get lucky. How will you be fixed for manpower?'

Dan said he could always try blackmail to lever the personnel if bribery didn't work.

'Seriously, though, if you give me an idea of what we might be up against, I can start gauging my requirements.'

'I'm lined up for a sizable courier job. It means that a confiscation on this occasion could make a dent in supplies and finances, which is the kind of deal we've been waiting for. It also means that if my contact is tailed after he passes the drop to me, he might open the door on a few key people with their hands still dirty. This could be a *really* big one, Dan.'

'Are you saying we could nail Ballantine?'

'Chance would be a fine thing. If we ever get him it'll be by the back door. Don't rule that out, though. As for tonight, I reckon a bit of stylish tailing and swooping can make a big hole in Ballantine's operation and bag us a few bastards that are long overdue for a pull.'

'And the set up?'

'I'll be contacted at Chumley's. They want me to be in position at ten, so I suggest you get your people in place a bit before that, and make sure they're spread thin – police in homogeneous lumps tend to show.'

'You don't say.'

'I'll need tailing to whatever and whoever my destination is, but tell them to be careful on the way, I'll likely be covered by somebody. Given even average luck, I think you can be sure that after my contact leaves Chumley's he'll lead one of your posse back to where he came from.'

'Could be worth stopping up for. We're not being premature, are we, just because there are certain pressures imminent?'

'Well, we could wait till later, of course. There's always later, with the chance of a bigger bust when they're ready to let me handle the heaviest deals of all. I've thought about that in the last few minutes, but I think too much could go pear-shaped in the meantime. So, since this is a big job anyway, I think it's best we make it the one where we confiscate the confectionery and boot some arse into custody.'

Dan was silent for a minute while he made a note.

'You said there was a second item, did you?'

'Very much up in the air. It's speculative, Dan, but I'm going to push the situation for all I can get out of it, and as fast as I can. This could be the really significant collar, if my hunch is right.'

'Tell me what I should do, then.'

'Do you still have the pen-bleeper I gave you?'

'I've still got it, and I still don't know what it does.'

'I should have sent the whole lot back to London long ago. I'm glad now I didn't – we might have a chance to try it out in battle conditions. All you do is adjust the clip on the side until the little red window says "on". OK? Now leave it that way and keep it with you. If I don't call you by midnight and tell you to forget all about it, keep the bleeper beside you all night, and make sure you've got some back-up muscle on standby. If the bleeper goes, look at the long window on the barrel and it should be showing an address, or at least a location. You and your lads get there as quick as you can.'

When he had finished talking to Dan he went back to the flat to check the mail. Stick was there, eating cornflakes in the kitchen with a newspaper propped on the milk bottle.

'They all look like bills,' he told Spender, pointing to the letters on the drainer, without taking his eyes off the paper.

Spender went through them. Two were junk mail from insurance companies, one was a card telling him all he had to do was sign and return it to get his first pack of twelve cookery cards, and the final one was a note from London reminding him that his annual firearms proficiency test was tabled for late July.

'Not one bill among them,' he told Stick.

'Well, it was just a guess.' Stick swallowed a wodge of cornflakes, gesturing with the spoon. 'Any word about my uncle Archie's stamp collection? I'm skint, you know. I could be doing with liquefying that capital.'

'I'll let you know,' Spender said. 'How are things with you and Donna? Still an item, are you?'

'We're fine. So're Keith and Dory – though I think he's worrying a bit over some demo or other she's getting involved in.'

'Like what?'

'She wasn't specific with him, so he couldn't tell me very much. But it seems she's one of the real agitators in the local branch of Jude's People, and her and that Jeremy Fuller have cooked up something that Keith reckons sounds dangerous, the way she was talking.'

'Christ.' Spender shook his head, throwing the mail back on to the drainer. 'People don't half make their lives complicated. Why all the bloody agitation, eh?'

'Maybe so the bad bastards don't get complacent.'

'Forget I said anything,' Spender muttered.

The usual crumbling crowd were in Chumley's, adding to the gloom – the whores steeped in their hopelessness, the punters, terminally seedy, waiting for whatever misery they happened to prefer to boredom. Even the background music, bleeding muzzily through cheap speakers, set the kind of mood more likely to induce the blues than chase them.

Spender sat at a table near the door, pretending to read a paperback he had found on the way there. He was aware that one of the men acting sleepy-drunk in the opposite corner was a policeman, and at least two at the bar were also from the circus assembled by Dan. It was a tribute to improved acting skills within the ranks these days that he couldn't be sure how many others in the place were actually officers of the law. He hoped, fervently, that there really were more than he could see.

The contact, a woman, appeared at half-past ten. She sat down at Spender's table straight away, smiling as if she had known him all her life.

'Hi,' she said brightly. 'Sorry if I've kept you waiting.'

Under the heavy foundation make-up, laid on so

thick that the natural lines of her face had been submerged, Spender could still see she was a junkie. The eyes were a big giveaway, watery and red-rimmed. Her hands shook too, even though she clasped them tightly in an effort to keep them still.

'I'll leave the grab-bag lying by the chair,' she said, her voice quiet now. 'It's black, it won't attract any attention.'

'Where do I take it?'

'The address is on a bit of paper lying just inside the top. Pull back the drawstring and you'll see it. Your wages are under the paper.'

'What now, then? Do I buy you a drink?'

'No, you've got to take off. I'll sit here for a while until I'm sure you're well away, then I'll hop it.'

Spender pulled the grab-bag towards him with his foot and put it on his knee. It was heavy. He slackened the drawstring to save time when he was outside, then nodded to the woman, pushed back his chair and stood up.

Don't anyone else move yet, he prayed, and nobody did.

He headed for the door, casually elbowed his way outside and walked to the nearest shadowy corner. There he opened the bag and took out the piece of paper and the envelope with the money. Quickly he felt the bundle at the bottom of the bag. It had to be a sub-contract; there were deal-size packets, dozens of them, held together in one big bundle with criss-crossed elastic bands.

He opened the envelope and did a quick thumb count; two hundred pounds. He put it in his pocket, opened the slip of paper and held it out, letting the light from a street lamp fall on it.

Mr Bellamy, outside public toilet, Groat Market.

He crushed the paper into his pocket and started walking, conscious he was being followed, wondering how many goodies there were, and if there were more of them than baddies. In the darkness the tread of his own footsteps was all he heard. That was something else that both the police and criminals were getting very good at: moving silently.

Approaching his destination he saw a man in a leather bomber jacket move from the shadowy frontage of the public lavatory. He looked both ways as Spender walked past, then he turned and fell into step beside him.

'And what might your name be, sir?' Spender enquired.

'I'm Mr Bellamy.'

And I'm Charlie Chan, Spender thought, passing the bag across. The man took it and immediately altered the tempo of his step, marching smartly ahead of Spender for fifty yards then disappearing down a side turning.

Spender kept walking, taking a wide route back to where he wanted to be. When he was sure he was on a street with no surveillance, he took out the mobile and tapped in a number. There was a momentary delay while control patched him through to the radio telephone in Dan's car.

'Boyd here.'

'Spender. How did it go?'

'Brilliant, so far. Can't tell you anything over the air, this band isn't secure. Is the other item still on?'

'No idea. I'll be in touch if it isn't.'

'Very good. And by the way – well done.'

'It was nothing. You'll remember to let me have a look at the medal after they pin it on your chest, won't you?'

Spender put the mobile back in his pocket, ran to the main road and hailed a cab. He got the driver to set him down on the corner of the street where he had put the Cosworth earlier. In the car he took off the shabby raincoat and changed his shoes. Tonight he had decided to put on the oxblood brogues, which he regarded as his only true indulgence, his one sinful luxury. In the dashlight he flexed them and saw the leather gleam darkly.

When he had shaved with a battery portable, he put on a suede jacket from a cleaner's bag in the back.

'Better,' he muttered, tidying the razor and the bag away and starting the engine. 'Much better . . .'

He drove to a quiet residential mews where he parked the Cosworth, then walked the remaining three hundred yards to his destination.

Cynthia was in the Three Elms, as she had promised. She waited until he had settled at a table, a different one this time, then she came across and sat down. The waitress arrived on cue, and Spender ordered a beer for himself and whatever the lady would have, just as before. This time the alleged Drambuie came to four pounds.

'I thought you weren't going to come,' Cynthia said. 'I could see this farewell performance of mine being a limp old anticlimax.'

'Has Shanko or his friend shown up yet?'

Cynthia moved her head a fraction, indicating a man in a white trench coat at the bar.

'That's Reginald. Tonight I made a point of watching – he *is* carrying something. It's under his coat, high up at the front.'

Spender studied the man. He was perhaps forty, with ash-grey hair and sickly yellowish skin. He had the kind of face that appeared to have been deliberately lined, the deep grooves geometrically measured, then etched with balanced precision on either side of his forehead, nose and mouth. He waved his hands a good deal when he spoke. At that moment he was addressing the barmaid; Spender could see what Cynthia meant when she said he was awkward and not good at anything human. To watch Reginald was to witness an overdone pretence of reality, the kind made by characters to whom the everyday gestures and reactions of ordinary people were foreign territory.

'Weird,' Spender said.

'What's the betting he molests domestic pets?'

'I think he's more a farmyard type,' Spender said. 'Your household cat fondler has kinder eyes than that bastard.'

'Oh God, how squirmy.' Cynthia did an elaborate shudder. 'He's kissed my cheek a couple of times.'

'Well,' Spender said slowly, 'I hope that when the time comes and some nice honest man wants you to marry him, you'll have the decency to own up to that. You'll be condemned to an outcast's life, mind, but it can be an honourable existence as long as you keep away from decent people.'

Cynthia shook her head sadly, enjoying the gag. Then she glanced at the door. 'Uh-oh. There's your man now.'

Spender looked across and saw Shanko saunter in. He wore a voluminous brown-checked wool suit, a cream shirt and bright floral tie. Reginald had already seen him and they were greeting each other with extravagant hand signals.

'The meeting of the clockwork toys,' Cynthia said, her lips scarcely moving. She looked at Spender. 'Tell me to mind my own business if you like, but how are you going to establish contact with them, assuming that's what you want to do?'

'Did you say I could tell you to mind your own business?'

She nodded.

'Well, mind your own business, Cynthia.'

She pouted authentically, capable of sustaining a joke, making him realize what good fun she would be if he ever got to know her better. But he would not do that. Spender truly believed that women like Cynthia would be wasted on the kind of man he had become.

More people were coming in. Cynthia was receiving eye signals from the manager, who hovered near the bar, fingering the lapels of his dove-grey tuxedo.

'Some of our better-heeled clientele have just arrived,' she told Spender. 'That means I have to circulate.'

'Fine. Enjoy yourself.'

'Well . . .' Cynthia stood up. 'I may be having my ear slobbered on by another, but my thoughts will be with you . . .'

'Women are always telling me that.'

She moved away. Spender watched Shanko and Reginald cross the room and sit down at the table where he had sat the night before. They took adjacent chairs and sat with their heads close, lost in what seemed to be desperately important conversation.

Spender made himself look away. He had no fear of being recognized, since at the time of their previous encounter Shanko was elaborately smashed and obviously unable to focus on the object of his outrage. The real problem was that Spender was less than half sure how he would breach the repugnant tête-à-tête taking place a few yards away. If he was to make things happen even roughly as he wanted, then a way would have to be found.

He ordered another small beer, to keep the management's attention away from him for a while, and to give him time to think. He hoped Dan would remember to stay available for a call. He also hoped that being lucky twice inside a twelve-hour period wasn't beyond the upper limit of today's horoscope.

12

'Was it something I said?' Stick asked, trying to make Donna look at him. 'Just tell us. A clue would do.'

'I don't know what you mean.'

'Sure you don't. It's all my bloody imagination, I suppose. I stood there like a pillock for twenty minutes while you played up to that chinless twat with the CND T-shirt on.'

'We were talking about something we're both enthusiastic about,' Donna said. 'English literature. We both studied it . . .'

'So that was the fascination, was it?'

'Yes, it was. We were discussing Joyce's use of interior monologue.'

'What are you on about?'

'Something that doesn't interest you.'

'Who says?'

'You do. When I mentioned James Joyce and asked you if you'd ever read *A Portrait of the Artist as a Young Man*, you made a joke out of it.'

'Did I? I don't remember.'

'I'm not surprised, you'd had a few at the time.'

'So what did I say?'

'You said you were writing one of your own, called *A Portrait of the Young Man as a Piss Artist*.'

Stick grinned.

'It's not really all that funny,' Donna said stiffly. 'Especially to someone like myself who believes that certain things are too important to be joked about.'

'If anything's really important, it'll stand up to a little joke, no bother.' Stick carefully prised the cap off a bottle of Newcastle Brown. 'Hand us over that glass, pet.'

They were in the kitchen at Keith's place, keeping a diplomatic distance while Keith and Dory had a row in the sitting room. It had begun in the pub towards closing time: Keith had started arguing with Dory over her plans for what she called a demonstration of solidarity with dumb beasts, around the time Stick began to get needled because Donna was pointedly ignoring him – or so he believed – while she talked a blue streak with a lad who had happened to put a battered old book called *Dubliners* on the bar while he waited to get served, thereby attracting her full attention.

'Maybe we shouldn't have come back here,' Stick said, hearing raised voices from the sitting room. 'I could see they were itching for a full-weight barney when we came out the boozer. We could've gone back to my flat. We could still go back there, come to think of it . . .'

'Sex is practically all you think about, isn't it?'

Stick paused with his glass almost at his mouth. He stared at Donna. She stared back.

'Who said anything about sex?' he demanded.

'You didn't have to. It seems to me any time we're on our own you've got your hands all over me.'

'It's the first time I've heard you complaining about it.'

'Maybe it's because I'm more attuned to the narrowness of your interests by now.'

'When you first met me,' Stick said, 'you told me you were intrigued – that's the word you used, *intrigued* – by my directness and what was it? My uncluttered appraisal of life as I see it.' He took a gulp of ale. 'What happened? Did it dawn on you that a bit of rough is just a bit of rough, whatever majestic reasons you give yourself for fancying it in the first place?'

'How dare you!'

Stick stared at Donna for a moment, then he began to smile.

'Nobody's ever said that to me before – straight out of melodrama that kind of chat, isn't it? *How dare you . . .*'

'You implied,' Donna said, 'that I was attracted to you by . . . by something purely physical . . .'

'It occurred to me that might have been exactly it, but you hadn't quite realized.'

All at once there were tears in her eyes. Stick softened immediately. He put down his glass and wrapped his arm around her.

'I'm sorry,' he said, pecking her forehead. 'I didn't mean to take it out on you.' He hesitated, then added, 'I was jealous, and that made me want to hurt you.'

'Jealous?' She said it huskily, nuzzling the front of his shirt. 'Of what?'

'Of the way you were getting on with the bookish lad.'

'He was just a boy, silly.'

'Aye, well . . .'

'Just because I have interests in common with other people, it doesn't mean I want to get emotionally involved with them.'

'I suppose not.' Stick drew back a little, putting his finger under her chin, making her look up at him. 'Tell me though,' he said, 'what makes the likes of you like the likes of me?'

'I told you—'

'No, but really, below the carefully thought-out reasons, what was the spark?'

'Just you, I suppose. Who you are.'

'But you're beginning to find me narrow.'

'Now listen—'

'It's what you said.'

'I was being defensive.' She kissed him. 'Let's stop quarrelling and talk about something else.' She eased gently out from his enclosing arm and picked up her glass from the drainer. 'Tell me about your friend Spender. You keep promising you will, then you go off the subject. It's as if you were avoiding talking about him sometimes.'

'He's been a pal for as long as I can remember.' Stick shrugged. 'There's not a lot to tell. What did you want to know?'

Now it was Donna who shrugged. 'I don't know – it's just that he's kind of a closed book. Dory said Keith avoids him as a topic too. You're both cagey about him. Has he done something you're ashamed of, is that it?'

'All we do is let him have his privacy. That's not the same thing as being cagey. He's a private man,

Donna, you must have noticed it. He's always that bit . . . separate. And Keith and I respect that. But the facts about him aren't special or terrible or anything else out of the ordinary. He used to be married but now he's not and he's got two nice daughters.'

'And he works for the Government, he says. What does that mean, exactly? What job does he do? A postman works for the Government, it's a job-description that covers a very wide territory.'

'He never talks about his work much.'

'You don't know what it entails?'

'Not really. Listen, Donna, you're not with the DSS, are you? You ask the same kind of questions and you've got that special stare they've got – it's the look you see on an Alsatian when it's watching somebody eating fish and chips.'

'There you go again.' Donna put down her glass and folded her arms. 'Edging off the subject, a bit at a time.'

The kitchen door opened. Dory flounced in, noticeably flushed, and picked up her bag from the table. She glanced at Donna.

'I'm off home,' she snapped. 'You coming?'

'Well . . .' Donna looked at Stick, then back at Dory. 'I suppose it's getting late . . .' She turned to Stick again. 'Would you mind?' The question was accompanied by apologetic eye movements.

'You carry on, love. I'll give you a bell tomorrow.'

Keith came into the kitchen when they had gone. He leaned heavily on his stick as he walked, the way he did when he was tired.

'You look worn out,' Stick told him. 'You don't

want to go arguing like that. It'd grind anybody down.'

'She just won't see sense.' Keith lowered himself on to a chair by the table. 'I can understand what it is to have principles that put severe demands on you, in fact I think I understand it a little bit more every day, now. But to act on impulses that could land you in serious trouble, without actually advancing your cause in the eyes of the public, is just self-indulgent and counter-productive. But she can't see that.'

'Then maybe she'll have to learn the hard way.'

'But I don't want that, Stick. I don't want her hurt. She needs protecting from herself, and that's a bloody fact.'

'Do you think if I had a word with Donna it would help? She's her mate, she could maybe talk a bit of sense into her easier than you.'

'Donna's right behind her. They're allies as well as friends, remember. Politically, whatever one of them's in favour of, so is the other one. They've got solidarity.'

'Any idea yet what she's planning to get up to?'

'I've more than an idea.' Keith looked at the clock by the cooker. 'Do you think Spender will be back at the flat by now?'

'He said he might not be back at all tonight. Some job or other.'

'Great. You can never find a cop when you need one.'

'It's that bad, then? A police matter?'

'It's bad enough that I need to talk to Spender about it. Warn him what's likely to happen. Who knows, maybe there's something he can do. Talking to him about it's the only thing I can think of right now.'

'We could bomb round there on the off chance,' Stick said.

Keith looked wearily at the clock again and yawned. 'No, never mind. It'll keep till the morning.'

'I measure my success in pounds sterling,' Reginald shouted. He was alone in the den, as he called it, and didn't give the impression his words were intended for anyone in particular. 'I would love an artistic success that made money, of course, but if I had to choose, I would take the dough.'

Spender had heard that before, somewhere. He examined his face in the bathroom mirror. Pretty good. For a man who wasn't fond of alcohol, he could certainly look like a lush.

Spender could still hardly believe he was right there, in Reginald's house. Not for the first time in his career, a combination of brass neck and good luck had swung things his way. His breakthrough moment came shortly after gatecrashing the two-some with the excuse that he wanted them to share his birthday celebration – a suggestion that Reginald had found acceptable and Shanko didn't really comprehend. As they talked, Spender noticed something go wrong with Shanko just seconds after he popped a pill and washed it down with brandy. Experts called it an awareness dip, a moment of sensory vacuum that occurs when the onrush of a drug's effect is too fast for the system to handle. Reginald had been tremendously impressed by the calm, practised way Spender had poured cold water over a napkin and administered it to the back of Shanko's neck, shocking him into something like alertness again. Reginald displayed both gratitude *and* relief, since he had believed his companion was about to die on him. Calmed and grateful – and clearly in a mood for more coherent company – Reginald began to call the shots while Shanko, no longer receiving light or sound in straight lines, just sat and stared, grinning occasionally.

Amazing luck, Spender thought. If he hadn't spotted Shanko begin to go under, he might never have made it to this stage. He wouldn't have managed it so effortlessly, that was for sure. In short order he had been asked to join Reginald and Shanko for a drink back at the house. What Cynthia – if she had been watching – no doubt viewed as great skill in people-handling had actually been terrific luck.

'Alex? Are you still with us, birthday boy?' The fruity voice came from the hallway beyond the bathroom door. 'You haven't done something daft like go home, have you?'

'Still here,' Spender said, opening the door and stepping into the hall. He remembered to stagger.

'Where's your drink, then? Left it in the bog?'

'No, it's in the den.'

Spender led the way back there, wondering what had induced him to adopt the name Alex.

'I like to see a chap that can enjoy his drink, and hold it every bit as well as he scoffs it.'

Since arriving here in a Daimler driven dangerously by Reginald, Spender had been drinking large amounts of flat ginger ale which his host believed was whisky, since he had put an entire litre bottle of Glenfiddich at Spender's disposal.

'Pity old Shanko had to drop out,' Reginald said as he sank into the chesterfield again, spilling gin on his knee. 'He'd had a bit more than he thought, I fancy.'

'A lot more,' Spender said. He had watched Shanko, dazed and minimally *compos mentis*, systematically blank himself with pills and brandy. The man was a biochemical disaster area. 'Hope the taxi got him home all right.' He paused then, letting a few seconds lapse before he said, 'Where does he live, by the way? I thought I heard him say he doesn't have a place.' It was what the prostitute, Margo had said. 'I'd hate to think he was sleeping it off in a doorway somewhere.'

'Nah . . .' Reginald screwed up his odd puppet-like face and shook his head emphatically. 'Even his nearest and dearest, his mother, gets told the same story, that he doesn't have a permanent place to live. It's complete hogwash, of course. A blind. He's got a very nice little house. Well out of the way, at Cullercoats. I must be privileged – he told me I'm the only person he's ever shown it to.'

Spender silently acknowledged that as a ploy it was excellent: a man with a home who told everyone he had no fixed address was as hard to pin down as a genuinely homeless person – and he was in a better position to go missing.

'How come you're such good mates?' Spender said. They had reached a level of intimacy that permitted such a question; closeness had been accelerated by Reginald's intake of gin and Spender's adherence to the First Law of Ingratiation: Always Go with the Other Man's Flow. 'You're not exactly matched types . . .'

'That's the secret, I suppose.' Reginald mopped at the damp patch on his knee with the velvet cuff of his smoking-jacket. 'Perhaps we're not so different as we seem, though. Shanko has a certain loutish air when you first meet him. He can seem thuggish, even. But the man's an original, it soon becomes evident when you get to know him. A free spirit, that's what he is.'

And a relentlessly sweet-talking arse-licker, Spender had noticed. Every time Shanko addressed Reginald, doped as he was, the honey fairly dripped; it was badly done, too, but Reginald didn't notice, he basked in the praise and the badly cobbled adulation – a variation on the decent-and-pally technique that had put Spender right here, right now.

When Reginald had insisted Spender stay in their company and Shanko immediately agreed, it had been obvious that this odd soul was the fountain-head of something Shanko needed badly, and which he would run no risk of losing.

'He's a genuine friend, too, you know,' Reginald drawled over the rim of his glass. 'He's the loyal kind.'

From the start, Spender had suspected a drug connection. He had thought it possible that the weird-looking contact in the Three Elms was the chemist, or a line to the chemist, he had been hoping to track down. Now he found it harder to believe, but the nagging fact remained that a psychopathic bully-boy like Shanko, a man with no genuine feelings for another human being – apart from maybe his mother – placed great value on Reginald. What was the attraction?

'This is an interesting room,' Spender said, trying a new direction. 'You've obviously taken a lot of time and trouble furnishing it and filling it with so many nice things.'

Almost as good as Shanko, Spender thought. The room was ghastly. It was overfilled with ill-matching heavily padded furniture, covered in material that Stick would have described as bedroom rug in eight shades of dung. There were bad-taste miniature sculptures, lamps that did nothing but bother the eye, and a monstrosity of a desk piled with mothy old clothbound books.

'It's been my sanctuary since boyhood, you know. My father's before me. I always loved the way it became the whole world, the second I closed that big door. It still has that feel, a safe place, all the space I'll ever need . . .'

His voice trailed off. He poured more gin and raised his head unsteadily to look at Spender.

'What did you say you do again, old chap?'

'I'm what you'd call a perpetual student, I suppose. I dabble in psychology.'

It was the first time Reginald had asked, although he obviously thought it was the second. Earlier, he had been keen to know Spender's age. When he told him the truth, that he was thirty-seven, Reginald had insisted he wasn't much older himself – forty-two, he said, which might have been true, but his speech and manner belonged to a man approaching his seventies.

'Psychology, eh? Not *psychiatry*, I trust? I've had some bad encounters with those fellas . . .'

'No. Just plain psychology.'

'Fascinating stuff.' Reginald tapped the side of his nose. 'Don't like to talk about your researches, I suppose? I quite understand.'

'And what's your line, Reginald?'

'Ah, now you're asking . . .' Reginald wrapped the fingers of both hands around his glass. 'There's what I am in my heart, and there's what I am by dint of hard learning. In here . . .' He paused and tapped his chest. 'In here I'm a poet, a dramatist, a philosopher of sorts and a man who would dearly escape from himself at times, if only I could . . .'

Spender watched a change come over Reginald. His voice had deepened and he wasn't slurring his speech any more. He shifted on the couch, pushed himself upright.

'I've had a terrible life, Alex.' He touched the side of his head. 'Too much brain coupled to too little opportunity. It's a bad equation.' He smiled balefully. 'It can send a chap mad.'

Reginald got up and went to the desk. His newly sombre tone seemed to affect his movements, too; he walked with his feet very close together and held his head at a tilt, as if something wide was perched on his shoulder. Spender was reminded of something he had been taught at a seminar, about behavioural shifts in disturbed people, but there wasn't the time to think back and remember clearly.

Reginald fished among the old books and pulled out a single sheet of heavy paper. He held it up in front of his chest, showing it to Spender.

'That's what I am by training.'

Spender looked at it and felt his heart thump. Reginald was holding the membership certificate of the Pharmaceutical Society of Great Britain.

'You're a pharmacist?'

'Indeed. A good one too, I don't think I flatter myself to say so. But when my illness came . . . Did I mention, I became ill? I had to give it up. To be accurate, the authorities *insisted* I stop practising.'

Now Spender's mind was racing. He wanted to ask four questions at once but made himself stay quiet. Reginald was opening up at his own speed.

'I had what's called an impulse control disorder, you see. Classic manifestation.' He pointed to his head. 'Trichotillomania. A recurring failure to resist the impulse to rip out my own hair. I was pretty bald for a time.'

Reginald stepped away from the desk briskly. He was still very much a drunk man, but he was a different kind now, he had the agitated movements of the quarrelsome drunk, the man impatient with the air around him. When he turned to Spender again he looked hostile.

'Then the focus shifted,' he said. 'The diagnosis changed, accordingly. They couldn't seem to grasp – the doctors, that is, the self-styled experts – they couldn't understand that the limitations of everyday existence were the root of my problem. I was effectively a Renaissance man living in a society that mistrusted originality and anything else resembling adventurous thought.' He let out a laugh like a yelp. ' "Increasingly perfectionist and inflexible," that's what they eventually put on my record.'

Watching the wild-eyed way Reginald scanned the books on the desk, Spender remembered more of what he had been told about psychotics, how alcohol in excess could undermine the civilized barriers they erected around themselves. Tonight Reginald had probably drunk much more than usual; he had been frightened, first, by what happened to Shanko in the Three Elms, and the subsequent relief made him drink very fast; later, exhilarated at having new company, he had been drinking neat gin non-stop for hours.

'Did you meet Shanko when you were in hospital?'

Mistake! Spender took an involuntary step back as Reginald spun on him.

'Hospital? Are you patronizing me by any chance, Alex?'

'No, no, I—'

'You know bloody well it wasn't a hospital! It was a containment facility! And yes, I did meet Shanko there, we had a certain inter-dependence. Does it make your little psychology-fixated ego feel smug, guessing that much?'

He took a step nearer and jabbed a finger hard on Spender's breastbone. Spender showed no reaction.

'While we're on the subject of your preoccupations, I'd like to know how you came to ingratiate your way into our company tonight.'

A bit late to be wondering, Spender thought. And even now, it was only alcohol-induced paranoia that was forcing the point.

'It was deliberate, wasn't it? I'm usually alert for that kind of thing, for intrusions by the curious . . .'

'It wasn't like that, Reginald. If you'll remember—'

'No, it was just a coincidence that someone like you, entertained by oddities, stumbled across two men like us, ho, ho, ho . . .'

Reginald appeared to deflate suddenly. He slumped against the desk, supporting himself with stiffened arms.

'Shanko said it once and I never forgot – trust nobody, he said, for they only want to take from you. Nobody gives. I came to understand that. *Nobody gives*. There's only Shanko, with his friendship.'

'Reginald . . .' Knowing he was already in error by asking a question, Spender decided to go for broke. 'What do you give Shanko?'

The whole front of the desk moved outward as Reginald gripped it and stepped back. It was a vast shallow drawer, covered with neat partitions, each filled with different coloured packets.

'My skill. That's what. You guessed as much – you're only asking so you can have it confirmed. I give him my skill. Both Shanko and I were acquainted with a man who had limited talents in the field of recreational-drug manufacture. He wasn't a good man, he used to steal from other patients in the facility. So Shanko stole from him, he stole his entire illegal stock of a particular crystalline compound, which I had analysed, and which I eventually manufactured for my friend. There you have it . . .' Reginald smiled thinly, dangerously. 'Happy? Got it all now?'

His hand came up from the drawer with a small yellow packet. He tipped it and white powder fell in a thin stream on to the desk. His other hand came forward holding a cutthroat razor. It was opened, the edge of the blade pointing down. Skilfully, he chopped the patch of powder into four thin lines.

'Be my guest. Regard it as a prize for sniffing out the breed of quarry that fascinates you. Have *another* sniff.'

'Ah, well no thanks, Reginald . . .'

'Don't offend me, now . . .'

In his pocket Spender pressed the button on his transmitter. He had entered the address when he was in the bathroom, just in case. He hoped Dan was on the other end.

'You should consider yourself honoured,' Reginald said. 'This stuff is running out, you know. It's base is pure cocaine hydrochloride . . .'

'Mixed with baking powder, among other things.'

'*My*, but you're sharp!' Reginald waved the razor in the air a few inches from Spender's nose. 'As I say, it's running out. When I finally stopped practising, under pressure, I took away a number of substances I had been setting aside, a little at a time over a period of years – against an emergency, that's how I thought of it. Well, I haven't told Shanko because I don't want to see him disappointed, but soon there'll be none of this left, and to date I haven't worked out how I'll come by any more.'

He flipped the blade of the razor suddenly, putting the edge close to Spender's cheek.

'I've used one of these before,' he said, his voice flat, entirely convincing. 'If you don't avail yourself of my kindness, I'll use it on you. Rejection offends me to the point of violence – I don't even try to fight it any more.'

He handed Spender a short copper tube. 'Don't pretend you don't know what to do.'

Spender bent down over the desk, praying fervently for Dan and his troops to start battering the front door. But the silence in the room was not broken, it simply thickened as he snorted a complete line of the cocaine up through the tube and into the tissues at the top of his nose, making them sting.

The following minutes were a haze. The drug had hit him in a rush that didn't subside. His notion of time faded, cancelling his sense of continuity. He was aware of making himself stand still, his hand on the back of a chair, steadying him, while Reginald fell asleep on the chesterfield.

A long, long time later he was watching the room fill with men, taking the big drawer out of the desk, leading Reginald away, moving everywhere at once with plastic bags, small vacuum cleaners, cameras and popping flashguns.

He saw Dan's face, smiling kindly, being understanding as he helped Spender on leaden feet to walk through the hall, using movements he had to learn all over again and execute clumsily, like a child.

In the cold open air he was left to stand alone by the side of a car while Dan unlocked it. A darkness seemed to swell at the back of his head. He felt his chest heave, then his stomach swelled. There was a hot rushing in his throat and roaring in his ears. He buckled forward, hearing splashing. As if he were someone else he heard his own retching and coughing.

'That's it now. Just take it easy, we'll soon get you sorted out . . .'

The car door opened. He looked down from a great height and saw the mess on his lovely oxblood brogues.

13

'You look like you got off your death bed earlier than you should have,' Stick said. 'What's wrong with you, man? You've big loops round your eyes. You're the colour of margarine.'

'I'm fine,' Spender grunted. 'All I need's a bit of fresh air.' He pushed his way to the door.

'When did you get in? I was late back but you weren't here.'

'Four o'clock, thereabouts. I had things to do.'

The blood test and urine sampling hadn't taken long; the delays had been caused by a loss of physical control and intermittent memory shutdown. After assuring Dan he was in good enough shape to make his way home on foot, he had found himself wandering along a street he didn't even recognize. Later, after being guided by a milkman to a familiar stretch of the main road, he had got lost again, winding up this time on a river bank with a cold wind turning his hands and face numb.

When eventually he found his way to the flat and put himself to bed, he couldn't sleep. Stomach cramps kept him turning and restless until he finally got up, showered and dressed. Leaving the flat as quietly as he could, he bumped into Stick, when all he wanted to do was get on the streets and let the air blow on him until he was back to normal.

'It could be flu,' Stick suggested. 'There's a bit of it about.'

'I'm fine, man. Just leave me. I don't need all this fussing.'

'Right, right, don't boil your water.' Stick turned away, then stopped. 'Listen, while I remember – Keith wants to see you. It's important.'

'It'll have to wait.' Spender put his forehead on the door jamb. 'Tell him I'll look into the shop this afternoon.'

'I think he'd like it if you made it sooner than that.'

'Jesus. What's so important?'

'It's Dory, she's getting up to something with Jude's People and he's kinda worried about it. He really needs to talk to you, Spender.'

'Right.' Spender flapped his arm impatiently and began to move off. 'Fine. I'll see him soon. Very soon. I just want a walk in the air first.'

The police surgeon who examined him in the early hours of the morning had been keen to explain why he had been sick, and why he would continue to feel lousy for a while. The body, realizing rather late that it had been poisoned – late, because of the stunning by the cocaine and its suppressing action on his natural alarm systems – suddenly tried to chuck out every trace of the toxin. By that time it was in the system, of course, so the sickness was just an inconvenience, it achieved nothing.

'Normally, with unadulterated cocaine,' the doctor told him brightly, 'there would have been stimulation of the nervous system. You would have experienced a fair degree of excitement. But this batch was doctored with baking soda, in fact our initial tests on the residue picked up at the house suggest it was the pre-cook mixture for a batch of crack, the very mix that's been killing people, of late.'

Spender's condition, the doctor explained, was comparable to that of the drinker who turns to raw alcohol that has not been properly refined.

'Instead of elation there is depression and incoherence. Disorientation, too, and hallucinations, tingling in the hands and feet, and in severe cases irregularity in the rhythm of the heart, leading to death.' The doctor clucked softly. 'You're a big man, so that has helped you. You'll suffer, but you will be able to metabolize most of the threat out of your system without any damaging after-effects. Time is all it takes.'

And it was still taking time. Something like nine hours had passed since the poison entered his system and still he felt he had no control of himself. As he finished dressing it dawned on him that he had been crying, or doing something of the kind, for his cheeks were glazed with tears and his throat and jaw ached, yet he had not felt low at that point; he had not felt anything. Now, walking along the street with his hands in his pockets and his head bowed, he could not fix his mind on a point of destination. Walking was all he could do.

As he turned a corner a hand caught him by the elbow and drew him into a doorway. He let himself be pulled several yards before he could summon enough reaction to resist. He swung his fists, right and left, head down, meeting no resistance. Then he looked up and saw it was Dan.

'What are you doing, for God's sake? Folk'll think you're kidnapping me.'

'Who ever kidnapped anybody by pulling them into a coffee shop? I was across the street getting into the car and I caught sight of you. You still look terrible. You should be home in bed.'

'I can't sleep. Can't seem to settle at all. I'm better out and about.' He rubbed his neck disconsolately. 'I'm letting the air help metabolize my blues away,' he added, smiling weakly.

'Just sit down and I'll get us something.'

Very little time seemed to pass before Dan was back with two steaming cups of coffee.

'I'd have preferred tea,' Spender said.

'Just drink it.'

He did as he was told. The hot liquid helped. It burned at his throat and most of the way to his stomach, making him feel alert.

'So,' he said, 'we did all right yesterday. Or did I dream all that?'

'We did very well, thanks to you.'

'Tell me about it, I need something positive to hold on to.'

'Well, after you left Chumley's last night your contact went back to base, tailed by four of our people. They got three arrests including the contact herself, plus half a kilo of cocaine and sundry amounts of crack, heroin and a slab of old-fashioned cannabis resin. There was money too, about four-and-a-half grand. The person you delivered to—'

'Mr Bellamy,' Spender said, surprised he remembered the name.

'Real name John Walter Clements, a haulage contractor who had begun to fancy himself as a drug dealer with a roving commission. We picked him up in one of his garages together with the others, all employees of his. He was right in the middle of a share-out. One of them's coughed the lot already. They're drivers, and the idea was that they would peddle the stuff in pubs and clubs up and down the country, moving on each night to the next venue. Very hard to catch, that kind.'

'But you've caught these ones, haven't you? That's what matters in the present hurry-up climate.'

'Yes, and the word will get round that it's not such an easy number, not like some people might have been thinking.'

'And what's the score with Reginald Hume?'

'I doubt he'll ever get to court. Daft as a brush, according to the examining psychiatrist, although he didn't put it quite that way. The point is, the case has been broken. The toxic crack is off the streets and its source is eliminated. I don't think we've anything in the way of proof that'll let us nail the man who did the actual pushing, mind.'

'One way or another,' Spender said, 'Shanko will be attended to. How's Gillespie taking it?'

'Like a dog with two what's-its. He was on to London first thing, pulling the plug on the special squad, spilling all the details of the arrest and wind-up down the line without stopping to breathe. He's as elated as he's capable of being. I daresay he'll get in touch to congratulate you personally.'

'I won't hold my breath.'

'I was thinking about Ballantine earlier,' Dan said, rubbing his chin, the way he did when he was avoiding direct mention of a topic. 'He's not going to go away, is he?'

'And he's going to be after me.'

'Well yes, that's what I was thinking.'

'Don't let it bother you, Dan. Now he's served his purpose and helped us chop a lump out of the trade, I'm not going to wait around hoping the due process of law will get him before he gets me.'

'Scurrilous talk, Spender.'

'What are you going to do? Book me on intent?'

'Be careful. You've put your luck under a strain as it is.'

'My luck gave way the instant I snuffed that crap up my nose, Dan. I'll not be relying on luck when it comes to finalizing business with Teddy Ballantine.'

'All that apart,' Dan said, 'I think the very best thing you can do right now is take time off and forget about work. Why not take a week? Two weeks? Get a fresh slant on things.'

'I'll see.' Spender finished the coffee. 'Maybe you were right to drag me in here. I feel better. I'm getting continuity from second to second. That's a definite gain.' Suddenly he remembered something. 'Last night, all those guys of yours, they saw me, didn't they? I didn't have the time, or come to think of it the ability either, to get out of the way when you showed up.'

'I arrested you,' Dan said simply.

'Really?'

'You were just another dope-head as far as the lads were concerned. As soon as I took you on as part of my workload they ignored you. Fortunately most of them were on loan from Durham anyway, so there wasn't much chance they'd know who you were. And then there was your rumpled and fuddled condition, with the red eyes and all that powder on your top lip – that made a pretty good disguise. What's up? Are you worried about becoming a known face?'

'Of course I am. The day I become a familiar character, that's the day a good percentage of my effectiveness evaporates.'

'Well, it hasn't happened yet.'

Walking back to Keith's shop, Spender thought again about the likelihood that got stronger every day. More and more people had to become aware he was a policeman, there was no way he could avoid it happening. Teddy Ballantine would be more than half sure by now, so would runners like Mickey Lawton, who would spread the word. A time had to come, Spender knew, when the only way he could maintain adequate competence in his job would be to move on. He could not delude himself about that, nor about the fact that when the day came, he would be a lot more miserable than he felt at present.

At the shop Stick was temporarily in charge. Keith had gone to the clinic for a check-up.

'He'd got so agitated about Dory he forgot all about it, until ten minutes before time.' Stick examined Spender closely. 'Feeling better now, by any chance? You've got a bit more colour. You look less like marge now. More a kind of peanut butter.'

'So what's the score with Dory? What's bothering Keith?'

'I think he'd want to tell you himself.'

'Stick, just for now, fuck the niceties. If you know the facts, then you tell me.'

'Well, I don't suppose it'll hurt. He filled me in on it this morning. Dory and Jeremy Fuller and Jeremy's second-in-command, a guy called Ralph Murray, they're planning this bit of sabotage, see . . .' Stick broke off, shaking his head. 'They must be mad as a box of parrots. Crazy. They want to get real, that bunch . . .'

'Are you going to tell me, or what?'

'Well, they're going to do something up at the MacIntyres' place. The abattoir.'

'Oh for Jesus' sake . . .'

'Got to be off their bloody heads, right? Just imagine it. They're actually planning to go out into the wicked world and take on the MacIntyres. Some picture that paints – a bunch of pimply faced protesters up against *them*? That pair's got muscles in their piss.'

Spender recalled Dory making a note in her book when she discovered the MacIntyres were in the slaughterhouse business.

'Any idea what it is they're planning?'

'She wouldn't tell Keith.'

'Dear-oh-bloody-dear.' Spender put his hands to his head and groaned softly. 'This is all we need, eh? The MacIntyres are enough trouble when they're left alone. Imagine what they'll be like when a bunch of jumped-up animal protesters twist their bollocks.'

'Keith's done nothing but picture it since he found out about Dory's plans. He's tried to talk sense into her, but she's determined. Thinks she knows it all.'

'Well, she's picking the hard way to learn something new.' Spender turned and looked out of the window. 'Where does your Donna stand in all this? Is she involved?'

'No, she's more of a theory type, if you ask me. She's behind Dory in principle, of course. One hundred and ten per cent. But there's no danger of her getting hurt, she'll never get close enough to the action for that.'

Spender turned and looked at Stick.

'Call me hyper-sceptical if you like, but do I detect a note of disenchantment?'

'What are you talking about?'

'I'm talking about you, Stick, and your feelings towards Donna. That was a kind of acid assessment you made of her just now.'

'I was being a realist, like I always am.'

'A realist? You?' Spender laughed mirthlessly.

'My relationship with Donna is as healthy as it ever was. And who's talking about us, anyway? It's Dory that's the problem. Her and her suicidal tendencies.'

'I don't see what I can do,' Spender said, 'apart from give her a warning – and she's not going to pay any attention to that, is she? Besides, warnings and the like aren't supposed to come from coppers like me, they're the territory of the other crowd, the ones with shiny buttons.'

Keith arrived, looking weary and drawn. Stick congratulated him on being so quick.

'I got the day wrong,' Keith said. 'It's next week. I'm getting so I can't think straight.' He turned to Spender. 'I'm glad you've shown up, mate . . .'

Spender explained that he knew about Dory's plans. He added that he didn't think he could do anything to improve matters.

'I was hoping you could mobilize something that would minimize the damage. The rebound damage, that is.'

'Maybe. But even if I did, even if I got some bodies lined up to blunt the edge of whatever Dory and her pals are planning, how can we be sure that's going to make the MacIntyres any less vindictive? If you so much as look at them the wrong way you're in trouble.'

'I'd be grateful for anything you tried, if there's even a chance it would help. I don't want Dory getting hurt. The thought of it makes me sick.'

'I'll see what can be knocked together,' Spender said, 'but I think the best hope lies with you. You've got to try and talk her out of it, tell her what dinosaurs the MacIntyres are.'

'I've tried, she won't listen. I'll try again, mind.'

'When does the balloon go up?'

'Saturday night.'

'I'll do what I can,' Spender said. 'You do the same.'

Before she left the house Frances prepared sand-wiches and sliced up a cream cake, leaving strict instructions with the girls that they were to let their father have the lion's share, or at least let him think he was having it, since he was doing her a real favour by sitting with them tonight.

In the event Spender didn't feel like eating, so the girls had everything to themselves.

There was nothing on television, and at half-past eight Kate, the younger one, decided she wanted to go to bed. Spender went up with her, tucked her in, and felt slightly miffed that she didn't ask him to read her a story. Things changed, he reminded himself as he went back downstairs. But no change was quite so traumatic, all round, as the transition of a female human being from childhood to adolescence.

He had not expected to get Laura on her own on this visit, so that much he could count as a bonus. Except he couldn't quite convince himself he was doing the right thing by giving her the third degree. The misgivings persisted as he settled down beside her on the settee. He pushed ahead anyway.

'A little bird tells me you've joined the animal liberation people.'

She looked up from the open exercise book across her knees. He could tell he had broached the subject the wrong way, though he didn't think he knew the right way.

'Who said?' she demanded.

'Is it a secret, then?'

'It's *my* business.'

'Aye, I understand that, but what's wrong with other people knowing? Is that in the rules? That you've not to tell people?'

'Nobody said that, no.'

'So you don't really mind me knowing.'

'I suppose not.'

'That's fine.'

Spender would have preferred it if the television had been on. That way, he could pretend to be distracted from time to time, coming back to the questioning in an offhand way, as though his interest in Laura's membership of Jude's People was a marginal item. Without television an awkward silence thickened around them. Spender cleared his throat.

'Did you have to sign anything when you joined?'

'Only the pledge.'

'Pledge?'

'The pledge to do all in my power at all times to act in the best interests of animals, and to take what steps I can to preserve their well-being.' Laura glared at him. 'That's all right, is it? I mean, it's not something that'd give the police a reason to pull me in, or harass me?'

'So who's been talking to you about the police harassing you? Do you get instruction about things like that – confronting the police, and so on?'

'Not instruction, no.' Laura became intently interested in her exercise book.

'What, then?'

She looked up, her eyebrows high, all uncomprehending.

'You said "not instruction". Does that mean they've talked to you about coming up against the police at demos, that kind of thing?'

'What's this all about, Dad?'

He felt he was too far in to try for a look of puzzled innocence. So he tried to explain.

'I've got experience of these people you've joined up with, Laura. They're well meaning, I know that, but just a few of them are hotheads, you know what I mean? They believe in making trouble to make their point, and, of course, whatever they do, it rubs off on the rest of the members.'

Laura performed an artificial yawn.

'Some of the things they've done already have been very serious. They've broken the law. And I happen to know they're planning something else quite soon. Do you know anything about that, love?'

Laura looked at him pityingly.

'Do you? It's important that you tell me.'

'I reckon you must be thinking about somebody else,' she said. 'It's Jude's People that I've joined.'

'That's who I'm on about. If you ever heard about something they were planning, something that might be against the law, you'd let me know, wouldn't you?'

She looked down at her exercise book.

'Laura?'

'I'm not a spy, Dad. And I don't want to be one.'

'I'm not asking you to spy.'

'Yes you are.'

'No,' he insisted, 'it's nothing like that. All I'm worried about is you being mixed up with the wrong crowd. You can't blame me for that, can you?'

She said nothing. At that moment Frances was creeping in by the kitchen door, home early and ready to startle them with a surprise entrance. She closed the door soundlessly, tiptoed to the lounge door, and heard Spender say, 'Do they ever talk about civil disobedience or anything like that at the meetings?'

Frances pressed herself to the wall, delaying her entrance.

'They talk about all kinds of things,' Laura said. 'I wish you'd stop asking me questions about them, Dad. They're my friends, you're going on like they're crooks.'

'No I'm not, love. I'm just trying to find out how they conduct their meetings and things like that. I like to be well informed about groups like Jude's People. Do you know Mr Fuller? Jeremy Fuller?'

'What if I do.'

'Well, is he one of the people who talk about confrontations with the police, or anything like that?'

Frances decided not to make her entrance a surprise after all. Feeling troubled, and a little angry, she let herself out of the kitchen again and went round to the front of the house. Using her key she opened the door noisily, making sure they heard her.

'Hello, you two,' she said, poking her head into the lounge, catching the uneasy look on Laura's face. 'Been having a nice time, have you?'

'Not especially,' Laura said.

'Just nattering,' Spender muttered.

Frances would say nothing for now, she decided. Not until she had taken time to think it over, and had given her feelings time to settle down. As matters stood at present, she would find it hard to be civil to her great lump of an ex-husband. What kind of man, of all the men she could have tangled with, would actually sit there in her home and grill his own child as if she were a common criminal?

At a few minutes before twelve that night, in the vehicle yard at MacIntyre Brothers' Abattoir on the north-eastern outskirts of Newcastle, three large purpose-built articulated meat-transport wagons caught fire and were completely burned out before the flames could be brought under control. The damage to the vehicles was estimated at a cost of a quarter of a million pounds.

The fires were clearly the result of sabotage, and although no organization claimed responsibility, a number of placards stuck into the ground at the scene gave an adequate indication of the saboteurs' animal-liberationist sympathies.

'I thought you said it would be on bloody Saturday?' Spender yelled at Keith as soon as he found out.

'I thought it was Saturday. I got it wrong, OK?'

'Christ. I'd got my spiel all worked out for the brass. I could have got men up there and they might have staved off the worst of it. All you had to do was get the day right.'

'She told me it was Saturday.'

'Well, she lied to you, Keith. That's some foundation of trust you've got going there, I must say.'

'She was protecting the interests of something that means a lot to her, I can see that and respect it, even if you can't.'

'She was lying – period. She can't be trusted – full stop.'

'Aw bollocks!'

Keith limped off to the back of the shop. Spender stared out at the street. As he stood there tapping his foot to no tune at all, he wondered just what it would take – short of a miracle – to forestall a backlash from the MacIntyres.

14

'When somebody jumps the gun on me I don't usually approve,' DCS Gillespie said. 'This time, however, I'll overlook it.' He switched on his tight smile and switched it off again. 'Five minutes before you called, I was trying to clear a place in my appointment diary so we could have lunch some time.' He looked around the roof of the Castle Keep. 'A very impressive venue, I must say. I understand this is the "new castle" the city took its name from.'

'Built by Robert Curthose,' Spender said. 'He was the bastard son, or *a* bastard son, of William the Conqueror.'

'Well, I'm impressed, and now I've caught my breath from the climb . . .' Gillespie held out his hand. 'Congratulations, Spender. You did a splendid job.'

'Thank you, sir.'

'Did it all work out to your own satisfaction?'

'Well, the law was served, I suppose.'

'You don't think that's enough?'

'It's all the rules cater for,' Spender said, 'but it leaves plenty to be desired. Ballantine's still a free man. The pusher, the man that actually sold the toxic crack to the kids and is therefore, technically, a triple murderer is on the loose as well. They've both suffered some damage, but it's nothing much. And they'll be back in business before we know it.'

Gillespie moved to the parapet. He gazed out over the panorama of the quayside and the Tyne bridges.

'There'll always be loose ends, Spender. You know that well enough. That's why it's necessary to take the positive view of every circumstance. We have won this round, right? Our cohesion as a policing body has been preserved, and not a minute too soon. Furthermore, our rating in the efficiency league has gone up. You were a key figure in achieving all that, and you accomplished it in the course of one night. What the hell else do you want?'

'I'd like to feel I'd really served justice,' Spender said. 'But I can't feel that without kidding myself, can I? Like I just said, the two real bastards at the back of both cases we sorted out are still in place, and they're in the same old position to go on doing harm and making a bomb out of it.'

'Dear, dear me.' Gillespie sighed heavily. 'Talk about knocking the gilt off the gingerbread.' He turned and stared at Spender. 'Have you ever read *Don Quixote*, by any chance?'

'No, sir, I haven't.'

'You probably know about the character, all the same. He was so besotted with the notions of justice and chivalry that he believed he was required to right the wrongs of the entire world. You and the old Don have a lot in common, I think. He was also known as the Knight of the Rueful Countenance. Another mark of similarity, if you'll pardon my saying so.' Gillespie stood away from the wall and flexed his elbows.

'It's bracing, but I'm sure you didn't get me up here for the sake of my health.'

'No, sir. It's about the fire at the MacIntyres' abattoir last night.'

'You know something about that? Your investigative breadth astonishes me, Spender.'

'I've a few suspicions, I won't put it any closer than that. My worry at present isn't so much about catching the villains as containing the reaction of the victims.'

'The MacIntyre brothers? Hard nuts, I gather.'

'They're certainly that, and I think they might create a nasty backwash.'

'And?'

'I wanted you to sanction extra manpower to keep an eye on Gerry and Alfie for a while, at least until the steam pressure drops.'

'Have you any idea who carried out the arson attack?'

'The animal liberation lot.'

'It doesn't take the sharpest mind in criminology to figure that out. I mean do you know *specifically* who might be involved?'

'Maybe. Proving it would be hard.'

'So yet again the guilty parties are likely to escape the net, eh?' Gillespie spread his hands. 'Wouldn't it do something for your sense of justice if the MacIntyres did have a go at the perpetrators?'

'I can't make myself think of the MacIntyres as real victims of anything, sir.'

'Mm. They wouldn't know who the culprits are anyway, since the attack was carried out at dead of night when they were both in bed, according to their statements. And think about it, in the absence of a specific target, their vengeful feelings couldn't be focused, because our experience tells us that anger projected against a vague target – in this case the whole animal liberation movement – is never particularly potent nor long-lived.' Gillespie spread his hands again. 'I don't think there's anything much to worry about, Spender. Certainly not enough to justify me putting a surveillance team on the MacIntyres.'

'But I think they *do* know who torched their wagons,' Spender said.

'How could they?'

'Well, the brothers might be closer to the apes than a lot of us are, but they're also clued-up techno-freaks. They run their business with the help of every kind of state-of-the-art technology you could imagine – including a nifty new darklight video-surveillance system that would put the wind up the Pentagon.'

'You think they have tapes of the guilty party or parties, then?'

'I wouldn't doubt it for a minute.'

'I see.' Gillespie put his back against the parapet and folded his arms. 'I'll see to it that my men are briefed to be wary of reprisals. That's about all I can do.'

'But Mr Gillespie, with respect—'

'I'm stretched, Spender, and recent events have produced overtime levels that have to be balanced out over the next few weeks. We have to ensure a tidy equilibrium in the departmental spreadsheet come the year's end.'

'How about maybe a two-man tail?' Spender suggested. 'At least you could get an early warning—'

'My men will be briefed to stay alert for possible trouble from the MacIntyres. I said that once already because it was the decision I had made, Spender. It wasn't being thrown open to debate.'

'Well, if that's your last word . . .'

'It is.'

Spender stared out glumly over the roofs of the city.

'And once again,' Gillespie said, 'congratulations on the outcome of recent events.' He turned towards the spiral stairs and paused. 'I'd be interested, incidentally, to read the report on the matter you'll no doubt be submitting to your masters in London.'

Spender watched him disappear down the stairs.

'If you want to do that,' he muttered, 'you'll have to be bloody telepathic.'

At the age of fourteen Billy Harper had been apprenticed to a commercial signwriter in his home borough of Leytonstone, in London. After only a few weeks' service, his boss was saying that it was a rare example of natural talents being fitted to exactly the right job; the boy was a natural. Billy could see a typeface alphabet just once, and after staring at it for a couple of minutes, he had it locked in his memory and could reproduce it in paint on any reasonable surface at virtually any size. That talent alone would have been enough to see Billy through a working lifetime in reasonable comfort with adequate security in his retirement. But Billy had two other characteristics as powerful as his talent with a brush: he had a sense of adventure, and he had envy.

Painting shop signs and showcards wasn't adventurous work, and it paid only modestly. On the other hand, making copies of valuable original paintings, with a sideline of naughty nude pictures of beautiful women, was highly adventurous stuff back in the thirties, and there was always a ready market for top-quality fakes and limited-edition erotica. By the time Billy was twenty-one he was living in a nice little detached house in Wimbledon and making more money in a day than his original job would have earned him in a month.

By the time he was twenty-two, however, Billy was in prison, convicted of designing, etching, printing and distributing illegal lithographic prints: the prints in question were replica ten-shilling, one-pound and five-pound notes.

After serving eight years of a fifteen-year sentence, Billy came back to the world a genuinely reformed man. He moved to the north-east, away from old associations, and began a new and honest life as a dealer in postage stamps.

'People from all over the world consult me now, you know,' he told Spender. 'The time I did in the Scrubs turned out to be the most profitable years of my life. I studied, I absorbed and I applied myself. I used my natural eye for line and colour, plus my strong memory and my knowledge of technical processes, to turn myself into a philatelic authority. Everything about this trade was foreign ground to me until I went inside. I discovered stamp collecting and the appreciation of rare and fine specimens while I was in prison, and I learned to make it my profession in the self-same place. I've never stopped being glad of that. Never.'

'You're one of maybe three people I've known in my life that have dabbled in fakes and fakery at one time and another,' Spender said. 'What's the reason for it, Billy? Why the fascination with counterfeit things?'

'It's a way of bending the world the shape you want it, instead of suffering it the way it is,' Billy said.

He grinned, his curiously weathered-looking face transformed as if a light had gone on inside. Billy could always be relied on for a candid answer, even to a policeman – which he knew Spender was, though he had never asked and had never been told.

'Theatre, the movies, they're the same thing,' he said, 'falsehoods, counterfeit versions of people, times and events.' He winked. 'It's safest to limit it to that, mind you. Get into the realm of Cup Final tickets and currency, and the next thing you know, you're facing a hard chunk of the reality you were trying to side-step.'

Spender looked round the modest shop, with its framed testimonials from eminent clients, the showcases with individual stamps in their semi-transparent envelopes, the ivory cards bearing the descriptions and prices beautifully handwritten in Indian ink, and the shelves of boxes and albums, reaching from waist height to the ceiling, all along the wall at the back of the counter.

'You must be one of the few happy men I know, Billy.'

'As long as I've got my little place here and my job to absorb me, I'm smiling, ta very much.'

The underlying odour of the place was warm dust, like the schoolrooms of Spender's childhood, with a mellow tang of scented pipe tobacco. Spender loved coming here as much as he liked to hear Billy Harper talk. In a world awash with depressing mediocrity, Billy was a man of sparkling depths, and he had knowledge to spare.

'I hate having to get down to business,' Spender said at last, 'but have you had any thoughts about the album I left with you?'

'It's a fascinating item.' Billy reached under the counter and brought it out. He ran his hand caressingly over the cover as he put it down. 'One of the thoughts I had was, I wouldn't mind owning it.'

'Well, I told you the story I got – it belonged to an old man who'd made it his life's hobby, and so on. An inheritance, that's what I'm told it is. What do you reckon?'

'There are thirty individual specimens and twelve distinct sets of stamps in there,' Billy said. 'They're not collector sets – by that I mean they don't ramble the way a collection does, with all kinds of odds and sods, some kept for their appearance, some for their memories, others because they're worth a few bob. No, these are small, definitive sets. And they're all noticeably good commercial entities.'

Billy opened the album. 'Look at this Monaco set. All with imperfect corner blocks and worth about fifty quid each.' He turned the page. 'There, one stamp on its todd – but what a stamp. It's a Bermuda 1938 ten shilling. Very fresh condition, look at the green and the pale emerald, good as when it was printed, a beauty. The gum's a bit wrinkled but that doesn't detract from the value.'

'How much?'

'Hundred and forty minimum.' Billy turned the page again. 'That's a Canadian 1959 threepenny. Exceptional quality, and it's a scarce stamp anyway. At an auction it would easily fetch eight hundred.'

'So.' Spender looked at Billy. 'What do you think this is, really?'

'Looking at it, at its contents and the way they're laid out, and taking into account the exceptional quality of the little album itself – I wouldn't hesitate to say it's a dealer's nest-egg.'

'You mean a stamp-dealer's rainy-day collection?'

'Exactly. Items held back over the years, lucky finds and astute investments. Dealers of all kinds do it, you're bound to know that.'

Spender nodded. In Hatton Garden he had met a gem-dealer who carried his life savings around with him in a pocket; approximately two hundred thousand pounds' worth of seed diamonds wrapped in a square of black velvet no larger than a lady's handkerchief.

'So this is definitely nicked?'

'Somebody somewhere probably doesn't know it's gone yet.'

'Any idea who it might belong to?'

Billy shook his head. 'It's not a collection any dealer would admit having. It's compact, worth a few thousand, easy to lift and shift. And because the album's a luxury one-off, it doesn't give any clues about whose it is. I'd swear it belongs to a dealer, like I say, but that's as much as I can guess about ownership.'

Spender picked up the album. 'I'm grateful to you, Billy. What do I owe you for the evaluation?'

'Get out of here. I should pay you for letting me handle such beautiful things.'

Driving across the city centre, aware that he now had another headache in his collection, and reflecting simultaneously on the things he sometimes put up with in the name of friendship, he braked the car suddenly and swung in to the kerb. For the space of only two or three seconds he had seen a girl walk around a corner and disappear into a launderette. Her face was badly bruised and she was limping. Daylight and altered appearances could play tricks, but Spender was sure he knew her.

He locked the car and marched smartly across the pavement to the launderette. He pushed aside the bead curtain and looked inside. She was alone in the place with her back to him, bent over a bag she was loading from a machine.

'Margo?'

For a couple of seconds she stiffened and remained motionless. Then she slowly straightened and turned her head. Under the fluorescent lights the damage to her face looked worse than it did on the street. One eye had swelled nearly shut, the other had a bruise under it like a smudge of violet ink. Her lips were both split and swollen. On her throat were the unmistakable imprint of two thumbs, one on either side of her larynx.

'I don't want to speak to you,' she said, her voice dry and hoarse. 'Please stay away, don't come in here. I got this because I talked to you.'

'How could that be?'

'He's good at putting two and two together. He don't need proof. Somebody told him I kissed a punter goodbye. Next thing, his operation goes down the pan. In his book that's as plain proof as he could get – I was behind him getting shafted.' She drew a shaky breath. 'I thought at least he might have got picked up. But he's still about and acting vicious with it.' Margo glanced past Spender's shoulder. 'Please, go away will you? It's bad enough . . .'

He nodded and let the curtain drop shut. Back in the car he sat still for a moment, letting his intent harden. As he drove away the mobile rang. He pulled into a side street, turned off the engine and took the phone from his pocket.

'Yeah.'

'It's Frances.'

Two words, and he knew already it was more aggravation. You learned things about people when you lived with them, things you never realized you were picking up. There were maybe ten different inflections to Frances's opening voice, each with its own signal of what was up and coming.

'Hello . . . So what can I do for you?' he said brightly.

'In future,' she said, 'when you're with either of your daughters on your own, I'll be grateful if you will *not* play coppers with them. They're your family, for God's sake, your flesh and blood. Have you sunk so low you can't muster the humanity to behave decently even for a couple of hours with your own kids?'

'Just hang on, Frances. I don't know what Laura's said to you—'

'She answered a couple of questions, which were the legitimate kind, the kind a concerned parent can ask when she's worried.'

'Listen now—'

'Don't try to play it down. I'm not just responding here to something my daughter told me. I'm reacting to what I heard you say, and to your tone while you said it, and to the unstated but nevertheless very clear intention behind that tone and the nature of the questions.'

She paused and Spender was about to cut in, but she beat him to it.

'I took my time over this, I weighed the facts, I considered both sides, I took everything into account that I should. Then I let it all cook and I found I was getting madder and madder. So take notice, Spender – it is not on. You do not behave like a policeman when there is no good reason for it, not with the children, you don't. Be like a real father to them, nothing else. Do you understand that?'

'Yes, but—'

'Fine. I think you should leave off visiting for a while, until Laura begins to forget what you were like the other night. If I need anybody to mind them in the meantime, I'll ask one of the sitters.'

She hung up. Spender switched off the receiver

and put it back in his pocket. On the point of turning on the ignition again, he removed the key instead and got out of the car. The sensation pushing him out on to the pavement was hard to isolate, but it was something like not wanting to be shut in a small space with himself.

He walked along slowly, looking in the windows of little shops, seeing nothing, using the displays as somewhere acceptable to turn his distracted eyes. At one window a little old lady looked back at him and smiled. Startled and grateful, he smiled back a little too hard, disconcerting her.

It was turning into a fed-up-to-the-bumpers day. He was beset with a flurry of notions about making amends – flowers and chocolates for Frances, a trip somewhere special for the girls. It faded as soon as he imagined the looks – the half-resigned one from Frances that told him he was too corrupted by the job ever to change now; and Laura's eyes with the just-visible light of perplexity, wondering why it was so hard for him just to act like a dad.

Being a policeman, he told himself by a chemist's window, gave him a certain immunity to other people's bad wishes and their hurt feelings, but when it came to how the family felt he was like marshmallow.

Or so you tell yourself. If it's such a pain, how come you could grill Laura like that? Eh? How come, big shot?

He walked on, believing that what he sought, ultimately, was some kind of consolation. He couldn't stop the taint of being a policeman from seeping over into his private life, because his job was more than a job. Seepage was what it was all about. He suspected it had seeped into his soul long ago, turning it into a soggy apology for itself, a cowpat of compromises.

If there was a hope of consolation, he supposed, it lay in the fact that he had serious doubts about himself. So many policemen he knew gave the clear impression that they believed themselves to be complete men, measurably above average, to whom self-doubt would not only be alien, but wildly inappropriate.

Spender didn't believe himself to be a complete man; far from it. With his little home-grown panel of critics, he would probably never get beyond feeling much better than tolerable.

The last stragglers of the forensic team packed their gear back into the black van, slammed the doors shut and drove out of the vehicle park at the abattoir, watched all the way by Alfie MacIntyre. He had watched them collect fragments of twisted metal, bags of ash, chunks of burnt rubber and shovelfuls of shattered glass; he had witnessed the collection of brick dust, puddle water, dead leaves, twigs and a dozen other types of debris unconnected, as far as he could see, with the outrage that had been committed against property belonging to himself and his two brothers.

He was turning back to the house when Gerry drove his Land Rover into the yard and parked near the husk of one of the burned-out trucks.

Alfie waited as his brother jumped down from the cab and strode across the yard with his customary arms-akimbo menacing gait.

'I passed them just now. Finished, are they?'

'For all the good it'll do,' Alfie said.

They walked back to the house together. In the stone-flagged hallway they hung up their jackets on brass hooks. Alfie jerked a thumb towards the sitting room.

'Pearson dropped the tape off half an hour ago.'

'Did he do a decent job?'

'I didn't look yet,' Alfie said, opening the sitting-room door. 'But he reckoned it didn't want much editing or enhancing, so he must be happy with it, and he's a hard bugger to please.'

The tape lay on a low table beside the big television set. The label on the sleeve said, PEARSON ELECTRONIC SERVICES – SPECIALISTS IN SECURITY.

'He reckoned if the smoke hadn't blown across the number-three camera we wouldn't have had any problems.'

'The sods that install things always find something to blame,' Gerry muttered.

He put the tape in a video machine under the set, switched on and sat down. Alfie pointed the remote control and punched the video-channel button. He sat down beside his brother.

They watched in silence as eerily luminous figures moved across the screen, three of them, carrying nearly full lemonade bottles with tampons stuck in the necks. The shooting angle kept changing, switching to show the optimum view of the intruders as they moved close to the big wagons.

'Like sunlight, isn't it?' Alfie said grimly. 'The fuckers are tripping all over the place and bumping into each other, and yet the cameras are watching them, following them . . .' He shook his head at the awesome technology. 'Magic,' he breathed.

Gerry shifted in his seat and began to grin in an intense, humourless way as the petrol bombs were put in place; he leaned forward, hands clasped together tightly, as the conspirators lit the tampon strings and started running. Alfie turned off the video as the trucks caught fire.

'Pearson is bringing over stills in the morning,' he said. 'Total computer enhancement, he says. No trouble at all making identifications.'

'I wouldn't have much trouble anyway, if I watched the tape a time or two more. One of them's that bird, isn't it? The mate of the mouthy one that was in the pub.'

'I'd take money on it.'

'There you go, then. Who needs expensive prints? We'll soon work out who the other two are.'

'With something on this scale,' Alfie said, 'it's best to be dead sure, eh?'

The telephone rang. Alfie answered it. After identifying himself he stood for nearly a minute, just listening and nodding.

'Well, thanks for letting me know so soon. Yeah. Well, if that's the way it is, then that's the way it is. Cheers.' He put down the receiver and looked at Gerry. 'We both need a drink,' he said.

They went to the kitchen. The housekeeper, a woman who had worked for the MacIntyres' widower father while they were still children, ignored them. She had cordially despised them for thirty years and the displays of dislike were by now automatic and largely unconscious. Alfie eased around her where she stood chopping liver at the worktop. He opened the refrigerator.

'Export?'

'How bad's the news?' Gerry said.

'Bad enough.'

'Make it a German special, then.'

They went out on to the patio behind the kitchen with their cans.

'That was the insurance bloke on the phone,' Alfie explained.

'I thought it might be him.'

'He said the best we can expect, after all the back-and-forward paperwork gets finished, will be seventy per cent of the value. Because we went for group cover, and because it was less than three months since the renewal at the new terms, we get less.'

'Seventy per cent.' Gerry seemed to be trying the sound of it, to see how much he hated it in his mouth. 'Seventy per cent.'

He walked to the edge of the lawn. As he did, a heat sensor locked on to him and a camera in the eaves tracked his movements. He took a long swallow from his can, then he turned to face his brother.

'Seventy per cent,' he said, and shook his head. 'Somebody gets an idea in his shitty little brain, and next thing we know, we've got mess and aggro, and what we get in exchange is seventy per cent of what we lost, with sod all thrown in for the mess and the inconvenience and all the other buggering about.'

'That's about the size of it,' Alfie agreed.

'Right then,' Gerry said solemnly. 'The picture's plain enough, there's no complications. People have fucked us over, so now we fuck them back.'

15

According to the newspaper Spender was skimming, recent figures showed that in the last year more than 45,000 notifiable offences had been reported to the police in Cumbria, which was an increase of 35.2 per cent over the previous year.

'It's a flaming scandal,' the lady behind the counter had said, summarizing the story as she took the money for the paper. 'Crime on the increase and the poliss on the decrease, far as I can see. We're getting something wrong somewhere, isn't that right?'

Spender looked at the figures again. The breakdown analysis was revealing: 70 per cent were crimes for profit – theft and handling, theft from vehicles, from shops, from the person; burglary to dwellings and non-dwellings, with 3 per cent accountable to fraud and forgery.

He folded the paper and stuck it in his pocket. Either crime really was on the increase again, he thought, or the police just weren't up to the challenge these days. Not long ago he had seen a confidential report that described how a policeman, posing as a citizen with an urgent need for a gun, was able to buy one – a Smith and Wesson .38 with bullets – after two days of simply asking around in pubs.

Something was badly wrong – but then something had always been badly wrong, hence the need for people who had to lock other people up. In the present move towards another crisis, the facts piled up day by day and led to certain conclusions, which varied according to your outlook and the mood you happened to be in.

'So how do you feel about it right now?' he asked himself absently.

The answer was ready and waiting. He believed crime was such an attractive, blossoming, profitable and well-organized business, with so many specialist branches, that the police would be overstretched for years to come, just keeping up.

'That takes care of the Thought for Today,' he murmured, wondering suddenly if this habit of talking to himself was really as widespread as psychologists made out. He didn't know anybody else who did it. On the other hand, he didn't know anybody who knew *he* did it.

An old man was looking at him, he noticed. There was a nod and a frowny little smile; he wasn't sure who Spender was, but Spender knew him, all right. Recognition was another topic he would think about when he got the time. On days when he would be glad of a friendly face he saw none. On a morning like this, with things to do and no need of interruptions, he had been out of the flat less than ten minutes and here was a face right out of his long-ago past.

'Mr Morrison, isn't it? You lived at the end of our road.'

'Bull's-eye, son,' Mr Morrison said, brightening.

'I remember you now. I lived at number two for twenty-six years, right up until eight weeks after the day the wife went off with the insurance man. You'd been away from home by then, but I'm sure you must have heard.'

Spender remembered being told. The rumour had reached him by some means or other – Mr Morrison's missis had run away to live somewhere near Scarborough with Greasy Peters the insurance collector. It had made a stir, but at the time anything unusual did, because so little ever happened.

'We'd been wed thirty year when that bugger came along with his Brylcreem waves and his Ford Zephyr. Talk about a whirlwind romance!' Mr Morrison laughed, showing a tobacco-stained tongue. 'Folk were ever so sympathetic, son, but the truth is, I was relieved. Since the time she went through the change she'd been bloody murder to live with. It was a relief, I swear to God it was, and to celebrate I made the break complete – I got myself a caravan on a nice friendly park and moved out of the old house. I've been in the caravan now for twenty-two years and I've enjoyed every peaceful minute of it.'

Two things were happening to Spender. He was genuinely enjoying the wry little story, realizing all this time later that Mr Morrison had never been the abandoned, desolate soul people had said. There was also a distraction, something troubling the corner of Spender's eye; there were two men a couple of hundred yards away whose movements were so concentrated and in some way aimed in his direction that Spender believed they were watching him. He reminded himself he could be mistaken. He knew he wasn't.

'It was you that lost a brother, wasn't it?' Mr Morrison was saying. 'That was a terrible sadness. A waste.'

'It certainly was.' Talking about Peter was never the same as thinking about him. Exchanged words meant nothing; thoughts and memories were what cut Spender. 'Look, I'm sorry I haven't longer to stop and chat to you, Mr Morrison, especially since it's been so long . . .'

'Oh, I'm sure I'll bump into you in another twenty-odd years, son.'

Spender forced a laugh. The men had disappeared. He turned and looked. A car was driving away from the roadside, very slowly. He believed it was them.

'Nice to see you looking so well, anyway.'

'You too, lad. Take care now.'

Spender raised his hand in farewell, swinging round to sprint to where the Cosworth was parked. He was three steps into the road when he heard the car accelerating sharply on his left.

He kept moving, aiming for the side of his car, aware they were speeding now, coming for him at a rate that tortured the engine. The effort of diving across the ten feet to the far pavement tore at his back and shoulders. He curled in on himself as he landed and rolled across the pavement's edge. The momentum carried him in among the feet of passers-by. He braked painfully with an elbow, rose to his knees and saw the car speed past.

People asked him if he was all right. He told

them thanks, he was, and let a woman dust down his jacket with her daintily gloved hands. Panting and feeling his heart pound, he looked across the road and saw Mr Morrison waving frantically. He was shouting something. Spender cupped a hand to his ear to catch what it was.

'I got the bugger's number!'

They had tea and scones in a nice chintzy tea-room while Spender waited for a response on the car registration. He had put the request through a London number; the search would be more detailed, so the comeback would take longer.

'No doubt about it, he was trying to knock you down.' Mr Morrison had said that three or four times. The fact still startled him. 'Imagine, in broad daylight.'

'That's when most hit-and-runs happen,' Spender told him.

'Is that a fact? And why would anybody want to do that to you, son?' The old man glanced at the portable lying on the table. 'Is it something to do with your job?'

'Maybe. Who can say?' Spender wondered what he thought the job was. Something odd, that was bound to be the assumption, since nobody in a normal job would carry one of those objects around with him. 'It's hard to tell nowadays who's your friend and who's out to hurt you, Mr Morrison. I'm grateful you were so alert, anyway.'

'Were you on to the police when you phoned just then?'

'That's right.'

'They'll want to see you, I expect. A statement and all that. I hope they catch the bloody villains. I've lived a long time, but I still can't understand one man wanting to do that kind of harm to another man.'

For a bloke whose wife ran away with the insurance collector, Spender thought, that was a very humane statement. He was trying to think of some adequate response when the portable rang. He snatched it up.

'Yes?'

The woman on the other end asked him to verify the car registration number he had given her. When he had complied, speaking quietly so Mr Morrison wouldn't hear too much, she read him the car's current ownership details. It was registered to a company, TEBAL removals, with offices in Newcastle, Durham and Sunderland. Secondary information was that the car had been stopped on two occasions and the driver – a different person in each case, neither of them known to Spender – had been warned, but no charges laid. Otherwise the vehicle had a clean history.

Spender made a few notes as he listened. When the call was over he apologized to Mr Morrison.

'That was work,' he said. 'With one of these gadgets they can locate you anywhere.'

He glanced aside and suddenly found his attention divided again. Their table was towards the back of the tea-room; his chair faced outward. For just a couple of seconds he saw someone come close to the window and cup his hands around his eyes, putting his face very near the glass to see inside. Spender recognized him straight away; it was Mickey Lawton. In the same instant, for reasons that were obviously – but oddly – connected to Mickey's sudden appearance, Spender realized that TEBAL stood for Teddy Ballantine.

He looked at his watch and staged a sharp intake of breath.

'This time I do have to rush, Mr Morrison. I'll get shot otherwise. You take your time, have more tea and another scone, I'll square it with the waitress.' He stood up, giving the old man no time to formulate anything that might cause a delay. 'Thanks again. I'll see you soon, I hope.'

'Remember,' Mr Morrison called as he left the cash desk and made for the door, 'I'm always available if the police want a statement. Tell them that, won't you?'

Spender promised he would. As he left he didn't step out on to the pavement but stayed close to the wall, sliding along it sideways until he was at the flapping side of the canvas awning. He stuck out his head and quickly looked along the street. Mickey Lawton was about a hundred yards away, moving slowly. Unusually for him, he was walking with his head down.

It took Spender less than two minutes of serpentine weaving around pedestrians to get himself close enough to Mickey to slap him suddenly on the shoulder, making him jump. When he turned Spender took him by the elbows and swung him out to the edge of the pavement.

'See that bus, you scabby-eyed little bastard? I'm going to throw you under the front wheels right now if you don't talk to me and give me answers I like. Got that?'

The bus was thirty feet away and accelerating. Spender swung Mickey closer to the edge of the pavement, getting him off balance.

'What's it to be? Intensive care or a quiet chat?'

'Fuck's sake!' Mickey screeched as he was shaken into the path of the bus. 'I'll talk to you! I'll talk!'

Spender shifted his hold to the shoulders of the loose coat. He dragged Mickey across the pavement and into a doorway.

'It's a hell of a shock when the worm turns, eh, Mickey?'

In spite of his fright and the disjointing pace of the past minute, Mickey looked surprised. His eyes for once weren't flat and sullen, they were alert to Spender and his movements, they were re-assessing.

'How come you were looking for me just now?'

'Who said I was?'

Spender gripped Mickey's ear and jerked it. The pain brought tears to his eyes.

'Tell me why, or I'll find another bus for you.'

'I wanted to know what had happened.'

'After the car missed me, you mean?'

'I was curious. I saw it was you and I just wondered what was going on, that's all.'

'Mickey . . .' Spender's voice had a taut edge of impatience. 'If you don't stop pissing about and answer my questions straight, without the pathetic little fibs, I'm going to kick your bollocks till your nose bleeds, and *then* I'll chuck you under a bus.'

To Spender's surprise, Mickey began to cry. He

wasn't the kind of lad anybody would suspect of harbouring emotions, yet there he was, sobbing like a child, big hot tears rolling down his cheeks.

'I'm in right deep shit,' he snuffled.

'I know. I just put you there.'

'With Ballantine.'

'Oh. Go on, then. Tell me.'

'When the courier deal went bad the other night he blamed me. Reckoned I should have clocked you weren't kosher. I got a kicking. Then he said if you don't catch it before the weekend it's going to be my dick in the wringer.'

'Tell me about the deal with the car. That wasn't your idea, was it? I can't imagine you organizing anything mechanized.'

'The two lads were collecting premium money off the tailor up the road there when you showed.'

'What's premium money?'

'Insurance. You know, protection. Ballantine does a lot of that.'

'I should have guessed. So – what about the two guys with the car?'

'Well, I fingered you to them. You can see the position I was in, I had to try something. They got on the car blower to Ballantine, he told them to run you down.'

'They nearly managed it too, Mickey. You owe me for that.'

'I'm fucking history,' Mickey groaned dismally, wiping his nose on his sleeve. 'Ballantine's going to crucify me. I'm grounded, he's seen to that – I don't have a tosser, none of the crowd dares say a word to me, never mind help out . . .'

'OK, I'll amend what I said – before he crucifies you, you owe me.'

'What can I do?' Mickey pleaded. 'Tell me. By Saturday he'll have some knuckle-dragger handling my case. I'm one of the expendables now, Brycie. I reckon the cock-up with the car means I finally blew it. Not my fault, but he'll blame me. So don't talk about me owing or helping, all right?'

'I'm getting my pound of flesh one way or another.'

'Like I said, what can I do? I'm not connected any more.'

'Just tell me things.'

Mickey shrugged.

'Does that mean you're going to try?'

'Listen, Brycie, who the fuck are you really?'

'Can't I go on being Brycie?'

'You're not like that any more. You're not . . .'

'I'm not a raggy-arse you can shove around? No. Not any more.'

'Ballantine wants to kill you.'

'What, in person? He wants to do it himself? Do you mean that, or was it just something to say?'

'He said if he ever gets face to face with you again he'll gut you. When he says that, he means it for real. Gut you. He's got this eight-inch Sabatier knife, had a special sheath made for the thing. He already used it to jigsaw one poor bastard that was behind on payments.'

Spender turned his head aside for a moment, watching the people coming and going on the street. They could all see he was menacing this lad, but nobody wanted to know. That factor had to be added to any speculation about the reasons behind rising crime rates. He looked at Mickey again and tightened his grip on the narrow shoulders.

'I can save your scrawny neck. Do you believe that?'

Mickey didn't know what to say.

'I'm telling you the truth. If you give me the help I'm after, I'll see to it you have enough money to get clear away from here and set yourself up some place else.'

'That's easy to say.'

'I didn't offer it to persuade you to talk, Mickey. You'll talk anyway, believe me. I made the promise because I would like you to have some ray of hope in your heart while you're spilling your guts to me.'

'How do I know I can trust you?'

'You don't know. But try and have faith. It warms the cockles. Come on and I'll buy you a drink, and while you're supping it we can talk.'

'It's not as if I had a choice, is it?'

'That's right.'

'And I've sod all to lose anyway.'

'Now you're catching on, Mickey,' Spender said, leading him away by the arm. 'Now you're catching on . . .'

That evening the MacIntyre brothers had a visit from their solicitor. He had come to explain the procedural difficulties inherent in bringing an action the MacIntyres were anxious to take against a Midlands-based manufacturer of packaging material. The company in question had supplied polythene rolls which had twice snapped in machines in the brothers' processing plant, causing expensive hold-ups and fussy maintenance work that had cost, collectively, enough to cancel the profit on two sub-contracts being undertaken at the time.

The solicitor took half an hour and three dry sherries to explain the fine legal points of the situation. In essence, the MacIntyres couldn't sue because the material in question was not guaranteed for use on the brand of machines they owned.

'You saved a tidy sum at the time you bought the machines,' the solicitor concluded, 'but the fact that they are non-standard in design and operation means they can be expensive in the long run, like so much else these days.'

Gerry MacIntyre stared at the sitting-room door for a long time after the solicitor had shown himself out.

'Maybe there's a curse of some kind on us,' Alfie said, lying back in his easy chair and stretching. 'I've not heard one bit of good news in days.'

'The only curse I know about,' Gerry said, 'is the way we pussyfoot around with solicitors and accountants and the other nellies that cost us good money, when we should be out there kicking arses and getting direct results.'

'That doesn't work all the time.'

'It works more often than the other ways. Did you see that shithead sitting there, running off at the mouth about the ins and outs of why we can't sue them bastards in Daventry, and all the time he's drinking our best Tió Pepe, and before you know it his account'll hit the doormat, another couple of hundred for doing fuck all . . . ?'

The doorbell rang. They heard the housekeeper answer it.

'It'll be somebody to tell us our lads have to join a union,' Alfie said, laughing, 'and as of next week we've got to pay them a productivity bonus.'

Gerry didn't think it was funny. He frowned at the door. Finally it opened and the housekeeper came in, still wearing her stained apron from the kitchen.

'It's a young man to see both of you.'

'Who?' Gerry scowled at her. 'What does he want?'

The housekeeper ignored him. She pushed the door wider and beckoned Spender in from the hall. The door had hardly closed behind him before his face registered with the brothers. Alfie stood up. Gerry stayed where he was, spreading his feet a fraction wider, propping his knuckles on his hips.

'What are you after?' Alfie demanded. 'You're one of that animal lib bunch of bastards, aren't you?'

'No, I'm not,' Spender said. He came forward a few feet. 'I know some of them, mind. As for what I'm after – well, I'll get straight to the point. I'm here to try and persuade you that they don't really deserve the kind of punishment you might have in mind for them.'

'Is that right?' Gerry turned to his brother. 'He's a bloody comedian, isn't he?'

'What makes you think we've anything lined up for these people?' Alfie asked. 'The police are handling the case. It's arson. Serious stuff. We're not likely to tamper with a police case. It wouldn't be sensible, no matter how bad we felt about what was done to us.'

'Of course,' Spender said. 'But I've a feeling you might know more about who actually committed the crime than the police do.'

'And where does that feeling come from?' Gerry said. 'Do you read tea-leaves or the cards, or what?'

'I've seen your darklight equipment. That would pick out anybody nice and clear, if they weren't wearing masks.'

'And you think we'd go after them,' Alfie said.

'I think it's a possibility.'

Gerry slipped his hands into his trouser pockets, relaxing the atmosphere a shade, but continuing to stand where he was. 'What are you threatening to do to us, then, if we go after these shits?'

'Nothing.'

'Then why should we listen to you?'

'I told you, I don't think they really deserve the kind of revenge you could work on them. They're only silly kids . . .'

'Who cost us a bloody fortune,' Alfie pointed out.

'I appreciate that. I can't excuse what they did, nobody can. But I would ask you both to exercise some charity with them. There are worse people around than these ones, and they've a lot to learn.'

'I might be happy to teach them some of it,' Gerry muttered.

Spender had said all he could on behalf of the saboteurs. He had held out no hope before he came here, he had simply done what he could. Absently he looked around the room, knowing they wanted him to go, finding no good excuse to linger. On the sideboard he saw a picture of George MacIntyre, the brother who was in prison. It was his wedding picture. Spender looked at the smiling bride. A bell rang dully somewhere in his head.

'I'll be off, then, gentlemen. Sorry for the intrusion, but I felt I had to say my piece.'

'Yeah, well . . .' Gerry went forward and opened the sitting-room door. He followed Spender out into the hall. 'Take my advice, next time save your breath. Whatever me and my brother decide to do about these jumped-up schoolkids, it won't be influenced by anything you've said.'

Gerry slammed the door shut behind Spender and went back to the sitting room.

'Cheeky bastard,' he grunted, throwing himself into the chair opposite his brother's. 'It never dawns on clowns like that, does it? If somebody puts one across you, you've got to hit back. We'd look like a soft touch if we didn't, right?'

'I suppose so.'

'The trio that shit on us, they're going to regret the day their mams had them.'

'We could go to jail,' Alfie pointed out.

'They'd have to prove we'd done anything. And any road . . .' Gerry nodded at the picture of his brother on the sideboard, '. . . our George don't reckon jail's so bad. Not when you're the one that's calling the shots.'

Outside in the yard, belting himself in and starting the car, Spender suddenly remembered where he had seen the face of George MacIntyre's wife before. She was the woman – he would swear it – the very same woman he'd seen in the photograph DI Gunter had forced on Dan Boyd that lunchtime in the Parish Arms.

16

The early sun, glancing low over the beach at Cullercoats, put a bronze sparkle on the chain collar of a spaniel as it dashed from the sea and bounded around its master, a tall youth in oilskins and a yellow woolly hat. He leaned down and said something to the dog. In response it shook itself, showering water in a fine spray, momentarily creating a rainbow.

'When I was a kid,' Barry Lennox said, watching the boy and the dog move off towards the north end of the beach, 'I used to be like that. A loner with a faithful hound. We went everywhere together until I was about fifteen, then I started getting crumpet-hungry and my poor dog got neglected.' He looked at Spender and sighed. 'Thick bastard, wasn't I? Imagine giving up the companionship of a good and loyal dog for the treacherous and costly company of women.'

'You're an embittered old cynic,' Spender said.

'Of course I am. And you can't say I haven't plenty to be bitter and cynical about.'

Lennox was in his late thirties, a man of solid girth with the kind of cheery, chubby face that made it hard for people to believe he was a policeman, with all the stern and unfunny obligations the job entailed. He had known Spender since schooldays when they kicked a ball round together and they had joined the police force at roughly the same time. Nowadays Lennox was one of the few officers in the north-east who knew something about Spender's status and his method of operation.

'I appreciate the peace I have nowadays,' Lennox said, reminding Spender of Mr Morrison. 'I notice if I complain a lot, people tend to back off and leave me alone. I like that.'

They were parked by the seafront in a black Granada, a CID car in which Spender had joined Lennox in the predawn when the beach had still been dark.

'How long have you been living on your own now, then?' Spender asked.

'Five years. I'm used to it, and nowadays when anybody asks me about my situation I just say I'm a bachelor. It saves a lot of effort and awkwardness.'

A detective sergeant whose wife had left him was no novelty among policemen, but Barry Lennox's case was different, his wife had run off with another woman.

'You've been on your own for a while now yourself.'

Spender nodded. 'I still see the kids, and I think I see more of Frances now than I did the last few years of the marriage. I'm a bit like yourself, I suppose. I like the flexibility of being on my own, although seeing my daughters growing up near me but *separate* from me, having nothing to do with the circuits of my life – that's hard to accommodate, sometimes.'

'I nearly took up with a lass a couple of years

back,' Lennox said, 'but it was that same thing, the good old flexibility, that made me change my mind. It dawned on me at three o'clock one morning just what a mistake I was making.'

'Night anxiety?'

'Well, no. I'd actually got out of bed and gone on to the landing to fart. Isn't that ridiculous? I was in my own house, for Pete's sake. I was within my rights to fart as often and as noisily as I wanted, but there I was, dangling in the dark, hoping I didn't wake up the little dear and shock her with my barbarity, or give her a touch of brain death from the fumes.'

The slant of blue-gold sunlight had shifted, dazzling them where they sat. Lennox leaned back, putting his eyes in shadow.

'If he behaves according to form,' he said, checking his watch, 'he should be out and about any time now.'

Spender had called Lennox the night before, telling him he was after a man who had a hideaway house at Cullercoats. He described Shanko. The details rang a bell with Lennox, who patrolled this area with the kind of regularity that made the smallest change in pattern stand out. He told Spender that a man answering that description was in the habit of strolling alone on the beach early on Tuesday, Thursday and Sunday mornings, whatever the weather.

'It was funny, you calling about him like you did,' Lennox said now. 'Only two or three days ago I was talking to one of the pensioners the council employs part-time to clean up the beach.

He was on about the way some people lose their civilized behaviour when they get on to the sand – like littering, throwing everything away even though there are bins. And this old fella says to me, he says, "That's one thing I'll say for the angel of death, he never drops a thing on the beach." That's their nickname for him, this guy you're looking for. The angel of death. It's because of the odd way he looks, all sombre and glassy-eyed, and the way he never glances left or right and never speaks to anybody.'

'Is he active locally, do you know?'

'Only on the beach, and only three mornings a week. He doesn't go anywhere around here. As I said, I'm not sure where he lives. The thing about him is, even though he behaves low-key, you can't help noticing him. He's such an enigma.'

'That's a hell of a word for this time of the morning.'

'A paradox, then. A conundrum.'

'A riddle?'

'That, too. On the one hand he looks like a tear-away, a right bloody oaf with his near-shaved head and the hair bleached lifeless, and all the finger rings like an old-fashioned hippie. But there's something about the way he carries himself that makes him more than a dead-head, and his clothes are maybe weird, but even I can tell they cost real money.' Lennox glanced at Spender. 'You haven't actually told me what you want him for.'

'No, I haven't. And you think because you've been a real help, I could at least tell you what the SP is on this one.'

'That's about it, yeah . . .'

'Well, if we're talking about the same man, he's a criminal nutter that I don't believe I can touch under the law. Not with anything that's more than circumstantial, which the courts would kick out even if the case ever got that far.'

'But you plan to touch him anyway.'

'Could be.'

'That's fine.' Lennox put up his hand. 'Don't tell me anything else. Save your breath, I'm made of wood anyway so I can hear bugger all.'

For half an hour they sat and watched the morning develop along the sea front. A few people began to appear, wrapped up against the wind, smiling at each other and waving, performing the opening pattern of their day.

'There he is,' Lennox said, pointing to a figure walking towards them along the beach. 'Is that your man?'

Spender took out the binoculars and spun the magnification-ring all the way round to 12x. He fitted the cups carefully to his eyes and stared.

'That's him.'

A few minutes later Shanko passed opposite the place where they were parked. He wore a pale-blue silk-finish tracksuit and white buckskin boots. A green towel was wound around his neck. In the clean sunlight his hair was a luminous fuzz.

'You can see where the angel of death notion comes from,' Lennox said. 'What do you want to do now?'

'Follow him back to where he came from. Can you do that without him catching on?'

Lennox gave Spender a withering look.

'Could Michelangelo paint ceilings?' he said.

The sun had warmed the streets by the time Shanko got back home. His house was a white and honey-gold stone bungalow, shielded by a tall hedge at the front and high walls to the sides and rear. The wrought-iron gates were electronically controlled. Shanko let himself in with a swipe of a card in a slot by the ornamental handles. Twenty yards away Spender watched through the binoculars and noted the presence of a dog's leaping paws just beyond the gates. They were brown and black paws, a Dobermann's.

'It's a lovely place, isn't it?' Lennox said.

Spender nodded. 'The dirtier and more sordid a man's life, the more he wants to surround himself with nice things.' He undid his seat-belt. 'If the rule holds true, the inside of that place must be like a palace.'

He opened the door. 'Give me an hour. I don't think I'll need anything like that, but plenty of slack keeps me from feeling pressured. I'll meet you in that café we passed as we turned up here – the one with the seats outside. If I'm up to it, I'll buy you breakfast.'

'Spender, seriously now . . .' Lennox leaned across as Spender stepped out on to the pavement. 'Do you expect trouble? Say the word and I'll back you up. Who needs a job and a pension anyway . . .'

'I'll see you later.'

Lennox drove away. Spender turned up his coat collar and crossed the road. He walked slowly, noting how quiet the road was, how self-contained in that middle-class residential way, a special quiet-ude that suggested the community stood in no need of the rest of the world.

He reached Shanko's tall iron gates and broke step for just an instant, glancing through the bars. There was no sign of life, but he would bet the dog was still out.

He kept walking until he was at the corner. Turning right he walked faster until he was round the next corner, on the long rear access path. Shanko's house was the only one with a wall, the rest were hedged. Spender remembered Gillespie's remark about taking the positive view of every circumstance: no doubt he would point out, in this case, that it was a lot easier to clamber over a high wall than to fight a way through a mature hedge. Spender, having done both in the past, didn't believe there was much to choose either way.

The wall was coarse-textured and put together in a way that mimicked the old-fashioned drystone technique, although in places the use of mortar was glaring. Sizing up the job, and taking into account one or two good grips and footholds, Spender decided he might lose the odd patch of skin and would probably ruin the knees of his trousers, but there was no obstacle substantial enough to stop him.

'A piece of piss,' he concluded.

It took less than two minutes. He was at the top and straddling the wall before the dog realized he was there. On the way up he had glanced ahead and noticed something that might help if the beast started barking. Now it did bark and he was forced to put his theory to the test.

Carefully standing upright, balancing himself on the uneven edge with his arms spread wide, he jumped off the top of the wall and landed in a tangle of leafy branches at the centre of an old tree. He hung on tight and pulled himself nearer the centre, the leaves closing around him.

Moments later he heard footsteps on the gravel below. He looked down and saw the top of Shanko's head. The dog had stopped barking and was leaping around by the wall, its stub of a tail flailing.

Shanko muttered something and moved off. The dog went with him. Spender heard a door close and began disentangling himself from the tree. He noticed that the knees of his trousers had come off badly, as expected. So had his coat. He cursed softly and then, like a good commando, remembered to add the blame to all the malice he already felt towards the enemy.

A few minutes later, Shanko opened the front door to answer an insistent ringing on the bell at the gate. His annoyance slipped into surprise as Spender walked up close against him and knocked him back into the hall.

'What the f—'

He staggered and swayed to regain his balance. The dog appeared from the kitchen and began barking and prancing around him. Before he had control of himself Spender pushed him hard, twice, getting him into the sitting room, following him in swiftly and shutting the dog in the hall.

'You're dead, you fucker—'

'Cheeky,' Spender said, and slapped Shanko's face. 'Sit down.'

'Piss off, bastard!'

Shanko took a swing and missed. Spender hit him on the forehead with the heel of his hand.

'I'm not here for a punch-up. We have to talk – or *I* have to talk and you'd better listen.'

It was hard to tell if Shanko was high, or if the impact of events had unhooked something vital to his control. He was walking backwards away from Spender, his jaw sliding from side to side, teeth grinding.

'Sit down, I said.'

'You . . . You were at Reginald Hume's—'

'Good memory, pal, considering you were well out of your brain before we got there.'

Without warning Shanko threw himself at Spender, landing on him and knocking him back against a coffee table. Spender's knees gave and he landed on his back, hitting his head on a chair on the way down. Shanko came down with him, punching and grunting. It was intense anger, but it was being channelled in every wrong way. Spender realized that his assailant, mad as he was, had no co-ordinated means of hitting back.

'I bet you just adore the seaside life.' Spender rolled over, putting Shanko on his back and banging his head twice, smartly, on the polished floor. 'Is the bracing walk along the beach designed to intensify the hit? Does it get the old Bolivian marching powder surging through the veins? I bet that's why you look so gone-out down there with the wind blowing through your stubble.'

Spender stood up and waited for Shanko to pull himself to his feet.

'Sit down. If you don't do it voluntarily, I'm going to hit you so hard you'll have to do it.'

Shanko looked behind him to make sure there was a chair, then lowered himself slowly into it. 'I don't get any of this.' He rubbed the back of his head. 'What are you doing here? Who the fuck are you?'

'I'm someone you better hope you never see again after today,' Spender told him. 'A little while back I decided I was going to leave you alone, even though I knew you were a loathsome heap of shit that should be done away with. I thought to myself, he's bound to fall foul of his own system before long, and meantime he's had a bad blow in the hip pocket because his supplies have dried up.'

Spender leaned down, getting his face on a level with Shanko's.

'That's the way it was until a couple of days ago,' he said. 'I was letting you get on with your putrid life, even though you were due a backlog of reprisal, including a kicking I owed you that you don't even remember giving me.'

Shanko was trembling visibly. Spender had seen that quality of tremor before. It was the result of neither fear nor anxiety; all this upheaval was playing hell with whatever Shanko had put into his bloodstream.

'Then I changed my mind,' Spender went on. 'I saw what you did to a girl called Margo.' Shanko's mouth made a fractional flinch at the mention of the name. 'And right now,' Spender said, 'you're thinking, wait till I get that bitch, just wait.'

'I don't even know any Margo.'

'She's the reason I finally decided to come here. So now shut up and listen, eh?' Spender moved a couple of inches closer. 'This is the health warning. If you ever hurt Margo again, or any other woman or man that can't fight you back, I'll know about it, and I'll make you wish you'd listened to me. You'll wish that, Shanko, because I'll hurt you. But more than that, I'll hurt the dear little person you love most in the whole world.' He took Shanko by the ears again. 'Look into my face and try to believe I wouldn't do that.'

It took the power of probability to make this work, to make Shanko believe that the loathing in Spender's eyes could spill out over someone he didn't even know.

'Do you understand what I've said to you?'

Spender looked hard and saw he was being taken seriously. Shanko believed this intruder could walk up to his old mum's house, knock on the door, and when she answered it he could grab her and thump the living daylights out of her. Shanko could fear that because he could imagine it clearly; he could imagine it because he was capable of doing it to anybody else's mother, or to their dog or cat – it would all be much the same when you were Shanko.

Spender straightened up and stepped back.

'I'm going now,' he said, jerking his head at the door. 'See to it that I get out without the dog molesting me.'

Shanko came with him to the hall and shut the

dog in the kitchen. At the front door he detained Spender with a cautious hand on his sleeve.

'I've got to know you won't go back on this.'

'What do you mean?'

'Tell me you won't do what you said you'd do, just for the hell of doing it. Tell me that.'

'You need to hear it, do you?'

Shanko nodded, one downward jerk of the head and one up. In the past, Spender had wondered why the innate superstition of criminals was never exploited more. Properly handled, those who placed their faith in omens and charms could be put through hell.

'I can't promise anything, Shanko.'

Spender walked to the gate and waited, without turning, until it buzzed and swung back. He stepped out on to the street and slowly walked away.

Shanko stood on the front step a long time after Spender had gone. Beside him the dog sat quietly, its stumpy tail twitching. It knew something was wrong.

'Diet,' Donna said, addressing Stick. She habitually prefaced a topic with a headline. 'You said you wondered why eating more vegetables and fruit could really do you all that much good.'

'I wasn't arguing, mind,' Stick said. 'Just wondering.'

He had brought Donna to the flat with the vague notion of spending idle time with her. No plans, just time together. In the event, she had begun tidying the place and keeping up a stream of information as she went.

'And I didn't really ask you for an explanation,' Stick added, 'not a full-blown treatise, any road.'

'Sure, sure. Let's just take cancer, then.'

'Christ, do we have to?'

'Listen.' Donna smiled reassuringly and her eyes softened. 'Cancer's a very human issue, Stick. It's got to be faced and understood. It's not something that just happens overnight. Most cancers are a long time coming, and it's believed now that at certain stages of their development they can be knocked out by stuff in the food we eat. Natural chemicals like beta-carotene, which you get from oranges, peaches, carrots, melons and bananas, and from a lot of other sources. Then there's the vitamins, like vitamin E – your body can extract that in good amounts from whole-grain bread, and from cereals and unsaturated vegetable oils.'

'Doesn't meat get a look-in at all?'

'Animal fats are alien to us,' Donna said flatly. 'Did you know that barbecued meat, that burnt-on-the-outside stuff that people seem to love, is loaded with carcinogens? Salt-cured and salt-pickled meats are believed to be responsible for a lot of different cancers, too.'

'Bloody hell.' Stick went to the window and looked out at the street. 'You're always learning, eh?' He took a swig from his can of beer and tried to change the subject.

'Did you happen to see that article, I forget where it was now, but it was by some famous doctor, he said that regular sex was absolutely essential for a strong heart and muscles?'

Donna was frowning, thinking about something else. Her face cleared as she noticed Stick was waiting for a response.

'Sorry?' she said. 'What was that?'

'Regular sex and good muscle tone . . .'

Donna sighed. 'Back on the hobby-horse again, are you?' Her frown came back, then she snapped her fingers. 'I know what it was I'd meant to talk to you about. Free radicals.'

'Aye, well hang on, there, Donna . . .' Stick put up both hands to demonstrate his reluctance. 'I've told you before, party politics is something that gives me a headache just to think about, never mind discussing it.'

'No, no, *free radicals*, they're molecules that contain an odd number of electrons. They've each got an open bond or a half-bond, they're highly responsive, and they're implicated in a lot of cancers. Certain food elements—'

'This isn't really man-and-woman talk, pet.'

Donna's mouth snapped shut in mid-sentence. She glared at Stick. She was still glaring when Spender came in. He apologized automatically and said he hoped he wasn't intruding.

'Not at all,' Stick assured him. 'As a matter of fact, there's something I want to talk to you about, urgent, like.'

'At a guess, I think I want to talk to you about the same thing.' Spender looked at Donna, who was doing a slow pan of the room, checking the general tidiness she had imposed since her arrival. 'Are you all right?'

'Yes, I'm fine,' she said, narrowing her eyes at

the curtains. 'Listen, do you two have a washing-machine, by any chance?'

Stick made some complicated eye-signs that Spender didn't understand.

'Look, I won't interrupt right now, but I want a word with you on your own Stick. It's more than a bit urgent, right?'

'So how urgent's that, exactly?'

'Some time later this afternoon.'

'I'm sure Donna wouldn't mind if we stepped outside, maybe went for a quick jar while we nattered . . .'

Spender saw the colour rise along Donna's neck.

'Don't be daft, man,' he said quickly. 'Later will do just fine.'

There was a loud banging at the front door. Spender went and opened it. Keith was there, leaning on his walking stick.

'They've done it,' he said, sounding breathless. 'Those crazy MacIntyre bastards . . .'

'Slow down and start again. They've done what?'

Keith took a deep breath. 'Last night,' he said, 'they were in the Archer's. Me and a couple of the lads dropped in for a last one after the gig and by the time we got there Alfie and Gerry were well pissed.'

Stick and Donna came to the door, craning their necks.

'Gerry was saying how the people that had cost them so much money and trouble were going to catch it,' Keith went on. 'He was telling all and sundry, waving his fist about, his brother doing the hear-hear bit alongside him at the bar. Gerry said they knew for sure the three that did it. Well, when he put a number on it I took him seriously . . .'

'So what's happened?' Spender said.

'Young Eddie, a kid that runs errands and does odds and ends for me and some of the other shops along here, he saw the MacIntyres in a Land Rover on Percy Street, about a quarter of an hour ago. They drew up halfway on to the pavement and snatched Jeremy Fuller and his second in command, what's-his-name—'

'Ralph Murray?' Donna said, looking shocked.

'Yeah, him. Eddie said Gerry was round them like a mad thing, then Alfie jumped out and they bundled the lads into the wagon and drove away with them.'

'What about Dory?' Stick said.

'She's in the shop. Under protest. I locked her in the back room this morning when she wouldn't listen to reason.'

For a moment the four of them were silent, looking at each other. Finally Stick turned to Spender.

'What do you reckon they'll do to the two lads, then?'

'I'm trying not to think about it,' Spender said, easing past Keith and hurrying away along the street.

17

In the view of other members of Jude's People, Jeremy Fuller and Ralph Murray made a strikingly good boss-and-servant team; those who liked them rather less referred to them as master and mouthpiece. Generally, it was agreed they were temperamentally perfect for the posts of Administrator and Deputy Administrator. Some members on the fanciful flank of the organization, mostly older folk prone to see the hand of God in everything, went so far as to say that the appointment of Jeremy and Ralph to their respective jobs had been divinely inspired.

Jeremy tended to dominate Ralph socially, too, which surprised no-one; his assertive nature had a perfect outlet in Ralph's eagerness to please. It was odd, then, that when the pair of them actually found themselves under extreme emotional pressure, the relationship appeared to change.

As soon as they arrived at the MacIntyres' abattoir, Jeremy and Ralph were hauled from the back of the Land Rover by two big men in blue overalls who threw them, without ceremony, over a six-foot wall. They did it as easily as they would have hoisted and slung a couple of sacks of potatoes.

The lads landed in deep, wet, foul-smelling straw.

By the time they had scrambled to their feet and spat out the worst of the loose dirt, Jeremy's assertiveness was beginning to show cracks.

'Let us out of here, you bastards!' he screamed at the wall. 'Let us out at once! If my father hears about this you're finished! Finished!'

'What'll he do?' Ralph said quietly, wiping scraps of straw from his chin. 'Use his influence to get their credit stopped?'

Jeremy didn't hear. He was looking around the walled enclosure, making a soft, breathless whining sound, like a spoilt child denied a treat.

'The bastards aren't listening.'

Somewhere near by an animal snuffled and grunted, then, further away, sheep began to bleat.

'Is this a farm?' Jeremy turned in a circle, as if he expected a sign to appear at the top of the wall. 'Ralph? What do you think? A farm, is it?'

'It smells too unwholesome to be a farm.' Ralph shook back his long hair. 'It's like *Nineteen Eighty-Four*, Jeremy – this is your worst fear, it's the slaughterhouse. It's the same stink as before, you can't mistake it.' He sniffed and made a face. 'Death. That's the smell, newly dead animals.'

'You're trying to upset me, aren't you?'

'You get the same pong in the butchers' shops in the summer, only not as strong as this.'

'Will you shut it?'

'I keep myself calm by talking, Jeremy. If I don't talk there's a real chance I'll panic.'

'What are they going to do with us?' Jeremy's face seemed to be drawn in tight vertical lines, as if invisible strings were pulling his chin and lower lip towards the ground. His wild, panicky eyes, combined with the straw in his hair, gave him a deranged look. 'This is against the law!' he yelped. 'They can't just abduct people like this . . .'

'They've done it,' Ralph said simply. 'And we know why.'

'But what are we here for? I mean they can't *harm* us, can they? They wouldn't dare . . .'

'Who knows what they'd do?'

Jeremy clasped his hands. His shoulders began to shake.

'Take it easy,' Ralph told him. 'In my experience of bullies and victimizers, they get really turned on at the hint of a bit of fright.'

'I'm not frightened!'

'Jeremy, you're practically shitting yourself. Get a grip.'

The tall wooden gate in the wall behind them swung open. A man in waders and a long leather apron stood in the gap. He wore a hessian cap shaped like a surgeon's and he held a long curved knife. It was caked at the junction of the blade and handle with hair and dark blood.

'You're to come with me,' he said, standing aside.

'Why should we?' Jeremy squeaked.

Ralph looked at him. 'Got any better ideas?'

'They've no bloody right—'

'Come with me, I said.' The man waved the knife. 'You can walk out, or we can do it the hard way.'

Ralph went first, keeping a careful distance between himself and the man. Jeremy tried to stand his ground, but when the man made to step into the walled enclosure he came out, moving quickly to catch up with Ralph.

'Go straight through there,' the man told them, pointing with his knife to a door in the side of a black-painted corrugated-metal building. 'Keep walking till you get to a barrier, then climb that and carry on walking on the other side. You'll be met further along, just keep walking.'

'This is fucking crazy!' Jeremy yelled.

'Better do what we're told, crazy or not.' Ralph moved towards the door. 'If I was you, I'd try to keep my mouth shut. We don't want them getting any madder at us.'

The door was stiff. Ralph put his shoulder to it and leaned. It gave suddenly and he staggered forward into semi-darkness. He stood still for a minute, letting his eyes grow accustomed to the gloom. He realized he was beside a pen with steel railings around it. It was empty, but on the floor there was a pool of startlingly bright blood.

'I'm getting out of here,' Jeremy said tautly, standing close to Ralph's shoulder. 'They can't make me stay here . . .'

'The only way out, I reckon, is to do what that guy told us.' Ralph pointed at the narrow concreted path ahead of them, a straight line between rows of empty pens. 'This way.'

They went forward, seeing a dim blue light ahead through a gap in the far wall. The air around them was warm and clammy. It left a moist film on their skin.

'There were animals filling up this place not long ago,' Ralph said.

'What?'

'Animals. I can feel the heat of them, and their smell's still here. They're probably all dead by now.'

Before they reached the blue-lit gap they came to a metal barrier about ten feet high. Ralph began to climb up it; he glanced over his shoulder and saw Jeremy leaning over the side of an empty pen.

'What's up?'

'I'm not going over there.'

'It's movement, Jeremy. It gets us somewhere, which staying here doesn't.'

'They're going to do something God-awful to us. I can feel it, I just bloody-well *know* they are . . .'

Ralph continued to the top of the barrier and swung his leg over the top. He waited until he was sure Jeremy was following, then he dropped to the ground on the other side and waited. At the top Jeremy slipped just as he began to descend and fell most of the distance to the floor. When he turned towards Ralph his nose was bleeding. Ralph decided not to tell him.

From where they now stood they could see that the blue rectangle of light was actually fluorescent strip-lighting shining through a wide doorway leading into the next building. The air round the doorway was dense with steam. On the floor at the entrance, in a thick trail leading from the left, there was churned-up mud with the clear imprints of many animal hooves.

'Oh Jesus,' Jeremy groaned. 'In there, that must be where they—'

Someone called to them from the blue haze of the

entrance. Jeremy recognized the voice and groaned again.

'Come on, then! Look lively, gents! This is a tour of inspection and discovery, not a sodding nature ramble.'

They approached the door. Just ahead, the sounds of distressed animals and strident human beings mingled with the rattling clamour of industry within the building. Alfie MacIntyre came forward, beckoning them urgently.

'You don't want to miss anything, now, do you?'

He walked right up to them with his arms folded tightly across his chest. He was in white overalls and a flapping white coat, with green rubber boots and glistening red rubber gloves that reached to his elbows.

'What we reckon, my brother and me, is that you lot wouldn't have been so ready to condemn us, or destroy our property the way you did, if you'd understood a bit more about what goes on inside our operation. So.' Alfie turned aside. 'We've laid it on, the full tour, with nothing left out. We're starting with the area where the cattle get slaughtered.' He jerked his head. 'Follow me. And don't dawdle. Dawdling in a place like this can be bloody dangerous.'

A number of times during the first five minutes Jeremy Fuller looked as if he would pass out. The temperature and humidity were high, and although huge ventilation fans were mounted at either end of the building, the powerful smells – excrement, blood and something like ozone tinged with burnt hair – were overwhelming. Men in overalls and stout rubber boots worked on grooved metal walkways, performing their skills on animals which entered one end of the building alive and healthy, and left at the other end as split and cleaned carcasses.

Alfie's sadism was all the more effective for being low-key. Every few minutes he would stop to deliver a calm and reasoned explanation of some visually harrowing procedure. Neither Jeremy nor Ralph took in much of what he said. The things they saw, on the other hand, would never leave them.

'The electric tongs they put on the beasts' heads, they're to stun them,' Alfie explained.

Before Jeremy's stricken gaze, a cow with big, soft, brown eyes let out an anguished bellow and leapt in the air as the tongs closed on its skull; a second later it lay twitching on the floor as a man dug a hook into its leg.

'We're very humane here, you see,' Alfie went on, 'and it's the law anyway. So once they're stunned they get hung up, like that, by a hind leg, then the fella with the knife there, see, he cuts open the jugular veins and a couple of the arteries – carotids, are they called? – something like that. Any road, he opens their necks and bleeds them, and while they're draining into the troughs the conveyor moves them along to the next stage.'

'Please,' Jeremy said, his voice so faint he could scarcely be heard. 'Stop this. I don't want to see any more . . .'

Blood surging from the freshly opened neck of a cow splashed across his shoes. The heat of it seeped through the leather. He put a hand over his mouth and moved on, bumping into Alfie.

'Steady, now, no jostling. You'll get to see every-thing in good time.'

Ralph, in his turn, was almost sick when he caught sight of the next phase, the skinning. He bit hard on both lips and pinched his arm, hurting the nausea down, swallowing hard to suppress it. As he averted his head from the place where air-powered knives and hide-pulling equipment were being used, Alfie nudged him and pushed him round again to face the activity.

'Don't want you missing anything . . .'

They turned a corner and were suddenly in the midst of the evisceration line. Here the cows' bodies were slit downwards the entire length from between the hind legs to the throat, then men pulled and hacked out their insides – livers and pancreases, hearts and lungs, intestines and spleens, stomachs and bladders, all tumbling forward and down in a steaming mass. The slippery organs, which minutes before had been functioning and supporting life, were sent along a separate channel for individual processing.

'The intestines get washed and thoroughly cleaned for making sausage casing,' Alfie explained to his pale and shaken guests. 'The fat surrounding the kidneys – it's called leaf fat, by the way – gets cut away by hand, and so does all the other fat and gristle the butchers don't sell nowadays. Once the carcasses are empty, they go along here . . .'

Alfie pointed to where the lower legs were being cut from the hollowed bodies with electric saws; further down the line the carcasses were split in half along the backbones.

'Smell the colder air, do you?' Alfie said. 'That's from the shrouding and chilling area. Shrouding's what we call the business with muslin there, see . . .'

Muslin from cold-water tanks was being skilfully stretched over the split carcasses and held tautly in place with metal clips from a dispenser that looked like a pistol.

'They're hung for twenty-four hours in the cooler, then the shrouds are taken off. The treatment keeps the carcass fat smooth and trim.' Alfie winked. 'Just a little trick of the trade.'

When they had gone past the side of the cooling area Ralph nudged Jeremy, who looked as if he might be in shock.

'We're outside again,' he said, gesturing upward with his chin. 'We're out, Jeremy.'

Alfie had walked away, leaving them in a small, roofless bay. Jeremy looked around cautiously. They were alone.

'I'll never get that stuff out of my mind,' he murmured. 'Christ, it's twenty times worse than I imagined . . .'

'Ah! There you are, lads!'

They turned. Gerry MacIntyre was coming towards them from the adjoining building.

'You've had a look at the cattle side of the processing then, is that right?' Gerry rubbed his hands, smiling with manic amiability. 'You'll be ready to see how we deal with the sheep now. And after that, of course, there's the pigs . . .'

Spender took the north road around the perimeter of the MacIntyres' property, putting five minutes on the journey but giving himself the bonus of dense woodland to hide the car and cover his approach.

He walked through the wood carefully, quelling the impulse to hurry, and after five minutes he emerged close to the rear boundary wall of the abattoir.

As expected, there were darklight cameras, mounted high up by the stanchions supporting stretched-out coils of electrified razor tape. He gazed at the bastion-like proportions of the security arrangements, wondering absently who might want to break into a place like that. A second later he was reminding himself that like every other policeman in the area, he knew next to nothing about the extent – or detailed nature – of the MacIntyres' business.

'Sightseeing, are we?' Alfie MacIntyre came out of the edge of the wood behind Spender. He wore jeans and trainers and a white T-shirt. 'If you are, I can recommend the view facing the other way.'

Spender looked past MacIntyre into the darkness of the trees.

'How did you know I was here?'

'Normally I wouldn't tell you.' Alfie smiled. 'But, considering what we paid for the set-up, I think I'm entitled to a bit of bragging. There's a pair of overlapping thermal-image units in the wood, another pair trained on the slope at the front. I saw you and your car arriving. You look better as a rainbow man.' The amiable smile slid away from Alfie's face. 'What are you after?'

'You abducted two men. Where are they?'

'I don't know what you're talking about.'

'Bullshit.'

'Believe what you want. Go on believing it while you get in your car and drive away. Which you'll do right now.'

A door in the wall opened and three men came out carrying a wrapped carcass between them. They moved with it towards a small van parked ten yards away. Spender looked at Alfie, then at the men, then at the door, which was still open. It was like throwing a switch. He told himself to go and all at once he was doing it, he was racing for the door, his hands out ahead of him, gripping the edge as he swung inside and slammed it shut after him.

He took ten seconds to check his surroundings. He was in an open, grassy area covered across the top with wire mesh. Opposite the door he entered by was another door, let into the side of the nearest of seven or eight corrugated-metal buildings. From where he stood, he could smell blood.

The handle of the door he had used turned. He ran forward into the building. When he was inside he kept moving, aware that he was on a concrete path but able to see practically nothing.

He stopped and clamped his eyes shut for a count of twenty. He opened them again and saw three goats in a pen. They were all in one corner, huddled, staring at him. He walked past and their heads followed him. One of them made a sound like a baby calling out. Spender started running again.

He came out into daylight, stopped to look around, then went straight into another building. Inside the door he stopped dead. At his feet, lying in the dirt and caught in a shaft of dim light from under the door, was an eye. It was a near-perfect sphere with pupil and pale-blue iris, the optic nerve and flat rectus muscles trailing away from it like limp streamers. For just a second Spender thought he knew that eye, swore he had seen it stare out of the head of Jeremy Fuller . . .

Watch it, he warned himself.

Going forward, he saw men working on what looked like mutton carcasses; it dawned on him he had come in at the finishing end of the process, so the further forward he moved, the closer he would come to the truth of it, the point of interface between commodity and living creature.

He froze as a calf somewhere bellowed.

Keep moving. Find them.

The smell of blood hit him again, blood and excrement and burnt hair. If there was a hell, he thought, it would be like this, a heartless place devoid of compassion or hope.

'Can I help you, pal?'

The man who spoke had a blood-smeared face and arms as thick as a wrestler's. He seemed puzzled to see Spender standing there.

'I'm looking for Mr MacIntyre . . .'

He hurried on, realizing from the sounds and the heat and the terrible intensity of smells that he was reaching a place where he might see things that would punish his mind for the rest of his life. He kept moving, trying to pump up his concern about Jeremy Fuller and Ralph Murray, in truth wishing to God he had never set foot in this place.

Three hundred yards away, at the very moment when Spender was about to be an accidental witness to the stunning of a terrified calf, Jeremy Fuller and

Ralph Murray were being shown off the premises by Gerry MacIntyre. They were grimy and they looked defeated. Jeremy had vomited twice and now, as well as resembling a drunk, he smelt like one.

'You've got off light, the pair of you,' Gerry MacIntyre told them at the gate. 'Make no mistake, we could've topped you. Slow, like. Kosher killing, draining the blood right out. Nobody would ever find a trace, not once you'd been processed.' He winked as he pushed them both out on to the gravel. 'Bear it in mind, eh?'

When the gate was shut behind them Ralph took a grip on Jeremy's shoulder. 'Are you going to be all right?'

Jeremy didn't answer. He stared down the road.

'It looks like we'll have to walk a fair part of the way back, at least until we get to a phone.'

'I want to go home,' Jeremy said, and for a moment he looked as if he might cry.

Spender found Stick and Keith facing each other across the table in the kitchen at the flat. He looked at them, reading their glum expressions, imagining them communicating wordlessly with some miserable angel hovering just above the table.

'I'll make us some coffee,' Stick said.

'No, I'll do it.' Spender went to the draining-board. 'It'll be one for each of you, I'm not having any. My stomach's a bit dicky. I just popped back here for a quick word with a pal of mine that likes dropping me in the shit.'

Stick pretended not to guess who Spender meant. 'Did you hear about the lads from Jude's People?'

he said. 'They got back in one piece, but pretty badly shook up, according to one of the girls at The Happy Carrot.'

'I heard,' Spender said. 'In a round-about way.'

He had called at Jeremy's house and had spoken to Ralph, who appeared to trust him enough to outline what had happened. Jeremy was in bed by that time, sedated with Valium.

Some time earlier Alfie MacIntyre, catching up with Spender in the cattle-dressing bay at the abattoir, had been pleased to tell him that the visitors hadn't seemed to enjoy the guided tour he and his brother had laid on for them. Alfie added that he thought Spender was looking kind of peaky himself.

'What happened to the lads, exactly?' Keith asked. 'Dory couldn't get anything out of either of them.'

'They were brain-battered,' Spender said. 'It'll be all the rage one of these days.'

He finished making the coffee and brought the mugs to the table. He sat down, looking at Stick.

'You don't mind me mentioning a certain legacy of yours in front of Keith, do you?'

Stick shook his head firmly. 'No sweat. Talk away.'

'I've had the item looked at. It's worth a few quid.'

'That's what I thought.'

'A few *thousand* quid, in fact.' Spender put his elbows on the table and leaned very close to Stick. 'Whose is it?'

'I told you—'

'Bugger what you told me.'

273

Stick looked at Keith, who was shaking his head already.

'I might not have explained too clearly about ownership . . .' Stick looked at the table. He made a finger-pattern in a coffee puddle beside his mug. 'Listen, now.' He looked up at Spender. 'Nobody knows about it. I mean it's not something that's likely to be missed from anywhere, not that I'm saying it came from anywhere where it would be—'

'Be quiet and let me explain something to you,' Spender said. 'In the course of time, the true owner of that collection is bound to notice it's missing. When he does, he'll call the police. When they arrive, they'll all sit down together and go over the owner's videotape records – any bets he's got videotape records, eh? – and they'll look at a few mugshot albums, too. Now then, what's the odds that between recorded tape and prompted memory, a certain browsing punter is suddenly going to stand out with the clarity of a big sore thumb?'

Stick sipped his coffee sullenly.

'So.' Spender sat back in his chair. 'I've had a bloody awful day, one of my worst, and I'm in no mood for being pissed about. Just give me a name, Stick, and we'll get on with talking about something else. Like how you two are coming unstuck from your girlfriends.'

'And what makes you think that?' Keith demanded.

'I know commiseration when I walk in on it,' Spender said.

18

'The hobby used to be less specialized than it is now,' Mr Thurston was telling a lady customer. 'Booty's and Gray's catalogues a century ago listed two thousand four hundred varieties, but that included what we call nowadays postal stationery – envelopes, wrappers and letter sheets – as well as a lot of local stamp issues.' He pointed to the stack of thick volumes on the counter beside him. 'The standard modern catalogues like Yvert and Tellier in France, Michel's in Germany, Minkus in America and, of course, Gibbons' in Britain, they exclude all that extraneous stuff, but even so the total listings, if you include the minor varieties, comes to more than a hundred thousand.'

You learn something every day, Spender thought. He moved slowly across the opulent little shop, adopting the gaze of the curious expert, rather than the gawp of the outright novice. The whole shop exuded the notion of costliness. From the rich red-and-blue Indian carpet to the mahogany showcases and miniature gilded chandeliers, this was a place for enthusiasts who had real money to put into their hobby.

Spender stopped by a showcase and examined two stamps mounted side by side on black card, sharing the soft beam from a polished, brass picture light. The label beneath the one on the right said: CANADA: 1852-7 10d DULL BLUE ON THIN HANDMADE WOVE PAPER, LARGE MARGINS AND EXCEPTIONALLY LIGHT CANCELLING. HIGHLY ATTRACTIVE AND RARE; £800. The one on the left had a more detailed label: CAPE OF GOOD HOPE: 1861 'WOODBLOCK' 1d BRICK RED, VERY LIGHTLY CANCELLED WITH GOOD MARGINS AND EXCEPTIONAL FRESH DEEP COLOUR. TINY NATURAL PAPER FAULT AT APEX, WELL CLEAR OF DESIGN. A BEAUTIFUL RARITY; £1800.

The album tucked under Spender's coat began to feel hot. Bringing it back in when the shop was open had seemed like the best proposition, though now he was here he couldn't imagine where he would plant it. Apart from catalogues, nothing was lying around. All horizontal surfaces were clear and uncluttered. In a place where prices could run into hundreds and even thousands for tiny rectangular pieces of paper, that was a wise precaution, but it was a bad situation for anyone wanting to do a reverse-klepto act.

'Can I be of help at all, sir?'

The young assistant folded one hand over the other as he spoke. He ventured a tiny polite smile as Spender turned, realizing he had been addressed.

'Uh, no, not right at the moment, thanks. I'm just looking, if that's all right.'

'Of course, sir.' The assistant turned away and lost interest at once.

Having moved close to the counter, Spender could see into a small ante-room beyond the spot where Mr Thurston, the owner, stood talking to his female customer. There was a safe (the make and type registered automatically: John Tann, key and combination, fire-resistant, four-corner bent-banded construction) and its door was half open. On the top shelf Spender saw perhaps twelve or fifteen little albums exactly like the one under his coat. Mr Thurston obviously believed in having his nest-eggs by the clutch.

For a moment Spender fantasized strangling Stick. He had done it before, at moments like this when facts didn't line up with information supplied. Stick had said nothing about a safe, or that it was out of reach in a little room behind the counter. He said he just lifted the book when the moment was right. He was curiously modest about his ferret-like abilities, his talent for dodging in, lifting, then dodging out again without anyone being aware he had moved. It was superstition again, Spender reminded himself: Stick, like others with his skills and inclinations, felt it would shrink his luck if he boasted about his talent, or even discussed it in any detail.

There were four members of the public in the shop and three of them, including Spender, were browsing. Behind the counter were Mr Thurston, a portly woman Spender took to be Mrs Thurston, a hook-nosed elderly man who appeared to be visiting and who watched the browsers suspiciously, and the young assistant. Trade just wasn't brisk enough for any funny business.

Spender began a third circuit of the shop, pausing even longer by the cases this time, racking his brain. If he didn't get the plant made today it would be on his mind like a lump of lead, an unwanted job waiting to be carried out. He was determined it would be done and off his plate before he left the place. Somehow. He wondered how long he could hang about browsing before the management got shirty.

Then providence marched into the shop in the shape of a sallow-skinned, half-toothless old woman with a battered brown stamp album under her arm. She marched straight to the counter and waved the young assistant forward.

'I want this lot valued,' she said, slapping the album on the counter.

People were watching. The woman's style was loud and unconsciously comic. At a street stall she wouldn't have rated a second look, but in here she was an event. Spender edged towards the counter.

'They've been in the family a lot of years,' she said, echoing Stick's heart-clutching little story. 'I don't want to part with them, but if I'm offered even half what I know they're worth, I won't say no.'

'And what do you believe they're worth, madam?' The assistant was turning the pages with the very tips of his fingers, as if there might be a risk of contamination.

'Ah, well now, I don't know if I should be talking about that.' The woman looked about her uncertainly. 'I mean, it's a very private matter. Best if you make me an offer and let me decide if it's fair.'

'We don't normally buy collections like this,' the assistant said stiffly.

'What do you mean?' Sharp indignation had entered the woman's tone. 'It's a good and valuable collection, lovingly put together, too, I might tell you.' She stepped back from the counter and pointedly looked up and down the shop. 'Is there anybody older I could talk to? Somebody that knows more about these things?'

Mr Thurston asked his customer to excuse him. He moved along the counter to deal with the small scene that was developing.

'How can I help you, madam?'

Spender slid into the space between Thurston's customer and the end of the counter. In straight-line terms he was six feet from the open safe door. He eased the book from under his coat and held it just out of sight, waiting for things to warm up. When the lady customer glanced at him he smiled eagerly at her, which made her turn away.

So far so good.

'Your assistant tells me you don't buy collections like this,' the little woman said, her voice now dripping disbelief. 'I explained to him it's got considerable value, and not just sentimental, neither . . .'

Everybody was watching. Mr Thurston cleared his throat carefully, turning the pages of the tatty album exactly the way his assistant had done, with the merest tips of two fingers.

'Well, I'm afraid Mr Simpson was correct, madam.' He closed the album and pushed it back towards her. 'This is not, strictly speaking, a proper stamp collection. Not by philatelic standards, you understand.'

'So what is it, then?'

'It's what I would personally describe as an agglomeration . . .' Thurston smirked to the shop at large, making Spender suddenly dislike him. 'Or, indeed, I might even say a gallimaufry.'

All eyes were on the little woman. Spender lifted the album to chest height, leaned forward across the counter and spun the volume like a Frisbee towards the gap in the safe door. He was standing upright again and peering through the glass top of the counter at an expensive Great Britain set before the book landed. When it did there was the merest *pop*, a sound without character or force. In the tension of the confrontation between Mr Thurston and the little woman, nobody noticed a thing.

'I don't know about any gally-whatever-it-is,' the woman said haughtily, sticking the album under her arm again. She strode to the door with all the dignity she could muster, and paused momentarily. 'I'll tell you this much, though,' she said, 'you lot in here just talk out the back of your arses.'

She left and the tension dropped. Thurston, pink-cheeked, apologized without directly looking at any-one. He went back to his customer. As he reached her he glanced aside, frowned, and ducked into the ante-room. Spender watched him pick up the album and put it with the others in the safe. He came out again, smiling politely, ready to resume business. The tiny matter of the album mysteriously finding its way to the floor had been forgotten.

A short time later Spender sat enjoying a cup of tea and a biscuit in a café round the corner from Thurston's. Thinking back over the last twenty minutes, he silently revived the exhilaration of what he had done.

'Great,' he whispered.

In order to reverse a crime he had actually gone through the motions of committing one. That was where the buzz came from. Breaking the rules and getting away with it produced a thrill that was completely divorced from the motive. Every civilized strand in Spender was aligned with law and order, and he would risk his own safety to uphold the law. That much being asserted, he still knew that at the centre of himself there was a wild character built for adventure and the sheer kick of flouting the rules.

More than that though, he thought.

What sometimes worried him was that he saw the opportunities villains saw, and worked out perfect ways to take advantage of them. Often, he stood in court and inwardly sided with men and women who committed acts that breached the law. The sense of being two people – two kinds of person – was not always pleasant. There was, too, the worry that one day the balance in his nature would shift, and the law-abider in him would have to take second place.

Thoughts of crime and its link with adventure stayed in his mind as he got in the Cosworth and headed out for the suburbs. At his destination one more wrong waited to be put right, and he wasn't going to kid himself – the means he planned to use could easily be interpreted as criminal.

By the time Gerry MacIntyre got to the Archer's Arms he was already past the stage most landlords would call fighting drunk. To Bunny Nicholls, a former coal-miner who had been guv'nor of the Archer's for twenty years, Gerry's condition was the human equivalent of weeping gelignite: desperately unstable.

Gerry parked himself as usual on a high stool at the end of the bar. He bared his teeth at the landlord. It could have been a grin, but Bunny, who had seen a lot of expensive pub fights generated by misunderstandings, decided to respond with absolute neutrality.

'A pint, is it, Gerry?'

'Thank you, Bunny my old pal.' Gerry flashed his teeth again and looked at the drinkers around him, all of them studiously trying to be invisible. 'I suppose you're wondering why I asked you all to come here.'

He laughed noisily at his own joke. One or two men smiled, not sure what to do, while the others pretended they hadn't heard.

'Tell you something else you're wondering,' he said, and paused to slurp from his pint. 'Where's my brother? That's what you're thinking. Where the hell's Alfie MacIntyre? Well, I'll tell you. He's at home in a fucking huff, that's where he is.'

He stopped talking and watched a young couple come in and sit down with friends in the corner. He stared at them for nearly a minute, until finally the young man looked up. Gerry gave him a V-sign. Fortunately the young man didn't respond.

'Bastard,' Gerry muttered, turning back to the bar. 'Anyhow, our Alfie, he went all moody because I put my foot down. I told him we've got to go the whole bloody hog and do what we set out to do, instead of settling for piss-arsed half measures. He doesn't see it that way.' Gerry swayed on his stool and had to grip the bar to stop himself toppling. 'Enough is enough, that's the line he takes. Except I reckon what he calls enough isn't enough at all. When the job's well and truly done, then *that's* enough.'

He slurped more beer and watched over the rim of his glass as more people came in. Some had musical instrument cases with them. They got themselves arranged around a table, and Gerry noticed that the last one to sit down had a walking-stick.

'*Aha!*' He snatched up his drink and slid down off the stool. Swaying over to the table he stopped by Keith's chair and tapped him hard on the shoulder. 'I've seen you before, pal. I never forget a face, especially if I've got a real strong reason. Know what I mean?'

Keith looked up at him. He didn't say anything.

'Last time I saw you, you were in company with a lass. Me and my brother fell out about that same lass this very night. Know the lass I'm on about, do you?'

'I think so,' Keith said.

'Fancies herself as a bit of a terrorist.' Gerry made a sour face. 'Really hard, she is. Like the two that helped her to burn our wagons. Hard as custard.' He did a wide malignant grin. 'They'll not be the same again, them two. And neither will the lass, when I get hold of her.' He prodded Keith's shoulder again. 'You tell her that. She has to take her medicine too.'

Keith sat still, giving off no messages, but Gerry was determined to follow through. He leaned down, getting his mouth close to Keith's ear.

'I'm told she's the girlfriend of a guy that's got a funny walk,' he said. 'A gimp, you know? You're the only funny walker I've seen her with, so if she *is* your bird, give her the message – her lesson's still to come. Nobody's exempt.'

'You'll leave her alone,' Keith said, so quietly that Spender, who had been standing near the bar for a couple of minutes, could hardly hear him.

Gerry was motionless, his pint clutched in his hand as he stared down at Keith.

'I hope I heard you wrong, kiddo.'

'No, you heard me right.' Keith looked up at him. 'Pick on somebody as big and ugly as yourself, just for a change.'

Gerry let go of his glass. It hit the floor and smashed. The beer frothed out from the shattered glass in a dark fan across the carpet.

'Get up, you pony-tailed fucker.'

Keith half rose, pushing back his chair. Others at the table tried to restrain him. He tugged his sleeve free and stood up, supporting himself with one hand on the table.

'I'm just about your target, I suppose. Go ahead and show everybody what you're made of, loud mouth.'

Gerry bunched his fist and drew it back. Spender materialized behind him and caught his elbow.

'Don't be a bigger shit than you can help.'

Gerry wrenched his arm free and turned. He peered at Spender as if there was fog between them.

'You,' he grunted. 'The fucking bad penny.'

They stood a yard apart, Spender motionless, Gerry doing a standing strut, swaying his body and waving his fists around in the air at either side. Finally, seeing that any move was going to be up to him, he spoke.

'Outside.'

As he left for the car-park, Spender threw Keith a hard, long-suffering look.

A few people followed them out but there was no spectacle to watch. Gerry landed a dirty punch when he sneaked up behind Spender as he took off his coat; the blow was placed so badly Spender hardly flinched. He stared at Gerry, making him feel uncomfortable as he weaved around, trying to drum up a response. Suddenly the agitated footwork got too much for Gerry's overloaded stomach and he had to withdraw to throw up.

Back in the pub, Spender apologized to Bunny and was assured, in return, that it was no trouble.

'I just hope he stays out of the place until he's sobered up.'

Spender ordered a light ale and took it to Keith's table. The others were leaving because the one giving them all a lift had to be home by half-past nine, and there were four of them to drop at various parts of the city. Spender and Keith were finally left alone at the table.

Keith made a wry, apologetic face and shrugged his shoulders up to his ears. 'What can I say?'

'You're a barmy bastard, Keith. That baboon would have decked you. Then what? I mean where's the chivalrous point in getting yourself knocked senseless, just because somebody threatens a little bit of revenge on a woman who cost him a few thousand quid in malicious damage?'

'Well,' Keith said, 'since you put it that way . . .'
He laughed suddenly and slapped Spender's arm.
'Did he hurt you?'

'Not a bit. He was badly pissed, mind. No saying
what he might have managed if he'd been able to
stand up straight and see right.' Spender sipped his
beer, studying Keith, evaluating his condition. 'Do
you feel even a quarter as rough as you look?'

'I've felt better,' Keith admitted.

'You've been having stress, right? You're not supposed to let that into your life. You were warned.'

'It's not always avoidable.'

'I'd have sworn Dory would be good for you.'

'Does it really look that obvious, then?'

'What?'

'That we're not hitting it off any more.'

'To me it's obvious. Whose fault was it?'

'Mine,' Keith said. 'Mine for letting her get away
with so much.'

'You'd make a politician, talking like that.'

'There's a saying that if you dissect something,
you've got to kill it first. That's what was happening, right up until two or three days ago. She
analysed and dissected everything we had going
for us. She never let up, forever working out the
why and how, breaking down my motives and
interpreting her own responses. Tell you the truth,
it near enough drove me up the bloody wall.'

'So what's the state of play now?'

'There's some restructuring at Jude's People.
Jeremy's pulling out of the job and Dory's scared
some moderate will sneak into the gap on a popular
vote. So she's out whipping up support for her own

candidate, some guy from Manchester. Which is my way of explaining to you why she isn't here. But the real reason is, she'd sooner be with her own crowd, after what I said.'

Spender nodded. He waited. He sipped his drink and waited some more.

'Do I have to kick it out of you?' he said finally.

'I'm not very proud of it,' Keith said.

'Tell me anyway.'

'Well, we had a bit of a barney and I said she would be happier picking over motives and motivation with some carrot-cruncher like herself, rather than a convert like me that was likely to lapse any time.'

'That was it?'

'No. I told her I respect what she does and what she stands for, but I admitted I have my misgivings, too. It worried me, I said, that to be really dedicated to the cause, I'd have to turn into a boring pain in the arse like her.'

'I can see how that would alienate her. Did she really bore you, then?'

Keith nodded. 'After the novelty wore off. And I was boring her just as much, except she would never admit it, because in her book, if you get bored with a cripple you're really fucked up, morally speaking.' He drummed his fingers sharply on the table. 'We were worlds apart, Spender. The whole thing was a mistake.'

'So you've actually split already.'

'No, not yet. I've still got that to face. And to save you asking, it's pretty much the same between Stick and Donna, but for different reasons.'

'He can be hard work.'

'Yep, he's just too much for her to take on. It's a job that needs broad shoulders.' Keith sat back. 'Enough, though, about the humdrum lives of young Keith and the lovable sociopath Stick. What have you been up to lately? Like tonight, for instance?'

'Can't tell you.'

'Official business,' Keith sighed.

'No. Unofficial. But I still can't tell you.'

Keith went silent for a minute. He sat tapping the table to a private rhythm, glancing at Spender from time to time.

'You lead a right fairytale life,' he said at last. 'It's a fact, when you take the time to stand back and really look at it. Be honest, you can do just about anything you want, can't you?'

'Sure.' Spender drew his hands down over his face. 'I'm the original free spirit. Unshackled by habit or convention, that's me. I do my own thing and I march to my own drummer. My existence is an unending carnival. I'm a deliriously happy bloke, I can't deny it.'

Keith nodded, his face as sombre as Spender's.

'You and me both,' he said.

Gerry MacIntyre woke up at the wheel of the Land Rover. For five seconds he panicked, thinking he had nodded off while he was driving. Then he realized the engine was switched off and he was parked tidily in a lay-by. It was pitch dark outside. He looked at his watch. Twenty past eleven. Where was he? Why was he there?

A throb at his temple made him touch his head and when he did, the sweat on his fingers stung broken skin. He sat upright in the seat, remembering. He had fought the big guy, the one that said he wasn't any part of the animal lib, but always seemed to show up on their behalf or when they were around. The light had petered out for some reason or another. He wasn't clear about why.

He remembered washing his face at an outside tap, then getting in the Land Rover and starting up. But this wasn't the road home.

'Shit . . .'

His head throbbed. He reached under the seat and found the bottle he kept there. *Yborova*, Polish pure spirit, so high in proof it evaporated on the tongue. He took a long swallow and felt it set fire to the whole of his mouth, then his chest and finally his stomach. Hardly able to breathe, he opened the door and stuck out his head, noisily sucking in the fresh cold air.

The soothing effect was more or less immediate. The pain left him. He felt in charge again. He also remembered why he was out there. At the point when the need to sleep had overcome him, he had been heading for the home of his brother George, out at North Shields. George was in prison, of course, but it was Carla, George's wife, that Gerry wanted to talk to.

'Good old Carla,' he muttered, starting the engine again.

She was a great girl, not just the sexily structured raver she seemed to be, but a woman with a head on her shoulders, the kind of woman that could see the reasons behind things.

'Carla can tell George why I fell out with our Alfie, next time she visits him,' he told his shadowy reflection in the rear-view mirror. 'She'll see the reason why, when I tell her. She'll understand and she'll agree with me. So will George.'

It had always been important to Gerry that he had George's blessing. Alfie was a good brother, no denying that, but George was the really strong one, the senior brother who knew the meaning of getting even and staying even. He had taught Gerry all about that. Now he had to know why Gerry couldn't go along with Alfie over this business with the animal liberators.

As he drew near the place where George and Carla had built their home he slowed down. His head was spinning again, which was probably because he was having to concentrate with so much drink inside him. Driving at twenty miles an hour, he watched for the turning, the long Tarmac drive to the secluded mansion George and Carla had christened Haven on the Hill.

He nearly missed it, but swung the vehicle round just in time to keep from mounting the grassy bank. Keeping the engine in low gear he let the Land Rover whisper up the smooth surface and round into the crescent of parking area in front of the house.

'Aw, bugger it,' he grunted as he switched off the engine, realizing he should have brought flowers or something. On the other hand, it was an on-the-spur visit, Carla would understand that. She was a very understanding person.

When he was out and standing by the flowerbeds at the front of the house, combing his hair, he thought about it again and decided he was right to come here tonight. Alfie had hurt him, the way he had called him a nutter and told him he didn't know when to stop. George had to know about that, he had to know and pass back the word: Alfie was wrong. That was very important to Gerry.

He went forward to the porch, smelling the jasmine flowers, noticing the sitting-room lights were on. He stopped and craned his neck. Carla was sitting on the couch, he could see the back of her head. For a second he was tempted to knock on the window and surprise her, but that wasn't a good idea, he decided, not when a woman was in on her own.

But she wasn't on her own. As Gerry watched a man came in from the hall. He was carrying a brandy bottle in one hand and a glass in the other. He wasn't wearing a shirt.

Gerry blinked and leaned closer. He knew the man's face. God, yes. It was him, that one that fancied himself, the handsome bastard, the copper he and Alfie had met once or twice at charity soccer matches and the like, Detective Inspector somebody.

What was he doing here? Without a shirt?

Carla stood up and Gerry heard his breath catch. She had nothing on but her pants, little black lacy numbers, hardly big enough to cover her backside. As he stared she put her arms round the policeman's neck and kissed him.

Gerry stood back from the window, hearing the rush of blood in his ears. Right at that moment he had no idea what to do.

He looked across at the lighted window again.

'I'll be buggered . . .'

He would need to give himself time to think, time to sort out his thoughts. This called for action, there was no question about that. Something would have to be done.

19

Ten days after Keith and Dory finally decided they would no longer be seeing each other, Stick was forced to admit that his relationship with Donna would have to be put decently to sleep. He brought matters to a head suddenly, because he didn't want her to be the one to announce it was over.

'It's trailed on long enough, pet,' he said. It was a Thursday lunchtime at The Happy Carrot, and Stick was at the window table he had come to think of as his own. 'I thought I might as well tell you now, and cut short the agony.'

Donna scowled as she unceremoniously banged down a plate of rice-stuffed cabbage in front of him.

'By *it*, I presume you mean our relationship?'

He nodded, little wrinkles of sadness at the corners of his eyes. She glared at him.

'I've been trying to tell *you* that for at least a couple of weeks, but you've kept hanging on.'

'I believe in giving things a chance, Donna. I know how you've been feeling lately, it's true, but I also know that you can be a victim of false emotions, they can mislead you so you don't know what you want.'

'Really?' Donna took a napkin from her apron

pocket and flicked away the crumbs of two bread rolls Stick had eaten while he was waiting for his meal. 'So does this mean you'll stop coming in here?'

'Well, I like the grub, but it might be kind of painful for you, seeing me day after day . . .'

'It would be agony,' Donna snapped. 'Will you be settling your account before you leave today, then?'

'God.' Stick shook his head slowly. 'You can be right mercenary when you feel like it, can't you?'

'Listen,' Donna said, moving closer and whispering, 'you're the only person who's ever been allowed credit in this place. It's gone on for weeks now and the total, including today's bill, is thirty-seven pounds eighty.'

Stick patted the front of his jacket and made a show of annoyance.

'I could have sworn I put my cheque book in my pocket before I came out.' He shrugged. 'I'll have to bring it in to you.'

Donna turned and flounced off into the kitchen. Stick attacked the plateful in front of him and when it was finished he had two sultana slices and a half pint of non-alcoholic ginger beer. As he wandered to the door, reflectively patting his stomach, Donna hurried through with a white envelope and put it in his hand.

'Our terms are seven days, net,' she said coldly.

Stick slid the envelope into his inside pocket and smiled at her.

'I'll miss you,' he said.

Donna looked around to make sure no-one was listening.

'And I'll miss what I thought we had going – but then I've been missing that for a while.'

'I was sure you understood me, you know. You brought something special into my life. A new kind of awareness. It's easy enough to like a bloke for his good points, but a real woman knows how to love him for his faults.'

'You read things into our relationship that weren't there at all,' Donna said. 'You fictionalized your own past and our present, and when it came to solid commitment you never even tried to meet me halfway.'

'Harsh words, lass . . .'

'How could any association between two people survive an alternating routine of myth-making one minute and neglect the next?'

'I think it's maybe easier for you to make yourself believe all that, Donna, than to bear the pain of the truth.'

'What? What are you saying?'

'Your conservationism – it's a praiseworthy approach to life, I'll not deny that, but somehow it threw a cold green light over everything. It was a terrible grind at times . . .'

'Christ!' Donna hissed. 'I don't believe this.'

'And while it's sad that you feel the way you do about us,' Stick went on, 'I've got to make myself look on the bright side. At least I'll get a chance to finish a pint in peace now, without you rabbiting on about saving the badgers, or telling me all the different dinners you can make out of a bag of chick peas.'

Donna jerked open the door and stood to one side, her mouth clamped shut. Stick smiled at her one last time and stepped outside. He turned to wave but she had shut the door and was gone.

He set off at an easy pace in the direction of the pub, thinking of what he had put behind him. It could have been lovely, he thought, but all that cold reason and commitment was bound to be a killer in the end. He was a lad who needed his elbow room, and he needed a good vulgar laugh now and then, too. So he supposed it was just as well it had ended sooner rather than later.

'All the best, Donna . . .'

Walking steadily with his hands in his coat pockets, he took a deep stoical breath and let his eyes turn towards the sea, and the horizon.

Not far away, Spender was paying a rare, reluctant visit to DCS Gillespie's office at Clayton Street police station. He had come in by a back door and had passed no-one on the way; nevertheless he was unhappy about having his face associated with this place and these people, and he told Mr Gillespie as much.

'Yes, yes, noted, Spender, but I'm pressed for time. That's why I summoned you here, instead of setting up the Len Deighton stuff on the roof of a hotel or whatever.'

'Fair enough.' Spender stood squarely in front of the desk, as he felt was expected of him. 'Before we go any further, have you given the OK yet on the exes I put in for?'

Gillespie's teeth came together with a soft click. 'Three hundred pounds,' he said. 'Rather a lot, when there's no adequate explanation of why you want it.'

'I'm entitled to four requisitions a year under the Exceptional Claims Arrangement, sir. This is the first one I've submitted to you.'

'Though not the last, I'm sure.' Gillespie opened the top drawer of the desk, took out a long buff envelope and handed it to Spender. 'It's all there, tens and fives as you asked.'

'Thanks.' Spender put the envelope in his pocket. 'So what's happened. What am I here for?'

'It's not so much that anything's happened, not particularly recently anyway. It's more a case of me wishing to carpet you while the cause – correction, the causes – are lying prominently on my plate.'

'And it had to be a real carpet, of course.'

'Don't be bloody impertinent, Spender.' Gillespie jabbed his finger on a sheaf of paper lying in front of him. 'Because of you, senior people have been seriously inconvenienced in the past few days.' He sat back, clasping his hands. 'I'm sure you remember a case involving a trade in wild birds, which blossomed into the discovery of a thriving fake-antiques industry.'

'I remember uncovering the whole thing very clearly, sir.'

'Quite. So you'll remember Mr Saddler, the man at the heart of the operation.'

Spender nodded.

'Well, two days ago, in court, just minutes after the case was adjourned in order to give the prosecution time to organize the full bulk of its evidence, a counter-motion against the police, claiming serious and malicious injury, was put before the judge by Mr Saddler's barrister.'

Spender held Gillespie's accusing stare.

'What do you have to say about that?'

'Nothing,' Spender said.

'Do you know how seriously you injured that man?'

'Not offhand.'

'Well, I'll tell you.' Gillespie reached for the papers and leafed through them. 'After you'd finished with him he had to be treated as a hospital in-patient. According to the record he suffered a fracture of the nasal bone, which led to a compression fracture of a lachrymal bone, which in turn caused a rupture of the naso-lachrymal duct, plus serious torsion-trauma to the trochlea, and a hairline crack to the nasal concha. In addition, as if all that wasn't enough, there was serious damage to the sclera and choroid of the eye itself, plus severe bruising of something called the zonular ligament.'

'All I did was nut him.'

'You could have blinded the man, for God's sake!'

'And if I hadn't acted when I did, he could have done a lot worse than blind me,' Spender said. 'In case the record doesn't show it, sir, Mr Saddler was carrying an illegal leather sap, shot-filled, which he was about to use on me. I don't know if you're familiar with the kind of injury those things can inflict . . .'

'I know about them. That isn't the point.'

'No,' Spender grunted. 'The point is that senior people have been seriously inconvenienced in the

298

last few days, as you said. The lamentable inconvenience caused to fat-arsed brass always takes
precedence over every other consideration, doesn't
it, Mr Gillespie?'

Gillespie started to say one thing then stopped
himself and said another, quietly, controlling himself with difficulty.

'The whole point, Spender, is that none of it
should have happened. Very senior people had to
put their hands on their hearts and tell a judge that
not only was the damage suffered by Mr Saddler
caused by some unidentified villain, but they had
to swear, in the face of very powerful scepticism,
that there was no irregular police presence on the
case – not before, not during, not after.'

Spender flexed his knees. 'You won't mind if I
don't keep up this naughty-schoolboy position, will
you? It's playing havoc with my back.' He walked
to the window, turned, and rested his hands behind
him on the ledge. 'What do you expect me to say?'

'You could at least show some regret for the
trouble you've caused.'

'But I don't regret any of it. I did my job. If that
means that some elements in the upper echelons
had to go to some trouble to preserve my cover,
well tough. They should feel better about doing
something to justify their money, for a change.'

Gillespie rested his face on the palms of his hands.
He looked up again after a few seconds.

'There's more, Spender. Some days ago, a
suspected drug trafficker, one Edward "Teddy"
Ballantine, suffered a string of grave personal
misfortunes.'

'Oh yes? What happened, sir?'

'You bloody know what happened! You were on to this bastard, weren't you? You were dug-in on his operation. In my presence you expressed regrets, after the clearing up of the toxic drug business, that he was going to get off scot-free. Don't deny it, and please don't underrate my intelligence by thinking I'd believe for a second that this might have been a coincidence.'

Spender waited a minute to let Gillespie settle down again.

'By the same token,' he said, 'I'm sure you won't expect me to be daft enough to put up my hand to something that could get my crown jewels converted to cufflinks if there was ever any scrap of proof that I did it.'

Gillespie was shaking his head and rubbing his neck at the same time.

'By Christ, Spender, there are times when I could make a crusade of putting you on your knees, and that's a fact.'

'I'll remember it, sir. Are you going to tell me what happened to Ballantine, at all?'

'Why not? Charades are what this job is all about these days.' Gillespie linked his hands at the back of his head and addressed the ceiling. 'The matter came to the notice of the police because the fire brigade reported things Mr Ballantine said and did. Otherwise we might never have known quite so much about the matter. It seems the gentleman was at his home, an opulent split-level in a quiet suburb of the city, watching television, when of all things a stream of burning petrol entered the sitting room from the hall and began to ignite his furniture and curtains. Within minutes the place was ablaze. By the time the fire brigade arrived the structure was virtually burnt down. But the worst of it for Ballantine, it seems, was that a huge rockery at the bottom of his garden blew up while the blaze was at its height.'

'Sounds bizarre,' Spender said, deadpan.

'Fragments of rock from the explosion were kept by the Chief Fire Officer. Very interesting they proved, too. They were not rocks at all, but a rock-like compound, fashioned into large rocks that would seem to have been hollow.'

'Maybe they were containers for something.'

'How astute, Spender. Containers they might well have been. Whatever they contained, and I'm sure it would strain no one's ingenuity to work that out, the loss sent Mr Ballantine into something like an epileptic seizure.'

Gillespie sat forward again, his hands flat on the desk. 'At the height of his hysteria and his wild jumping around – described by one onlooker as resembling tribal dancing – he paused long enough to swear he would mutilate the one who did this to him. And it would appear he *saw* who did it, probably because he was meant to. The phrase he used, actually, was . . . hang on . . .' Gillespie fished around in the papers on the desk and pulled out a yellow slip. '. . . "I'll slash the nuts off that two-timing junkie bastard Brycie, so help me Jesus I will." '

'A junkie, eh?' Spender sucked his teeth thoughtfully. 'That's the way they tend to be. Flaky and volatile.'

For a short time Gillespie seemed to withdraw into himself. He sat very still, one hand closed lightly round the back of the other. When he finally looked up at Spender his expression was almost sad.

'I don't like mavericks,' he said. 'I especially don't like the kind who already have a lot more professional leeway than anybody needs, and still decide they should take more. I got you here this afternoon to deliver a bollocking. But I might as well have saved myself the trouble – I think I knew that even as I was ordering you here. Whatever I say or do, you can offset it for yourself by going out and inflicting one more piece of anarchy on the system. It's quite amazing, when I think about it. You must get the feeling that nothing short of Kryptonite would bring you down.'

'Are you saying you're jealous of me, sir?'

Gillespie watched his own knuckles whiten.

'Get out of here,' he said.

Spender's mobile rang as he was leaving the back of the police station. He stopped beside the gate and answered it. Dan Boyd was on the other end.

'I just saw you leave,' he said.

'Ten spotter points, Dan, and well done. What do you want?'

'I've got a nice bit of cop gossip. Fancy a cuppa and a bun?'

'Round the corner,' Spender said. 'That place that does the sinful Danish slices. I'll be waiting with jam on my chin.'

The story was all over the division, Dan said,

when he had demolished his first Danish and had let Spender talk him into a second.

'Does it involve anybody I actually know? Remember I'm not exactly on the inside.'

'Of course you know him. It's your friend and mine, DI Kevin Gunter.' Dan wiped his mouth with a paper napkin. 'He's disappeared. Him and his girlfriend. And guess who the girlfriend turns out to be.'

'George MacIntyre's missis.'

Dan blinked. 'How do you get to know these things?'

'It's mostly expert observation and keeping my ear to the ground. What do you mean, disappeared?'

'There's been no sign of either of them for a week. Gunter hasn't been home, hasn't shown up for work, and wasn't known to be working on anything special that might involve him going out of sight for a while.'

'Are any theories being kicked around?'

'The consensus seems to be that Kevin and the fancy woman have run away together. Ruddick, one of the uniform inspectors, says he knew Gunter could never keep the relationship at a fun-and-business level. The way he put it was, Gunter's always been easy to lead by the dick. It seems a week or two ago, he admitted to Ruddick that he was falling in love with the MacIntyre woman.'

'So where are they likely to be?'

'General agreement puts them on a Greek Island, gazing into each other's eyes, smashed out of their skulls on ouzo.'

'I suppose there'll have to be an inquiry.' Spender

smiled as the waitress brought the second round of Danish.

'He won't be the first copper to run away and never come back.' Dan took a bite of Danish and chewed it slowly. 'Of course, muggins here has got the job of putting the report together.'

'Shouldn't take you long.'

'No, but it means I'll need to go and have a word with the MacIntyres about their sister-in-law.'

'Who reported her missing?'

'Her domestic staff, gardener and housekeeper. By now, the brothers should have worked everything out for themselves.'

Spender grinned. 'I can just picture the smoke curling out of their ears. Let me know how you get on, I enjoy a good laugh.' He wolfed down the remains of the second Danish and wiped his fingers.

'What are you chasing at the moment?' Dan asked.

'Well, following a severe chiding from DCS Gillespie, I've decided to be a better human being. Later on I'm going to go round Frances's house, pick up the kids and take them out for a pizza. After that I'll go home, get changed into something shabby, and maybe have a shot at reading myself to sleep.'

'Very civilized,' Dan said.

'Right. It's amazing, isn't it, the change that a rocket from the chief can make in a man.'

'What did he want with you?'

'Like I said – it was a disciplinary chat. The problem, I believe, is that in common with a lot of men tied in place with rules, regulations and the weight of their own authority, he's pissed off with toeing the line all the time. So he takes it out on a footloose bastard like me.'

Dan shrugged. 'You can't blame him, can you?'

'No,' Spender agreed, 'not in the slightest.'

At four o'clock, in the bar of a rundown pub near the railway station, Spender bought two half pints of bitter and took them to a vacant table in the darkest corner. He sat down, pulled a folded newspaper from his pocket and sat staring at it until the door opened and Mickey Lawton came in. After a nervous scan of the place Mickey saw Spender and came across. He sat down opposite.

'I really didn't think you'd be waiting,' he said.

Spender lowered the paper and looked at him. 'Are they all doubting bastards in your family, or are you the only one?' He pushed one of the half pints across the table. 'I hardly recognized you.'

Few people would have known it was Mickey. His hair had been cropped, he wore conventional jeans, trainers, a neat black T-shirt and a blue windcheater.

'Those mates of yours at the Sally Army, they talked me into all this. Said I was making the place look scruffy the way I was.'

'They took care of you all right?'

'They were smashing.'

'Good. I know it was a bit of a wait, but I always believe you should let the dust settle before making another move. So tell me. Are you fit for life's next great adventure?'

Mickey nodded at the grab-bag he had put on the

table. 'Me and all my worldly goods, we're ready for the off.'

'Fine. Now, I want to thank you for the griff you gave me on Ballantine. It was right on the ball.'

'I told you it was.'

'Yeah. People like him should realize that if they employ smart-arses like you to run their errands, they're not going to be able to keep any secrets.'

'I don't want to find out what happens to him.'

'It's already happened, but I wasn't going to give you any details anyway.' Spender took the buff envelope from his pocket and passed it across the table. 'Put it in your jacket. You can count it later if you feel like reassuring yourself.'

'Two hundred, like you agreed?'

'With a hundred on top,' Spender said, 'because your information was so spot on.'

'Jesus . . .'

'Don't go soft on me.'

They drank up and left the pub. On the pavement outside Spender gave Mickey a piece of paper with train times and a list of connections written on it.

'Remember, as soon as you get to Birmingham, ring the number at the top and they'll sort you out from there. I'll warn you, honest work isn't much fun, but at least you'll be able to sleep without the battery acid to hand.'

They parted at the entrance to the station. Spender found a florist's and bought Frances a bunch of red and white carnations. He had called her already to get clearance on taking the girls out for a treat. Now all he had to do was try to relax and enjoy himself.

*   *   *

At nine-thirty, with a good evening behind him and the prospect of a nice mindless downhill roll to bedtime, Spender decided to park the car near the flat then go for a gentle stroll around town, keeping to the quieter streets, soaking up the sights and sounds. It was therapy of a kind he didn't choose to analyse; he just knew it worked nicely on his nervous system.

Coming back towards the flat a few minutes after ten-thirty, he saw a familiar figure on the pavement outside.

'Hey,' he called out, 'does Doris have any idea where you are at this time of night?'

Dan turned, startled for a moment. Then he smiled. He looked relieved to see Spender.

'I haven't been able to settle,' he said as Spender drew level. 'I got halfway home, then I decided I wanted to talk. I tried to call on you – I remembered you saying you were going to have a kind of peaceful night . . .'

'I changed my plans and opted for another kind of peace. What's up Dan? You look agitated. Come on, I'll buy you a beer.'

They found a pub and settled with half pints in a corner.

'I've been up at the MacIntyres' place,' Dan explained.

'That would explain the state you're in.'

'Gerry was there on his own, his brother's in London on business. You'll never believe this, Spender . . .'

'Try me.'

'Gerry, he's drunk, but not ga-ga drunk, he's lucid enough, you know, but talkative . . .'

'Free with the verbals.'

'Right. So after I'd asked my questions about his sister-in-law, putting them to him as diplomatically as I could, he told me he knew all about her and Kevin Gunter. Had known for well over a week, he said. He told me his brother George knew as well – he'd gone to prison and told him. He said George took it very badly when he found out. Then he gave me that evil wink of his and said he had a video of Gunter and the girl together.'

'Together where?'

'At the abattoir.'

'The *abattoir*?'

'On a visit, so he says.'

They stared at each other.

'I played him along gently. Asked if I could have a look at the tape. He told me if the doctor ever said he was dying of something terminal, that would be the day he'd let me see it.'

Spender thought about that. 'What do you reckon, Dan?'

'I'm convinced he was telling me the truth. When I was leaving he seemed amused, but there was a terrible, hard glint in his eye, something deadly serious.' Dan looked around the room distractedly. 'What should we do?'

'Take advice, I think,' Spender said.

20

'I'm sorry if I was kind of tired and grumpy when you brought the girls home last night,' Frances said. 'I'd had a rough day but I shouldn't have taken it out on you. You did me a favour.'

'I enjoyed it,' Spender told her. 'So did the kids, I think. We had a giggle, and the pizzas were great.'

They were on the corner of Percy Street and Blackett Street, outside Top Shop. They had been moving in opposite directions, both hurrying, when Frances flagged him down.

'And you didn't mention Jude's People once.'

'Oh. You asked Laura about that, did you?'

'She volunteered.'

'So is my probation over? Can I see them a bit more often and take them out?'

'If you don't, they'll likely be round banging on your door.'

Spender looked at his watch before he could stop himself. 'Sorry,' he said, 'I didn't mean to be rude. It's just I'm a bit pressed—'

'I won't say a word about it. Pressure's getting to be the story of my life, too. I'll see you soon,' Frances said, and pecked his cheek before she hurried away.

The little kiss had been unexpected. It left a

warm spot on his face that he could feel all the way to the car. He got in behind the wheel and put on his belt. Then he sighed.

Staring out at the busy street, he thought of Frances, of her face that used to be so dear to him, the neat, appealing features that could look so wistful back in the early days.

He started the engine. It took an effort to think about the rest, the stuff that had happened since their young days together. Spender made the effort. He let out a little sigh of relief.

The mobile rang.

'Hello?'

'Dan. Any joy yet?'

'I'm in the car now, about to take off for Durham. He's lecturing at the university this morning so I thought it would be best to catch him between gigs. He sounded agreeable enough.'

'Well, let me know what he says, eh?'

'No, Dan.' Spender sighed. 'I'll be likely to keep it to myself, won't I? Of course I'll let you know.'

'Right. Sorry. I've hardly slept a wink.'

'Neither have I. But that's nothing new.'

'Did your friends show up after I left?'

'Not a sign. They were probably tucked away somewhere licking each other's wounds. Look, Dan, I've got to push off. I'll be in touch.'

It was a fine morning, the kind they showed in brochures of England, the countryside a dozen bright shades of green, with a rich blue sky and neatly marshalled stratocumulus clouds stretching to the horizon. A clock was chiming eleven as Spender parked the car off South Road, near the university library. He got out, stretched, and began walking south towards the botanical gardens.

There was an eerie sense of quiet grandeur about Durham, hardly the air of a city at all. It was more like a timeless, mythic settlement for heroic characters who laid down their legends elsewhere, then came here to rest and be silent. It was a special sensation, a mixture of feeling and image surrounding Durham that Spender could never shake, ever since the times when he had come here as a boy, impressionable and imaginative, to gaze at the cathedral (*Half Church of God, half Castle 'gainst the Scot*) right at the heart of the city, majestic on its peninsula in a bend of the River Wear.

The city was at his back as he walked, the river flashing in the sun across meadows to his right. It was the kind of day, he thought, to make you appreciate the richness of life and the mystery of being alive. In the circumstances, it was ironic that his business here this morning was with one of the country's leading experts on death and its causes.

In the precincts of Grey College he slowed down to a stroll and finally halted in the shade of an old laburnum tree. He leaned back against the trunk, feeling the warmth of the bark through his jacket. He closed his eyes, hearing bees somewhere near. There had been a time when he envied university students their idyllic lives; he was starting to remember why he had felt that way.

'Mr Spender?'

He opened his eyes and saw Professor Carroll standing a few yards away. He was tall and slim, with neatly clipped white hair and pale, almost translucent skin. In his dark suit, his tie neatly centred and his horn-rimmed glasses pushed squarely up on his nose, he looked the perfect emissary of his calling.

'I hope I haven't kept you waiting.'

'I think you're early,' Spender said, coming forward and shaking the professor's hand. 'It's nice to see you again.'

'And nice to see you, ah, Sergeant, is it, these days?'

'It is, but Spender'll do fine.'

'Shall we walk?' Carroll pointed in the direction of Trevelyan College, on the other side of the campus. 'My next appointment is over there. Perhaps we can resolve your problem before I have to mount the podium again.'

The last time they strolled together it had been cold and raining, though neither of them minded; they had been taking the air after Carroll's preliminary examination of a body that had lain undiscovered in a lodging house for three weeks. That had been in London. In the intervening years they had met two or three times; it was clear by now, without anything being said, that Carroll understood the background nature of Spender's work.

'A professorship is a wonderfully comfortable cloak,' Carroll said now, 'but the responsibilities can be irksome. In my work with the Crown I'm obliged, usually, to contend with the obscene realities of crime against the person. Here, I deal in complex theories of criminology and medical jurisprudence – intricate as sewing-machines, Spender, but of no use whatever to anyone wishing to go into the world and practise forensic pathology for a living. I sometimes feel like a fraud.'

'So what if you could only do one of the jobs? Which would it be?'

'I've thought about that, and I have to say I don't know. I can't make up my mind. The teaching is an *elegant* sort of pursuit, but it lacks the solidity, the mucky truth of real forensic work. On the other hand, I have to admit that dead bodies, especially the decomposed kind, give me the creeps.'

'Even after all this time?'

'Thirty years and thousands of autopsies since the first time I set foot in a post-mortem room, I have to say I'm still pretty squeamish. Some things you never get used to.'

'But you go on putting up with it.'

'I'm in the business because, frankly, I'm good at it. I have intuition and an armoury of special knacks that set me apart. All that just about balances the fact that the sights and smells of the mortuary have given me the worst moments of my life.'

Carroll paused and pointed to a wide meadow across the way. He suggested they walk across it.

'Any sensible individual,' he said as they reached the other side of the road, 'would have packed it in long ago, given the shocks and the various grades of nausea that I'm prone to. But I suppose I'm a shade masochistic, and I have to say that I love solving mysteries. The whole sphere of forensic medicine intrigues me as much now as it ever did.'

'Another compensation for the sights and smells.'

'Absolutely right. Back there a couple of minutes ago, when I saw you leaning on that tree, do you know the first thing that came to me? I thought, *Cytisus Laburnum*: toxic alkaloid is cyticine, a narcotico-acrid poison. Straight off, without having to try. So I'm a natural, I suppose.' Carroll smiled suddenly. 'You can tell why I like teaching, too. The pleasure I derive from talking is close to the enjoyment I take in good food. And I apologize for it, you've been very patient. You've taken the trouble to come all this way, so there must be something important you want to know.'

'As I mentioned on the phone, Professor, I'm after an expert opinion. To be honest, it's something I could have asked you there and then, but it's such a nice day, and lately I've had to tussle with so much downright ugliness . . .'

'I understand perfectly,' Carroll said. 'What's the problem?'

'Well, in your opinion, if somebody was deliberately killed in an abattoir, and assuming steps had been taken to cover the traces of the killing, would there be much chance of getting forensic proof that the crime had ever taken place?'

Carroll shook his head at once. 'No chance at all.'

'Even if maybe two people had died in the abattoir at the same time?'

'Even if twenty people had, there's still very little chance, in theory, of ever proving it, and in reality there's not a cat in hell's chance.'

Carroll stopped walking and stood facing Spender, his hands held out in front of him, palms facing, as if he were holding something that could be examined.

'Picture an abattoir. Because of the kind of place it is, with every imaginable bodily substance from animals being splashed on walls, ceilings and floors, with flesh and organs being smeared on every surface, you can bet the combinations of bacteria, viruses and tissue types are hard to calculate and impossible to count.'

Spender nodded, avoiding a wave of graphic memory.

'That's for starters,' Carroll said. 'Now, imagine introducing human elements to the scene – blood, membranes, body fluids, chopped flesh. Stir them up with what's already there. What have you got? A mess as near impossible to analyse and label as anything else you'll find in the place.'

'What would it take to prove humans had died there?'

'Torsos, heads, limbs, organs. All the things that any slaughterman worth his salt knows how to turn to mush and deprive of identity.' Carroll started walking again. 'I'll tell you this, Spender – if I wanted to kill somebody in a particularly cruel and horrifying way, a slaughterhouse is the place I'd choose to do it. The place is *designed* for wholesale murder, after all. And if my main concern was that the murder should never be detected, then it's the slaughterhouse again, every time.'

Spender nodded glumly.

'I haven't given you the kind of answer you wanted, of course,' Carroll said. 'No policeman likes to find himself investigating the perfect crime.'

'I don't even know if there's been a crime, Professor.'

'In that case you'll probably never know.'

'Unless I get to see the movie.'

'Sorry?'

'Thinking out loud,' Spender said.

Back in the car ten minutes later, he called Dan and told him what Professor Carroll had said.

'The top and bottom of it,' he concluded, 'is that human flesh subjected to abattoir procedures would end up indistinguishable from any other kind.'

'So what happens now?' Dan said.

'Write your report. Put in the speculative stuff about Gunter and his girlfriend being on an island somewhere. For all we know, they could be. Then file the report and forget it.'

'Easier said than done.'

'I know,' Spender said. 'But there's some you win, Dan, others you try not to think about. Men have gone off their heads living with less than this.'

Keith and Stick were leaning with their backs on the counter, looking at opposite ends of the shop when Spender walked in. Something mellow and a touch mournful was coming from a tape-deck on the shelf.

'I hate wakes,' Spender said, shutting the door.

Keith nodded to him. Stick did fractionally less.

'How long's this going to go on, then? Till one of you slits his wrists? Till both of you do?'

'We're all right,' Keith said. 'Just a bit down, that's all. It won't last.'

'We were talking about the girls,' Stick explained.

'All the weighing up we had to do. Well, Keith had to do, anyway.'

'It got too much,' Keith said, simply. 'Nothing was spontaneous in the end. Nothing.'

'And I did all I could to hang on to little Donna,' Stick sighed. 'I'm hurt about the way it turned out, but I'm not bitter. I could tell I was too rich for her palate. Too colourful for a woman that prefers her men monochrome.'

Spender came and leaned on the wall opposite them.

'You don't look too chipper yourself,' Keith told him.

'It's just business, mate. I'll get over it, same as you. All things pass away.'

'There were bonuses, I'll not deny it,' Stick said, unaware that the focus had shifted from him. 'I got my eyes opened. It's right what they say, isn't it?'

Keith looked at Spender, then back at Stick.

'What who says? About what?'

'Donna and Dory and them, the animal liberation crowd. We've no right to kill animals and eat them. It's murder.'

Spender had a flash of recall, a calf rearing, eyes wide, bellowing . . .

'Aye,' he said. 'Murder.'

'But what would happen to the economy if we all went vegetarian?' Keith asked.

Stick thought about it for a moment. 'It would collapse, right? No bad thing, maybe.'

'And if it's savage to kill animals for food,' Keith went on, 'what does that make all the men and women in the meat business? And all the men and women that eat it? Murderers?'

The tape had stopped. In the silence Stick and Keith looked at Spender. He shrugged.

THE END